CH.
(West C....................., ...,)

One would need to have lived in the townsland of Gurteen, to truly appreciate the concept, of a dreary September afternoon. Lost deep within the sap green hills of the western seaboard and dissected by crumbling stone walls, Sheep's Head Peninsula lay forgotten, shrouded beneath the fathomless weight of antiquity and the ominous dark clouds rolling in from the grey green sea. Isolated in the extreme, even the horrors of a war torn Europe seemed to have passed it by.

Kitty entered the kitchen, her face flushed, her school bag sagging on her back. Blackie, her collie jumped up to greet her, momentarily knocking her off balance. She patted him on the head.

'Who's a good boy?' she asked breathlessly.
The dog yelped and licked her face. She squirmed.
Grabbing his paws she lowered them to the ground and pointed to an old cardboard box nestled in the corner.

'Into bed.'
The dog reluctantly shied away. Kitty brushed down her blue school uniform, pulled on her elastic garters and straightened her wayward socks. Standing by the table she slipped the bag from her shoulders and dropped it to the flagstone floor. Though the kitchen was small and cramped, it was the heart of the cottage. Glossy grey paint covered the walls, peeling near the damp yellow stained ceiling. A pine dresser containing a selection of odd cups and plates stood by the door leading into the dark hall. A holy water font with a

chipped Virgin Mary, hung from a blue dado rail. Dull lace curtains drooped limply across the window in front of the Belfast sink. The constant drip of a solitary brass tap seemed to count away the seconds and minutes with monotonous regularity. Behind her a large black kettle simmered quietly on top of a small Aga cooker. The range was her mother's pride and joy. She loved to shine the two copper pipes feeding from it like a captain might polish the brass on his yacht, but in the few short days since her departure, the copper had already tarnished. An assortment of woolen vests aired on a makeshift line, sagging like a crescent moon above the range. A fly strip, brown and tacky, bespattered with countless flies hung by a brass thumb tack from a rafter in the ceiling.

Kitty was a pleasant looking fourteen-year old. Black curls framed her full face and sparkling brown eyes. She was sturdy, slightly plump and full breasted for her tender years. Her cheeks were still glowing and she tried cooling them with the back of her hand. School was a little over three miles away and she cycled there every day, hail, rain, or shine. Kitty loved school and was one of the brightest in her class. To her it was a social thing, a chance to be with girls her own age. Outside school hours she had little chance to spend time with them. An open newspaper, a half-empty mug of tea and an overflowing ashtray lay on top of the crumb strewn table. She cupped her hands and wiped the scraps away. 'Men,' she muttered as she glanced at the headlines.

**'Germany unleashes V1 bomb on London.
Hundreds killed.'**

Such articles no longer frightened her. She had become immune to the horrors of conflict. To Kitty, it was no different than reading the pages of a war novel. She folded the paper and put it to one side. Opening her school satchel, she grabbed some books, placed them on the table, sat down and began to do her homework. Blackie eyed her from his cardboard box, his head resting on his outstretched paws. The sound of the latch lifting and the distinctive grating of the front door distracted her momentarily. Her father had promised he would fix it, yet despite her mother's constant reminders and his genuine intentions, nothing had ever been done. Blackie lifted his head as the hall began to fill with light. A dark shadow fell across the grey coats hanging behind the door and Kitty heard the familiar sound of hobnailed boots

'You're back I see,' he said in a slurred voice. Blackie lowered his head.

'Hello Bill.'

Bill was in his late thirties, tall and powerfully built, some eight years younger than Kitty's father. He reminded her of a pirate, with his stubbled chin, high cheekbones, unkempt hair and weather beaten face. A black leather belt pinched his shabby trousers at the waist. He wore an old threadbare flannel shirt with rolled up sleeves and missing buttons, exposing his brown muscular arms and chest. In his hand he held a bottle. It looked like water but Kitty knew better. It was one of her father's bottles of 'poiteen'. She hated when he drank. He raised the bottle to his mouth and took a swig. With glazed eyes he looked her up and down for some moments, before muttering;

'Stick on the supper I'm starving and wash the dirty dishes while you're at it.'

He turned and left. The door grated, the latch fell shut and the little hall darkened once more. She could tell by the way he swayed that he had been drinking heavily and yearned for her mother and father's return. She felt nervous when he drank, his personality changed and he often became aggressive. She knew if her father was home, there was no way he'd be drinking like that. Pouring hot water from the kettle she began to wash the dishes piled in the kitchen sink.

Through the net curtains she could vaguely see him outside, chopping logs for the approaching winter. She watched him struggle for balance as he raised the heavy axe awkwardly above his head shuddering as he sent it crashing down with thunderous force, splitting the timber logs as if they were a matchstick's. Despite her misgivings, she genuinely feared for his safety. Finally he cast the axe aside, grabbed the bottle and returned to the house. Kitty busied herself with the dishes as he entered. He stood momentarily swaying in the doorway steadying himself with his free hand. He did not speak. She could feel his eyes upon her, but dared not turn to look. He stumbled into the kitchen and stood behind her. She could feel his laboured breath upon her hair.

'You must be tired, supper will be ready soon'
she said, avoiding eye contact.

'Is that what you think,' he mumbled?

'It's hard work,' she said, placing a plate on the draining board.

'I'll show you who's exhausted.'
He slapped the bottle onto the table. Kitty jumped with fright. Before she had time to react he grabbed her skirt and lifted it above her waist exposing her faded blue knickers, her white muscular thighs and the firm rounded cheeks of her bottom. She struggled to break free but his strong hands began groping her and tugging at her underclothes.

'Stop,' she screamed, 'I'll tell Daddy on you.'
Kitty in desperation splashed a mug of soapy water into his face. He let go, rubbing his stinging eyes.

'Ya bloody bitch,' he yelled.

Running to her bedroom she locked the door, hurriedly jamming a chair beneath the handle before huddling in the corner in a foetal position beside her unmade bed. The room was small and cluttered. Cardboard boxes packed with clothes lay stacked against the wall. A few of her favourite dolls rested on the window ledge. Despite its shortcomings, she loved her room; it was her sanctuary, the place she went when she needed to be alone.

'Kitty, I know you're in there.'

He knocked gently on the door; his voice now soft and warm.

'I'm sorry, Kitty. Please let me in, I just want to talk. That's all.'

Frightened, she did not reply.

'Let me in,' he roared. 'If you don't, I'll break this bloody door down.'

Glancing at the picture of the Sacred Heart above her bed she prayed he would go away. An almighty crash of a boot against the door told her he had not. The timbers split. The chair creaked beneath the door handle. Kitty trembled. Blackie began to bark. Bill's voice was animated now, full of anger and venom.

'Let me in, you little whore!'

Once more he kicked out. This time the timbers gave way to the force of his boot crashing against them. Splinters fell to the floor. Kitty picked herself up, ran to the window and flung it open. The door handle rattled violently.

'I'm warning you. You'll be sorry.'

Lifting the net curtains, she jumped out the window, knocking her dolls and grazing her knee in the process, as she made good her escape. With a crash the bedroom door flew open. Blackie barked excitedly. Bill stepped into the bedroom.

'I warned you,' he said in a slurred voice.

7

Blackie ran to the window. Only then, did Bill realize Kitty was no longer in the room.

'Bloody bitch.'

Turning, he stumbled over the broken chair and out through the shattered door swaying wildly as he followed the dog across the yard. Chickens cackled, flapping their wings and scattering in all directions as he approached. The cockerel raised its chest crowing defiantly before it too took flight.

For a moment he stood swaying in the middle of the yard, gasping for breath listening for a tell-tale sound.

'Kitty, where are you? I just want to talk.'

Blackie crossed the yard sniffing the ground.

'Good boy Blackie, go fetch.'

The dog headed off in the direction of a disused outhouse before disappearing behind an upright cart. Behind it Kitty sat sobbing holding her head in despair. The dog came and licked her face.

'Please go away Blackie' she whimpered as she tried to shove the dog from her. It was too late.

'Well there you are' he said in a softer voice.

He grasped the shafts of the cart to steady himself. Slowly he stepped forward, stooping down and patting the dog on the head.

'You're a great dog Blackie, do you know that?'

The dog wagged its tail and licked his hand. He spoke quietly to Kitty as he approached her.

'What's the matter? Why are you crying?'

She did not respond.

'Let's have a little chat, you and me. What do you say?'

Again she ignored him. He slid awkwardly down the crumbling whitewashed wall till he landed beside her.

'There's no need to be upset, everything's going to be fine.'

He raised a hand as if to wipe her tears but she turned her head away.

'Shush Kitty; everything is going to be fine. Your mother and father will be home tomorrow and you'll get to see your new baby brother, won't that be great? Tomorrow, everything will be back to normal. Now tell me, what's wrong with you?'

She wiped her tears with the back of her hands and despite her harrowing situation said.

'I never want you to do that to me again.'

Leaning his head back against the wall he closed his eyes and smiled. Kitty could see the perspiration running down his brow. She could smell the pungent masculine odour of stale sweat, emanate from his every pore. Opening his eyes he struggled to focus on her.

'Why are you so upset? There's no harm in it. It was just a little game, that's all.'

'I don't like that game and I never want to play it again,' she sobbed.

He lifted his arm and stroked her dark curls clumsily with his fingers.

'It's not just a game Kitty,' he said slurring softly, 'it's a way of showing people how much you love them.'

'But Daddy would never play that game with me,' she protested.

He smiled, shook his head and ran his fingers through his thick black hair. She noticed his grazed and bloodied knuckles.

'Your daddy is far too busy working on the farm. Don't get me wrong, he loves you too, just like I do. You have to understand that we all have to do things we don't like. I don't like having to plough the fields, or muck out the pig sty, but it has to be done. It's for the benefit of us all. Children don't like school, but their parents know what's best for them. In later years, they're thankful.'

'But I do like going to school,' she blurted.

'You're the exception, a very special girl Kitty. Sometimes, by doing things we don't like, for example, cleaning the kitchen floor, or washing the clothes, we are really saying, thank you. We are showing others our love and respect. That way we get their love and respect back and it makes us feel good inside.'

The cockerel strutted across the yard once more, crowing defiantly. Blackie turned and gave chase. Squawking in terror, wings flapping wildly, feathers flying, it reached the safety of the outhouse roof. The dog barked excitedly, jumping up in a vain attempt to reach the bird now defiantly ensconced on a rusted gutter.

'What a crazy dog you have' he laughed.

Kitty tried to smile.

'I see you've cut your knee.'

'It's nothing'.

'Here let me see.'

'Really, it's just a scratch.'

He lifted the hem of her skirt.

'You poor thing,' he said .kissing her gently on the neck. She could smell poiteen and stale tobacco on his breath and could feel his abrasive stubble rasping against her soft skin

'Trust me; everything is going to be fine,' he said inching his hand further up her leg. Petrified, she could feel the coarseness of his palm riding up her thigh. Finally his fingers touched her knickers and he tried to ease her legs apart. Kitty recoiled, struggling to break free but he was much too powerful for her and pinned her down, lifting himself upon her, while she tried to fight him off. In desperation she bit his arm.

'Fucking bitch,' he roared, slapping her hard across the face with the back of his hand.

She could taste warm blood trickling from her nose. He pulled manically at her knickers ripping them to shreds, then using all his strength he began forcing her legs apart.

'No stop. Please stop it!'

Her cries reverberated around the empty farmyard. Clumsily he unbuckled his belt.

'No. No,' she pleaded.

Fumbling he undid his flies and lowered his trousers partially exposing the milky white skin of his muscular thighs She could feel his hot excited state press hard against her.

'Stop' she screamed.

He grabbed her tightly by the throat. She gasped for air.

'Shut up you stupid bitch or I swear to God, I'll kill you. Do as I say and you'll be okay.'

Fearing for her life, she desisted.

'That's it, be a good girl, there's nothing to be afraid of, everything is going to be fine. I know you'll like it. I can see you're gagging for it. I can tell.'

He released his stranglehold. Kitty coughed and gasped for air. He arched his back, grasped his engorged and stiffened flesh and guided it towards the mouth of the pubescent hair between her legs.

'Please stop,' she implored. 'If daddy finds out he'll murder you.'

He grasped her bloodied face, squeezing her fleshy cheeks so roughly her bottom lip split. Clenching his yellow-stained teeth, he warned her.

'If you breathe a word of this to anybody, I'll kill you, do you understand?'

Kitty lay paralyzed with fear. One brutal thrust of his hips and he entered her, rupturing her soft virginal flesh, ripping her apart like some wild insatiable beast, frenzied by the scent of bloodied meat. Kitty screamed in pain.

'No. No Uncle Bill, you're hurting me!'

CHAPTER TWO
(NEW YORK CITY, 2001)

Though it was well past rush hour, Claire was relieved to find a seat. She was tired, having worked late the previous evening. Placing her black leather briefcase carefully on her lap she rested her head gently against the window pane. From the commuter train she could look out over the East River and Manhattan and watched the skyscrapers light up one by one, giant golden beacons on a backdrop of blue. She observed how the liquid glow, intensified before fading as each building in turn lost the reflected morning sunlight. Frowning she glanced towards the gaping hole and could see smoke still rising from Ground Zero where the towers once stood. Rescue crews still worked around the clock, clearing the debris, hoping to find people trapped in air pockets beneath the rubble. Less than a week had passed since the atrocity and most people knew in their hearts, it was a hopeless cause. What had been bravely called 'a rescue mission' was in reality nothing more than a recovery operation.

For over twenty-five years, Claire had travelled this line on her way to work in J.P. Golding's, Attorney's Office, on Liberty Plaza, in Lower Manhattan. The view across the water had never ceased to amaze her. She had grown to love this city, now it filled her with apprehension. Like so many other souls from the far-flung corners of the Earth she was drawn here, sucked in a vortex of hope, searching for a better life. Now as the world stood shocked in the

13

wake of this atrocity, the citizens of New York, despite their diversity, had forged a camaraderie, a unique bond that made them stand together in the face of adversity. One thing Claire knew for certain was, that despite this unique bond, this outpouring of goodwill, New York would never be the same again.

Claire had left Ireland in the mid-sixties to begin a new life in America. Initially it had been a massive culture shock for the young country girl who, despite suffering terrible homesickness, persevered, never wanting to return to that which she had run away from. She had grown up in a rural community near the Co. Wexford village of Kiltealy on the foothills of the Blackstairs Mountains. Only once in the intervening thirty-four years had she returned. That had been on a brief visit in the nineteen-seventies, to bury her mother. She gazed once more at the smoldering ruins and blessed herself. Taking her reading glasses and a file from her briefcase, she began examining the documents before her.

Claire was an elegant woman in her late fifties, smartly attired in a black pinstriped trouser suit. There was graceful serenity about her that was hard to define, and despite her hair being white and her face free of make-up, she exuded subtle beauty. The train came to a halt at City Hall and the doors shot open. There was the usual surge as commuters departed and entered the train. A small black girl rushed along the aisle and sat down on the seat opposite. Claire smiled. The child smiled back. The little girl's hair was neatly plaited and tied with pink ribbons complementing her pretty dress. She cuddled a Barbie doll proudly in her arms. Her mother, a tall black woman in her early twenties, dragged a large blue suitcase along the aisle behind her. Propping the suitcase against the seat she sat down beside her daughter. She was slim, attractive, short-haired with a pretty face. Though she wore dark glasses, Claire could see tell tale signs of bruising on her left cheek and lower lip. The young woman opened a newspaper, took a biro from her bag and began searching through the 'appointments' column. The little girl spoke.

'But Mommy, why do we have to live with Granny?'

'It's only for a short time Sweetie.'

'Is Daddy coming too?'

The mother ignored the question.

'I miss him.'

'You'll get to see him soon.'

'Does Granny know we are coming to stay with her?'

The strain was showing on her mother's face.

'No,' she said, her voice cracking.

'Great, we can surprise her.'

'Somehow I don't think she'll be that surprised' her mother said, casting a glance in Claire's direction.

Claire busied herself with the documents in her hand. The little girl continued to play quietly with her doll, speaking to it as she held it against the window pane. The doll was white and had long blonde hair. She produced a brush and began to gently stroke its hair. After a while she enquired.

'Mommy, why can't I have blonde hair?'

Claire peeped over the rim of her reading glasses. She was amused by the question and glanced to the mother who was engrossed in her job search, curious as to how she might respond.

'Cause you're a little black girl', she said impatiently.

'But I like blonde hair Mommy.' Her eyes widened.

'Daddy likes blonde hair too.'

The words seemed to cut like a knife. The young mother turned to her child, a painful smile on her face and pinched her daughter gently on the cheek.

'But you have beautiful black hair Sweetie.'

'But why can't I have blonde hair like my dolly?'

Her mother in exasperation folded the paper.

'Black girls have black hair. That's life, there's nothing we can do about it.'

The little girl pouted in displeasure, but a passing train and the gush of warm air momentarily distracted her.

She pressed her forehead against the window fascinated by the strobe of carriages zipping by. It vanished as suddenly as it had appeared. She turned back to her mother

'But Mommy I want blonde hair.

'Yes darling and I want a job.'

'But lots of girls have blonde hair,' she protested.

'But they're all, white girls!'

The little girl considered this for a moment and then blurted.

'How come, white girls can have black hair?'

Claire looked on, intrigued.

'That's just the way it is.'

'But why, Mummy?'

The mother turned away and lifted her sunglasses. Claire could see the purple green swelling around her bloodshot eye as she furtively wiped a tear from her face. The little girl waited impatiently for an answer. Smiling the mother summoned all her strength and touched her daughter gently on the cheek.

'When you grow up darling, you'll discover for yourself, 'there never was, nor will there ever be, justice, in this world.'

The child looked confused. The train came to a halt at Park Place Broadway It was Claire's new stop. In the distraction she had almost forgotten. Her usual stop at

Fulton Street was still sealed off since the disaster and now she had to walk an extra block to reach her office. She smiled warmly at the little girl as she packed her briefcase and made for the door. As she walked along the busy platform the little girl waved from the passing carriage. Claire waved back. Her mother's words echoed in her head.

'There never was, nor will there ever be, justice in this world.'

CHAPTER THREE

As Claire walked along the Manhattan streets, she placed a protective mask over her face to avoid the asbestos dust still hanging in the air. There was a pungent smell of burning and the acrid stench of a giant electric meltdown. Massive trucks rumbled in convoy from the site carrying their ghoulish loads of twisted metal and human ash. Everywhere she looked she could see the 'Stars and Stripes' hanging from street lamps, office blocks, and on the back of every car and truck that passed her by. At each street corner she was confronted by another hastily erected notice board covered with photos and messages for missing loved ones, nameless faces, staring back from beyond the grave, poor souls who had the misfortune of being in the wrong place at the wrong time.

As she walked onto the plaza in front of her office block, a blonde lady walking her dogs, approached. She wore a mink stole over her tight red dress. Two white poodles pulled hard on their leads almost dragging her along. Her hair was platinum but as they passed Claire could see the grey beneath the ill fitting wig and the craggy lines spreading from the corners of her heavy-set eyes. Her pale face was almost translucent, stretched like a drum skin, showing her veins and the tell-tales signs of surgery. The same shade of red, smeared her thin lips and her jewellery rattled on her wrists as she struggled to control her pets. Claire glanced down at the poodles. Each had a yellow ribbon tied around its neck and a doggy jacket emblazoned with the American flag.

Ever since the attack on the Twin Towers she felt a certain vulnerability as she entered the elevators and ascended to the office's of J.P. Golding's and Associates, on the thirty-sixth floor of the Plaza Building. Claire was a successful attorney in one of the most reputable firms on the East Coast. Financially she was independent, owned a beautiful apartment in the much sought-after residential area of Brooklyn Heights and though she loved her job and enjoyed her life in New York, something told her that perhaps now, the time was right for a change. When she first arrived in New York she was lost and alone. For five years she struggled, working at night to support her studies. Times were difficult and she often felt like giving up, but somehow she managed to persevere. Even now, those hectic early years seemed like a blur in her life. When she graduated she was offered work as a 'junior' in J.P. Golding's. That was over thirty years ago. Now she realized perhaps she had sacrificed too much in the pursuit of a professional career. Now that she was older she realized just how big a sacrifice it had been. She was single, with no family, no ties, and living alone.

There had been one special man in her life. She had fallen in love with Tim, about seven years after she arrived in the States. He was a wonderful man about ten years her senior. He worked at the United Nations as an interpreter and negotiator and spoke six languages fluently. He was born in Kenya, where his father worked as a diplomat for the British Government. His mother was the daughter of a German coffee plantation owner. His parents met on holiday in Mombassa and had fallen in love. Tim was their only child. Clare met him through mutual acquaintances. At first they were just good friends, enjoying each other's company; soon it blossomed into a relationship, then love. They got engaged on Christmas Eve 1971 and had planned an Easter wedding. In January, that winter, Tim was killed in a road accident in upstate New York. His automobile left the road in a severe snow blizzard. It was three days before the car was discovered buried under a snow drift. Tim was laid to rest in upstate New York, interred in the little graveyard of the church they had chosen for their nuptials.

For two years Claire lost her will to live. Had it not been for the support of her friends and colleagues she possibly would never have pulled through, but pull through she did. She never entered into another meaningful relationship after Tim's death. To her, he was irreplaceable. It wasn't that there weren't affairs, indeed she dated many men, but when they became serious she simply distanced herself. Her friends too, had tried to set her up with suitable partners, to no avail. Following Tim's tragic death Claire immersed herself in her work as a means of escape, often working twelve hours a day, six days a week. She studied law with a passion verging on insanity, becoming one of the most knowledgeable in her field. After two years of living virtually on 'auto pilot', she finally emerged from the darkest days of her young life stronger than before to become one of the most sought-after legal brains in Manhattan.

The doors of the elevator opened. The entire 36th floor was allocated to the Law firm. Claire stepped out on to the plush blue carpet emblazoned with the name J.P. Golding's & Associates and entered the reception area. It was about the size of a tennis court, adorned with lush tropical plants and wonderful flowers arrangements. The walls were covered in contemporary American Art giving it the impression of a Gallery more than a reception area. A white Italian marble fountain rose from the centre of the floor with three exquisitely sculpted cherubs adorning the centre column. According to rumour, it once belonged to a Monastery in Italy, but was dismantled at the behest of an American General who took it back to the U.S.A. in a B52 bomber.

Wearily, she tossed her protective mask into the trash bin and headed to the dispenser in the corner. She filled herself a paper cup of cold refreshing water. Kate, an attractive oriental receptionist greeted her with a handful of mail.

'Good morning Miss Conlon.

'Good Morning Kate. How was your weekend?'

Kate sighed.

'Good, under the circumstances.'

Claire sifted through the mail.

'Is Mike in his office.'

'No he hasn't arrived yet.'

Claire opened her briefcase, and handed a file over to Kate.

'That's the research on the 'Lee versus Merdith' case. Make sure he gets it the minute he arrives.'

Passing the files, she noticed on the front page of the 'New York Times'. a photo of utter devastation at the World Trade Centre

'What a horrid waste of life,' she said despairingly.

'I feel sorry for those left behind; they're going to have to deal with this for the rest of their lives,' said Kate.

'You know, you're right, by the way, how's your little girl Jessica?'

Kate smiled, revealing her perfect white teeth.

'She's great, back to her old self, crawling all over the place and giving my poor mother a torrid time.'

Claire laughed. The phone rang. Kate lifted the receiver.

'Good morning, J.P. Golding's and Associates, how may I help you?'

Claire slipped her mail into her briefcase, grabbed her drink and headed towards her office. As she walked along the brightly lit corridor leading to her office, she felt strangely alienated, as if she were looking at it through the eyes of a stranger. It was opulent, with all the trappings of financial success befitting a rich American corporation. That was one of the things she noticed when she first arrived in America, the obsession with wealth, or at least the perception of it. If you had it, you flaunted it. Brand names and logos were social statements, 'a must'. People bought into lifestyles as easily as buying tickets for a movie. Social standing was measured by the car you drove, the desirability of the man or woman on your arm, the size of your house, or the amount of credit cards in your pocket. Cards represented money, money represented class. If you didn't have money you were nothing. Sadly in America, it was as simple as that.

She stopped in front of her office door and observed the highly polished brass plate bearing the name 'Claire Conlon Attorney at Law. She had come a long way. Never in her wildest dreams could she have imagined the young girl from the backwaters of County Wexford, would make a name for herself in New York. She opened the door and entered. It was a modern office, minimalist in style with a large frosted glass desk surrounded by white leather chairs. The external walls were glass offering spectacular views of the city. An original Hopper hung on the wall behind her desk. Claire found an affinity with Hopper's work. She wasn't sure whether it was his vision of New York she liked, or whether it was the loneliness his painting seemed to portray? She placed her briefcase on the desk and went to the window. Sipping from the paper cup, she gazed out on Ground Zero. She could see the twisted honeycomb structures jutting from the rubble, like gothic pieces of sculpture on a base of glowing ash and smoke. She gazed upon the rescue workers below. From where she stood they looked like a swarm of bees in their black jackets and reflective yellow stripes searching for the nectar of life in a sea of man-made destruction.

It was from here she had watched in dismay as the North Tower burned, unable to comprehend the situation, assuming a plane must have suffered some catastrophic malfunction. She had wept despairingly as the poor souls above the impact zone waved their shirts and jackets from office windows through clouds of thick billowing smoke desperately seeking salvation. Half the staff had gathered in her office as the 'United Airlines' plane appeared from behind the Towers. Claire had never seen a civil aircraft flying so low above the New York skyline. They watched in horror as the plane altered course and headed directly towards the South Tower exploding in a huge fireball, ripping through the building like a knife through paper. The floor beneath their feet shuddered and the windows vibrated with the force of the impact. Screams of disbelief echoed throughout the office. Only then did the reality of the situation sink in and Claire, like the rest, fled in terror. As she hurried down Church Street sheltering from the debris falling like a ticker tape parade, she glanced at the mayhem above. People had climbed out onto the window ledges; some overcome by the intensity of the heat took what must have been the easier option and resigned themselves to their fate by jumping headlong to certain death. Everywhere she looked, total chaos reigned, streets were cordoned off, traffic gridlocked, cars abandoned, distraught souls wept as they searched for loved ones. Police, desperately trying to control the mayhem as fire engines and ambulances hurried to the scene, sirens wailing, competing with the screams of people running in blind panic, unable to comprehend the horrors they were witnessing.

The memory of that day still haunted her. She despaired at man's inhumanity to man and the cheapness of life. She questioned her own profession, recalling the numerous cases she had fought, defending clients she knew in her heart were guilty of murder, but because of her blinkered professionalism, her legal expertise, or the prosecutions technical ineptitude, those same murderers still walked the streets of New York, free to kill again. The law was an ass, and Claire knew it. Yet, despite her misgivings and the struggle between her professional and moral ethics, she continued to make a good living upholding an ideal, that was to all intents and purposes, a myth. Perhaps she was little better than a con artist, a legal prostitute, willing to bend like the law, in whatever direction her client might desire? She recalled her train journey that morning and the young black mother's words. Perhaps she was right.

'There never was, nor will there ever be, justice in this world.'

Sipping the last of the water she crushed the paper cup in her hands and tossed it into the waste paper basket beneath her desk.

CHAPTER FOUR

Claire was happiest in the confines of her home. She had bought the apartment in 'Brooklyn Heights' six years earlier. It was modern and spacious and she loved it. Like her office, the style was minimalist, tastefully bathed in subdued light. After her bath Claire poured herself a chilled glass of Sauvignon Blanc, her evening ritual after a hard day's work. It helped her to unwind. She walked barefoot across the highly polished cherrywood floor wrapped in her white cotton dressing gown, and picked up the remote control. After several minutes of flicking through the channels she stood up and made her way to her study. It was a small comfortable room with warm peach colored walls. The shelves were neatly stacked with reference books. On one shelf was a large bronze bust of James Joyce. She had spotted it by chance in a Harlem pawnbroker's window and was intrigued as to how it got there. Universally regarded as one of the most important writers of the twentieth century, she was ashamed as an Irish woman to admit that she had never attempted to read any of his works. She had heard how much of a struggle he was to read. She decided there and then to buy the bust. A week later she bought 'Ulysses'. Claire had not expected to understand it, let alone to like it, yet, upon reading it, she became a fan. Joyce's black humor surprised her, as did his insight and astute observations into the complexities of Irish society at the turn of the last century.

Hanging on the wall by the window was a sepia photograph of her parents. In it they stood like frightened rabbits holding hands and looking towards the camera. Her mother had told her it was taken on their honeymoon, a week after they were married. They had never been to Dublin before and everything about the place was daunting. The photo studio was no different. Though the photographer had tried to relax them, they were not prepared for the intense brightness and the pop of the sodium flash. It had taken the frustrated photographer several attempts before he finally calmed them sufficiently to obtain the photo now on view.

Behind Claire hung a large color photograph of herself and Tim, taken shortly after their engagement. Tim commissioned it to celebrate the event. He rested his handsome face on her shoulder as they posed playfully before the camera. In it Claire's face was young and radiant, full of joy and expectation. They seemed the perfect couple about to embark on a life together. Little did they know fate was to deal them a bitter hand. Above her computer was a small mahogany framed glass box, the sort you might use to display butterflies or insects. Inside resting on a gold brown velvet cushion was a single clamshell with a cream and speckled brown exterior. A little plaque beneath bore the inscription:

The Chocolate Flamed Venus
Clifton Bay 1963'.

Claire switched on the computer and sat down. Though she had left Ireland over thirty three years previously she found it easier than ever to keep abreast of the latest happenings in the 'old country'. When she had first arrived in New York communication had been haphazard to say the least. Most homes in Ireland didn't have a phone and Claire's parents were no exception. She was forced to write to them informing them of a date and time she would ring. Armed with this information her parents would drive down to the village of Kiltealy and wait outside the public phone box for her call, often with disastrous results. Finding the phone in working order was in itself an achievement. When it did work, more often than not some young local girl or boy was ensconced inside pouring out their undying love and adoration to some besotted recipient at the other end. Sadly this outpouring could last for hours on end. Often, her parents had to return home after a fruitless night, frustrated and disappointed. A few days later yet another letter would arrive and the saga would begin all over again. Claire was glad to see some things had actually changed for the better. Now all she had to do was log on to the internet and Ireland of the twenty first century appeared before her on her screen.

She was as much astounded as she was baffled by the transformation that had taken place. The country appeared so vibrant and wealthy. It had been turned on its head, transformed beyond recognition. Gone were the leprechauns and the gombeen men, replaced by a new breed of young educated professionals. She could never in her wildest dreams, have foreseen a day when the tide of emigration would turn. People from different countries were arriving daily. She was curious as to why they would choose a small rain-soaked island on the fringes of Europe to set up home. Was it really a better place than that which she had left? Could she retire there? Would she want to? Such questions had entered her head in the recent past. Though she no longer had family over there and despite the fact she had spent more than half of her life in America, she still considered Ireland her home.

Sipping her Savignon Blanc she waited as she logged on to some of Ireland's property market sites. She was curious as to what she might find and was appalled to discover the cost of property over there. For the price of an ordinary 'semi-detached' one could buy a mansion in the States. She sighed and raised her Sauvignon Blanc; perhaps she had left it too late. Gone were the days when you could find deserted homesteads scattered all over rural Ireland, gone too were the days when the Irish in droves, fled on boats to England, Australia, and America. Disillusioned, she decided to search the newspaper sites and logged onto the 'Irish Times' and began to read the headlines. Her attention was caught by an article on Child abuse in Irish Orphanages Apprehensively she logged on and began to read. Her face paled and she began to quietly cry. Once more the young mother's words echoed in her head. 'There never was, nor will there ever be, justice in this world'; This time, her words were laden with shame and guilt, a burden Claire had carried with her, for all those years.

CHAPTER FIVE

The following day Claire sat in a little Italian bistro Venetzia' on the Upper East Side on East 74th. Street just across from the Whitney Museum of Modern Art. She sat at a small table by the window looking out on the busy city. Tourists and young couples passed by on their way to Central Park a mere block away. Claire appeared upset and drawn. She glanced at her watch. It was now twelve thirty five. A waiter came to her table

'Good day, what can I get you,' he asked in a friendly New York / Italian accent.

Claire was lost in thought.

'Excuse me madam'.

Turning to him, she smiled weakly and apologized.

'I'm sorry I didn't hear you. I'm waiting for Mike Borinski, I believe you know him?'

'Ah mister Borinski the proprietor's brother?'

Claire nodded. The handsome young waiter grinned.

'I hate to say this, but punctuality was never one of Mr. Borinski's strong points. Can I get you a drink while you are waiting?'

Claire was amused by the accuracy of his statement.

'Yes that would be great. I'll have a white wine, Sauvignon Blanc please.'

Her mobile rang. It was Mike. He was running a little late. Mike was her closest friend in J.P. Golding's. They started their law careers around the same time and had worked together for over twenty years. They had become one of the best legal teams in the business having a near physic understanding of each other. He too was in his late fifties, tall and well built, with a full head of dyed black hair. Though he was not a particularly handsome man, he oozed charisma and had a love of life and a personality that was infectious. He made Claire laugh. His humor was black and outrageous. He had a fantastic ability to observe and ridicule the idiosyncrasies of life. He came from a Polish Italian background. His father, from Krakow, had emigrated just before the commencement of the 'Second World War'. His mother was born in the Bronx, to a second generation Italian family. Mike was raised there. He learned to be street-wise at an early age. In his teens he had many scrapes with the law, and loved to joke about it now. It had been Mike's idea to meet in Venetzia It had been bought recently by his brother Vincent and had become one of Mike favorite haunts.

On the weekends he loved to play poker here with family and friends. The gambling usually went on till the small hours of the morning, and substantial amounts of money were often won or lost in a single night. Luckily, Mike managed to hide the full extent of his gambling from his wife Gina. It was Mike more than anybody, who had helped Claire through her darkest days after Tim's death. He had worried about Claire's fragile emotional state. Though Gina and Mike were only a short time married when Tim died, they insisted that Claire should come to live with them till she 'got herself together' as they put it. She had intended to spend a week, perhaps two there, but Claire eventually ended up living over a year with them. Gina became like a sister to her, helping, supporting and encouraging her on every step of her road to recovery. She had practically become part of the family. Claire was Godmother to their only child,

Sophia. That was all of nineteen years ago. Sophia was now a beautiful vibrant young woman. She was a first-year student, studying law at Yale University. Over the years Claire had spent many holidays with the family in various parts of the globe, but the most memorable holidays always seemed to be spent in Italy.

On the first trip Claire had gone with them to meet Gina's relatives in Verona. Gina loved the place. She felt at home there. She pleaded with Mike to invest in some Italian property. He finally relented and bought a property in Venice, a beautiful twin apartment overlooking the Grand Canal, with wonderful views of the Rialto. While Mike enjoyed golfing with his mates in Pebble Beach and Augusta, Claire and Gina spent some wonderful times there together. Claire was simply besotted by the beauty of the place and adored the city and its people.

Mike entered the restaurant.

'Gees Claire I'm sorry, the traffic's a nightmare.' He kissed her on the cheek and sat down.

'How did your case go,' she enquired?

'The prosecution adjourned for a fortnight, thanks for the research.'

He raised his hand. The young Italian waiter came running.

'Yes Mr. Borinsky.'

'I'll have a cold 'Bud' Tony. Are you ready to order Claire' he enquired?

'Yes thanks I'll just have a main course Spaghetti Bolognese.'

'And the usual for me Tony, please.'

The little restaurant began to fill with local office staff on their lunchtime break.

'Looks like I got here just in time.'

She nodded in agreement. Time passed. Mike was finishing his starter of Mozzarella with sliced tomatoes.

'So what's bothering you?'

Claire smiled.

'You know me so well.'

'I've had to put up with you for over twenty years, I should know you', he moaned.

'Mike,' she said, her voice more serious now, 'I'm thinking of quitting.'

He was caught in mid swallow. He reached for his beer and took a mouthful.

'What?'

'I'm thinking of packing it in?'

'Your job,' he asked, trying to clarify the situation?

'Yes,' she said quietly. 'I've been thinking about it for some time now.'

Mike wiped his mouth with his napkin.

'Why?'

Claire shuffled uneasily on her chair.

'That's just it. I don't know.'

Mike tossed the napkin down, relieved.

'You're just having a bad day. You'll feel differently tomorrow, I know you will.'

Tony arrived with the main course.

'I'll have another Budweiser Tony.

He pointed to Claire's glass,

'Sauvignon Blanc?'

'No, I'm fine thanks.'

She continued.

'I don't know what's got into me Mike. It's just lately everything seems irrelevant. There has to be something more relevant in life than making money.'

Mike shook his head.

'There's not.'

She looked at him, surprised.

'That's it,' he said in a matter of fact way. 'That's what it's all about. You're born, and then you die. In the meantime, you work your ass off trying to survive, just so you can prolong the inevitable and before you know it, you're too old to enjoy what's left of life.'

He raised his hands shrugged his shoulders and flipped his palms.

'That's the real world I'm afraid.'

She twirled the spaghetti on her fork. Mike smiled apologetically.

'It's not quite that bleak. I suggest you eat something.' The sound of wailing sirens distracted her. It sent a shiver up her spine and a prayer to her lips. Looking out she could see the monstrous red fire engines weaving their way through a sea of yellow cabs, forcing them to mount the pavements as nervous pedestrians stood and watched. She continued.

'Maybe I've reached a crucial stage in my life? I don't know why I feel the way I do. Perhaps somewhere in my subconscious I've come to realize that I'm leaving nothing behind.'

He looked at her a little mystified.

'Gees Claire, I can give you the number of a good shrink'

She tried to explain.

'Don't get me wrong, it's not that I ever wanted children of my own.'

It was evident from her words she had. Mike was surprised. He didn't know her as well as he thought. He certainly never realized, that secretly over the years, she had yearned for a child. He watched in surprise as Claire struggled for words.

'I just feel all my life has been a waste. When I die......'

He stopped her in her tracks, genuinely shocked.

'Ah Gees, Claire. What in God's name are you talking about; you are still a young healthy woman, you'll be around well into your eighties.'

'I'm not sure if that comment is meant to be kind or cruel,' she said raising an eyebrow?

Tony began clearing some plates. She felt embarrassed that perhaps he had overheard their conversation; She waited for him to leave before she continued.

'I really have nothing to show for my life, it's been a complete and total waste of time.'

'Nonsense, you're a successful Lawyer. There are people out there who would give their right arm to be in your position.'

Claire shook her head despondently.

'God forbid, but if Sophia was kidnapped tomorrow and you were given an ultimatum; 'your daughter's life or yours, what would you do.'

Mike smiled uneasily.

'What sort of a question is that?'

'Please answer me honestly.'

Mike seemed a little perturbed.

'I'd gladly give my life, if that's what you mean?'

Claire smiled.

'That's just it. There are people out there who might give their right arm to be in my position, but in reality, I have nothing. Okay I have a career, but nothing worth giving my life for, that's a certainty. You have something more precious than yourself. I just wish I had. Can you understand what I'm trying to say Mike? My life lacks meaning.'

Mike placed his elbows on the table and rested his chin on his clenched fists

'You were always better with words than me' he conceded.

She looked out the window. It had started to rain and people dashed through a multicoloured sea of umbrellas seeking shelter .She smiled ruefully.

'I feel as if I too am running for cover.'

She turned to Mike, her face tinged with sadness.

'I need to find myself Mike, do something positive with my life, before it's too late.'

Mike lowered his hands and reached across the table, his voice warm and sincere.

'Why don't you just take a break, get away from the office, and go on a vacation. Chill out on some tropical beach in the Caribbean. Have a holiday romance.'

'What at my age?' she laughed.

'Take a sabbatical for as long as you need, the firm will understand. The last thing they want, is to loose you.'

'Am I crazy Mike?'

Mike released her hand and swigged on his beer. He smiled affectionately.

'Too fucking right you are.' She returned his smile taking a deep breath.

'I saw something on the internet last night.'

'A vacation?', he enquired.

He was glad that at last the conversation had hit a less serious note. He reached for a toothpick and began to clean between the gaps in his front teeth.

'No' she replied. 'I read an article on the Irish Times web site, about child abuse in Irish Orphanages.'

He made a sucking motion with his lips.

'Gees. How appalling.'

'Remember I told you, when I left school I had joined a convent?'

Mike nodded.

'I actually witnessed some of that abuse and I walked away.'

'Now Claire, I'm sure you did your best.'

He snapped the toothpick before discarding it, then raising his hand he ordered.

'Two cappuccino's, please.'

'No Mike I walked away, I did nothing. I turned a blind eye and walked away.'

'You couldn't have changed anything.'

'I could have tried Mike.'

She turned once more to the window.

'I didn't even do that.'

He watched her gaze out the window pane, through the raindrops, as through she was gazing into a window of years, back into some darker chapter in her life. Slowly she turned to face him. He could see tears welling in her eyes.

'I am as guilty as the rest. I'm like one of those sad silent cowards who knew about the 'Holocaust' but did nothing.'

'Don't be ridiculous, Claire.'

'I am. I know I am.'

'You're being too hard on yourself; you can't carry others guilt on your shoulders.'

'I know I have to go back there and see if I can help in any way. I owe it to them.'

He felt a tinge of pity and sadness for her. He felt perhaps she was right, that it would clear the air and put matters to rest Perhaps she should go back and confront her demons. The cappuccinos arrived. Mike dropped two sugars cubes into his cup and began to gently stir the coffee with his spoon.

'What about your apartment, what are you going to do with it?'

She sipped her coffee before speaking. She seemed relieved, like a burden had been lifted from her shoulders.

'I can lease it while I'm gone. It won't be hard finding a tenant.'

Mike sensed her determination. He had seen it so often over the years. He knew she was mentally preparing herself for a difficult trial.

'Maybe you're being too hasty; perhaps you should take a vacation first. Give yourself some time to think things over?'

She smiled warmly.

'Thanks Mike. I owe you so much.'

Mike felt uncomfortable. He found it hard to accept a compliment.

'Rubbish,' he replied.

She reached across the table and took his hand.

'You really are a true friend. Not many people have somebody like you to depend on.'

He laughed it off.

'Perhaps it's just as well?'

'You could bring Gina and Sophia to visit me when I'm over there. I'll give you a guided tour.'

Mike pondered a moment.

'I've always wanted to go to Ireland; you know, I think I'd like that.'

CHAPTER SIX
(IRELAND, 2001)

It was a wet Saturday morning as Aer Lingus Flight EI 104 made its final approach into Dublin Airport. Claire could hear the familiar sound of the undercarriage opening and the wheels locking into place. She felt a strange trepidation, perhaps a mild form of panic, as she contemplated the wisdom of her actions. She was here now. There was no going back, not for the moment at least. She was determined to give it her best shot. If things didn't work out she would simply return to the States. Through the fleeting clouds she caught her first glimpse of the Irish coast, followed by snatches of Ireland's Eye with its grey rocky headland, a short time later a brief flash of Howth Head before the clouds again closed in, then the white sandy beach of Portmarnock. The plane slowed and the whine of the jet engines almost ceased as the plane descended through the clouds. Her ears popped, she could see the grey slated rooftops of one of the many bland north Dublin housing estates flash by, surprised at the extent of the urban sprawl. The plane pitched slightly, buffeted by a strong easterly wind, the throttle opened, and the engines whined once more, making the final corrections before landing. As they crossed low above the motorway she could see the heavy morning traffic and the white plumes of spray rising in its wake. Rain ran sideways across the window and she glimpsed the perimeter of the airport and the runway lights. The plane hovered momentarily before landing with a gentle thud. She watched the water spray rise from the tarmac as the engines roared into reverse thrust, whining as they slowed the aircraft. Passengers clapped. She had seen it so many times before. Had they applauded the captain's skill, or the fact they were once more safely back on 'terra firma' or was it a joyous outburst of emotion at being back on home soil? The elderly gentleman beside her, obviously a nervous flyer blessed himself, relieved that his ordeal was over. The 'Airbus A320' swung a sharp right and taxied towards the terminal. A stewardess addressed the passengers on the intercom. 'Cead Mile a Flaite go mBaile Atha Cliath.'

It was Gaelic, the language of her forefathers, spoken by a small percentage of the population, mainly in the west of Ireland and on the Aran Islands. She had almost forgotten it still existed. It had been a compulsory subject in all Irish schools and she had hated it. For over twelve years she had struggled to learn it, now she had forgotten it all. Only in recent years had she come to realize how important language was to the cultural and heritage of a nation, and she vowed one day she would put that right. 'Welcome ladies and gentlemen to Dublin. Please remain seated till the plane comes to a complete stop and the fasten safety belt sign is switched off.'

She felt a certain security in the fact that her job at J.P. Golding's was still there for her if she wanted it. They had been so understanding and so supportive of her and had arranged a wonderful surprise party in her honour at 'The Algonquin Hotel' on 59 West and 44th. Street. It was one of the plushest joints in New York. All her friends were there and they wined, dined, and danced the night away. In a bizarre way it made the parting a much more traumatic and difficult affair for Claire. They had all wished her well, a safe journey and speedy return. Gina and Mike had insisted they drive her to the airport. Not since that morning thirty-six years before, when as a young woman, she boarded the plane at Shannon Airport, had she felt such a gut-wrenching emotion, such sense of loss. She was homesick for New York even before she boarded the plane in J.F.K. and cried unashamedly as she said goodbye. Now she sat looking out at the wet green fields of Ireland, emotionally confused as the plane taxied back to the terminal.

'Ireland is my home' she reassured herself, but little seeds of doubt began to creep into her mind. Perhaps she been gone too long? Would she like it here? Would she be happy? What was she going to do? Where was she going to live? Via the internet, she had reserved a room in the 'Westbury Hotel' just off Grafton Street. It would offer her an opportunity to discover the city and visit its galleries and theatres. Dublin was a city she never really got to know as a young girl, now perhaps she was about to put that right. She had decided to stay in the hotel till she found a suitable area where she could set up base and hoped that would be sooner rather than later. She was adamant she did not want to live in the city; she had done that in New York. Now she wanted somewhere tranquil, a rural setting, calm and secluded yet not too distant from the capital.

The terminal at Dublin was buzzing. It could have been Tegel, Orley or even L.A.X. It fascinated her how the modern airport had totally obliterated the culture of the country into which you now arrived. Airports it seemed were a country's first casualty in the inevitable tide of globalization. Each one, a clone of somewhere else, each terminal crammed with the same quick-stop coffee docks and fancy duty free shops, with the obligatory Hertz, and Avis car rentals, and foreign exchange counters. Claire grabbed her cases from the baggage carousel placed them on a trolley and headed to the foreign exchange. As she waited in line she compared the exchange rates. Europe was about to launch a single currency the Euro and put an end to the struggle of converting Lira into Deutch Mark, or Pesetas into Kroners. She could see the wisdom of a single currency. The banks and money lending institutions had been ripping the public off for years. If she were to buy a hundred 'Irish Punts' right now, it would cost her one hundred and twenty dollars. If she immediately sold the 'Punts' back without leaving the counter, she would get only ninety 'Dollars' for the exchange. It was daylight robbery. How did the banks get away with it, for so long she wondered?

Having been warned about the cost of living in Ireland, Claire decided to come prepared, and purchased one thousand Punts, to tide her over. She studied the strange looking currency and was thankful that at least the different denominations were a different size and colour, unlike American notes. She could never fathom why different dollar denominations were the same size and colour and unless scrutinized, each note looked the same. To the untrained eye a ten dollar note was practically identical to a hundred.

Pushing her luggage trolley out of the arrivals hall and towards the taxi rank, she felt for the first time in years, the Irish rain fall upon her face and kiss her lips. She could taste its purity. It welcomed her home, cleansing her doubts and breathed new life and determination into her. Sitting in the back of a taxi she gazed out at a rain soaked Dublin. The roads into the city were appalling and gridlocked and the weather didn't help. Traffic it seemed had come to a standstill. 'It's the road works on the M50' said the taxi driver apologetically, are they ever going to finish the bloody thing?' Claire felt there was something appealing about rain, not standing in it, but observing it. She recalled as a child, seeking refuge behind the timber shed, gazing out at stony walls covered in lush green moss, sopping wet and listening to the raindrops fall from rusted gutters above her head, their distinctive 'plopping' sound nurturing the soil while cattle grazed oblivious on far off hills covered in a misty gauze, as the sheets of rain drifted sideways in, like the strokes of an artist brush across a canvas of patchwork fields.

Through the window she could see the signs of change. Dublin seemed to be one big construction site.

'American, are ya' enquired the taxi driver?
He was a small balding man in his fifties with a flat Dublin accent.

'I live in New York,' said Claire.

'On holidays?'

'Sort of.'

What a nice word 'holiday' was she mused. It must have its origins in the words 'holy day'. To her it conjured up religious images of rest and relaxation, of family, prayer, and contemplation. She smiled inwardly as she compared the English word 'holiday' to the American equivalent 'vacation'. To her the word vacation had always conjured up images of someone vacating, a burning building or a train for example. It was an act of fleeing. How ironic, she thought, though both words describe the same thing, each appears to mean something totally different. As she sat in the back of the taxi looking out at the droplets slinking down the window pane and listening to the rain beat upon the roof and the wipers squeaking as they rhythmically flicked from side to side, she wondered was she on a holiday, or a vacation? She knew only time would tell. The taxi driver glanced in his rearview mirror. Claire could sense him looking at her. She was glad when the traffic eventually began to move once more.

Now she had a chance to observe him for a change. She could see his hardened features and cold grey eyes in the mirror. As he held the steering wheel she noticed the letters I.R.A. crudely tattooed on the back of his tobacco stained fingers. Was he, she wondered? Would somebody actually be crazy enough to advertise the fact? She couldn't imagine a member of the 'Taliban' or 'Al Qaeda' being that daft. Had he ever been involved, or was he just one of the thousands of armchair republicans, who sipped their beers and secretly gloated at the death of some young British soldier, or cheered the success of a bombing campaign on mainland Britain. She was well aware there were two sides to this pitiful story and that atrocity had happened on both sides, but how after three hundred years could there still be so much bitterness and mistrust, so much hatred and pain and so much fear amongst the two communities? He caught her looking. She quickly averted her eyes, feeling a little uneasy and embarrassed.

'Will you be staying for long?'
Claire had heard it all her life. 'You Irish are such a friendly race' but she had always been a cynic. The Irish weren't friendly at all. They were inquisitive and nosey. They had this insatiable curiosity that forced them into conversation. It was their means of extracting information. Foreigners, she believed, often confused it with friendliness.

'A couple of months, maybe longer', she replied.

In New York, when they spoke to you, it was different, it wasn't personal. They didn't want to know if you were the cousin or the daughter of some Tom,

Dick, or Harry. They didn't care. They just wanted you to listen to their story of misfortune, the true account of their marriage break up, or their time in Vietnam. They saw you as some sort of shrink, somebody they could pour their hearts out to, without having to foot the bill. The Irish on the other hand kept their thoughts strictly to themselves. They were more cunning and calculated. How naïve to assume that just because somebody speaks to you, they should be deemed a friend?

The traffic was moving faster now and Claire wished he would concentrate on the road not the rearview mirror.

'Are you thinking of living here?'
She took a deep calming breath.

'Well yes actually, if you must know.'

'It's not that easy anymore.'

'What do you mean' she asked, totally confused?
He eyed her in the mirror.

'They're getting a lot stricter ya know, not letting as many people in. Mind ya, you stand a better chance than most. We've always had a close relationship with the Americans.'

'I'm sorry I'm not following you?'

'Immigrants' the country is swamped with them. I walked the length of O' Connell Street last Tuesday afternoon and I swear to God I didn't heard a single Irish accent.'

Claire was taken aback; the driver had mistaken her for a foreigner. Memories of her early days in New York came flooding back. She was being treated as an immigrant yet again, this time in her own country. She realized it had been a long time since she left and that she probably did look and sound American, but still his words upset her. The taxi crossed over the Liffey at Butt Bridge. She looked down towards the dockland area. The skyline was dissected like some massive abstract painting by the black angular lines of the countless cranes cramming the quays. Large impressively designed buildings stood where old rundown warehouses once blighted the cityscape.

'That's the Financial Centre,' said the driver. 'Look at the size of the other buildings, small wonder only the banks can afford them?'

'Yes, I suppose.'

She was lost in thought, had she become more American than Irish? She had lived nearly two-thirds of her life over there. Perhaps unconsciously she had adapted to life in New York, changing like a chameleon does, blending unobtrusively with her environs. She knew inwardly she had not changed, she was still the same person who left these shore all those years ago. She wondered if she had the strength to outwardly change yet again and continue from where she had left off.

'I'm not actually an immigrant,' she said. 'I was born here and I still hold my Irish passport.'

The driver looked into his mirror.

'Ah Jaysus' you're one of us then. I got it all wrong. Sorry about that love.'

Claire was glad that she had sorted that little bit of confusion out, she sat back satisfied but the silence was short lived.

'Ya must have been away for quite a while then, I take it?'

'Thirty-six years,' she acquiesced.

She was relieved to finally close the door of her hotel room behind her. She was tired and had not slept on the plane. Standing by the window she looked out on Grafton Street. It was late afternoon. She could see the hustle and bustle of a modern city, but something was different, something was missing. She watched as people sought shelter in doorways while others wore plastic bags upon their heads dashing through the sea of vibrantly coloured umbrellas as they scurried from store to store. Despite the inclement weather everything seemed oddly refreshing. Finally she realized what had been missing. Noise. There was no noise. Grafton Street was a pedestrian zone, free from the snarling traffic and honking horns that epitomized New York.

She stood looking at the grayness outside, watching the raindrops beat against the pavement, distorting the window displays reflected along the wet street and wondered. Had she actually come here of her own accord, or was it part of some pre-ordained plan. Was there something greater, guiding her every step, a bigger scheme of things above and beyond her control, was she the master of her own destiny, or simply a pawn in the game of life?

CHAPTER SEVEN
(IRELAND 2005)

The first months had been a difficult adjustment for Claire. Fitting in, had been more of an ordeal than she had imagined. She was confronted by many painful memories of the Ireland from which she had fled. At times she felt alone and isolated. She offered her services to the victims of industrial school abuse, but the supporters groups were wary and took their time, before being finally convinced of her genuine desire to help. When finally she was accepted, she became deeply involved and immersed herself in this new challenge. Through her work, friendships blossomed, and Claire gradually began to feel fulfilled.

Finding the right house in which to set up home had taken up a lot of her spare time. Eventually she fell in love with a beautiful period cottage, Primrose Lodge on the outskirts of the village of Enniskerry in County Wicklow, and decided to rent it. It was a quaint granite building; on its own grounds, with ivy clad walls and white latticed windows, situated in the beautiful Dargle valley, named after the small river that ran its course along the southern boundary of her garden before flowing into the Irish Sea at the town of Bray some four miles away.

Claire had no family in Ireland and it was such wonderful news when Gina rang to tell her they had accepted her invitation and were coming over for Christmas. Gina, Mike and Sophia were her only family now and Claire was overjoyed to see them. Despite the harrowing attempts made by commercial enterprise to hijack it, Christmas was still a time for family, a time to be with loved ones and to savour their company. They spent a wonderful time together exploring the beauty spots of Wicklow. Mike was more interested in the abundance of excellent golf courses and spent much time on the fairways while Gina, Sophia and Claire explored the countryside stopping off to enjoy afternoon tea in the quaint 'old world' settings of Tinakeely House or Hunters Hotel.

Their visit had a strange galvanizing effect on Claire. She felt relieved in the knowledge their friendship was stronger than ever. Despite the distance that separated them geographically, they were still a tightly knit unit. That summer Claire accepted their invitation and joined them in Venice and so it continued, each spending as much quality time with the other as possible.

Four years flew by. Claire wondered where the time went. She had settled in well and was happy, happier than she had been in years. She loved village life and had bought the cottage. She loved the sense of community. She loved taking a stroll along the secluded tree lined pathways of the Dargle valley dappled in morning sunlight, or walking to the village to sit in the local café and read the morning paper or simply have a chat with some of the locals. Though she was known affectionately as 'the lapsed Yank' nobody dared call her that to her face. Claire didn't mind really, she had encountered similar situations as a child. It was an affectionate part of village life.

She could recall her father discussing the local publican, known to one and all as the 'Bulldog

Breen' because of his unfortunately flat face, to this day she still did not know his real name, or 'Rasher' O' Reilly, so named because he was a thin streak of a man, or 'The Daw', so called, because of his lack of intellectual prowess. On reflection she was content; there were a lot worse names than the 'lapsed Yank.'

Her favourite place and one real sanctuary was her garden. She loved to spend her free time pruning and weeding the roses, or sitting on the garden bench reading a novel while listening to the trickle of water as it washed over the smooth stones nestled on the riverbed. When Claire was not working in her garden she was busy researching files to help in the battle with the 'Redress Board'. The board had been established by the Government to investigate the claims made by former inmates of the industrial schools with regard to compensation. Apparently it was possible or so 'the board' seemed to think, to evaluate in monetary terms the amount of physical and sexual abuse inflicted on different individuals. Most of the 'abused' were in the 'forty to seventy' age bracket. She regularly sat watching and listening as people told their stories. She listened with revulsion to accounts of rape and buggery. She watched people break down, and turn to shivering wrecks as they tried to relate their unspoken horrors. She tried to comfort mentally scarred women, who had committed the unthinkable; becoming unmarried mothers in their teens, and subsequently ending up in the 'laundry rooms' incarcerated like common criminals, to be used as slave labour for the next twenty years of their lives. She listened to stories of how the individuals responsible were protected by Church and State. Now, the poor unfortunate victims were forced to face their adversaries once more, in

49

the hope of seeking compensation, but above all in the hope of seeking justice. Claire was doing all in her power to help them.

Individuals from the religious orders were called by the board to counter claims made against them. Though some were guilty of serious offences, under the agreement made between the church and state, no individual could be imprisoned or punished for his or her crime. Claire knew the Tribunal was just a shambolic attempt to pacify the masses.

'There never was, nor will there ever be, justice in this world.'

How prophetic those words uttered by that young black mother on a New York commuter train, all those years ago now seemed.

|Claire seized this opportunity to expose the wrongdoings of Church and State. Everywhere she went she brought the plight of the victims to the fore, often to the annoyance of older generation Catholics, who simply refused to believe anything untoward had ever taken place.

CHAPTER EIGHT

Bill O' Malley sipped a coffee in the canteen of R.T.E. the national television station. The early afternoon sun filtered in through the large windows and he was thankful the place was not busy. Spreading the Irish Times in front of him he began to read.

O' Malley was a handsome man in his late thirties, tall and well-built, having once played inter-provincial rugby before being forced to retire with cartilage problems. His hair, light brown and tightly cut receded at the temples and he was casually dressed in a 'Chino' slacks and light blue short-sleeved shirt. Employed as a researcher, he traveled the length and breadth of the country arranging interviews and checking out filming locations.

A graduate of Trinity College Dublin, he attained an honours degree in history. Realizing a degree no longer meant an automatic job he decided to seek work abroad and spent a year in Melbourne, working as a junior sports reporter for the 'Melbourne News' and found himself a nice apartment on the 'Toorak Road'. Though the job was boring, he loved Melbourne and had a wonderful time. Later he went to Argentina, and because he couldn't speak Spanish, spent the best part of a year and a half working as a ranch hand for a wealthy family. The ranch consisted of over four thousand acres of rich pampas. An affair with the boss's daughter Katerina, resulted in him being sent packing despite her broken-hearted pleas to allow him stay. Finally he ended up in America spending a summer in San Francisco working as a barman before returning home. He applied for a temporary position in R.T.E. as a 'Trainee Researcher' and was shocked

when he was offered the job. That was eight years ago.
Two years later he was offered a permanent position as
a researcher. Though he liked the job he felt it lacked a
challenge and once again he was beginning to get itchy
feet. His mobile rang. He lowered the coffee cup and
pulled it from his pocket.

'Yes.

He took a pen from his pocket and began to write
down an address.

'Okay. Two o' clock. I'll be there.'

He put the phone back in his pocket, checked his
watch, folded the paper, drank his coffee and headed
for the door.

Bill sat in the middle of a traffic jam cursing
his luck as he headed for Malahide, a seaside town
twenty kilometres north of Dublin. In two minds as to
whether he should take the coast road or the M1 he
opted for the motorway thinking perhaps it might be
marginally quicker. His task was to organizing a piece
to camera, an in-house term, for an interview to be
televised the following night on a current affairs
program. He rolled down the window of his silver
1977 Volkswagen 'Beetle' and lit a cigarette. He was
not a heavy smoker and reserved the use of cigarettes
mainly for social occasions and the odd nerve calming
emergency. He could feel the warm sun on his arm as
the car inched its way through the city traffic. At times
like this he dreamt of working for some big American
Television station with its own 'News' chopper. The
idea of being able to fly above the traffic enthralled
him. He vowed to get himself a pilot's license some
day. He hated traffic. He found it harder and more
frustrating to drive in traffic than any work he had ever
done in his life. He saw it as a form of torture,
invented by a series of sick Transport ministers, who
worked in cahoots with engineers, to ensure they

produced the most ineffective road systems imaginable He had read somewhere, that at the beginning of the twentieth century the average speed through Dublin city was twelve miles an hour and that was in a horse and carriage. Now over a century later, despite sixteen valve engines, man walking on the moon and the wealthy booking holiday flights to space, the average speed across Dublin city has dropped to eleven miles per hour. He exhaled deeply at the thought. Eventually he reached the M1 and traffic began to flow and gears other than first and second once more became an option.

As he neared the airport roundabout he noticed something strange, it appeared to be a person standing alone on the central island. At first he thought it was some student prank to attract attention to one of their many grievances. When he neared, he realized it was a lady and wondered how in God's name she got there and why? As he entered the traffic flow on the roundabout he could clearly see it was an elderly white haired woman. She looked surreal, out of place in her surroundings. She seemed distressed and his immediate concern was for her safety. Barging his way into the inner lane, he locked the steering. The old beetle rattled and the engine whined as he forced it over the kerb and unto to the central margin. A large truck slammed on its breaks. The infuriated driver pressed hard on the air horns and shook his fist.

'Fucking asshole' shouted a burly skin-head leaning from the passenger window.

Bill ignored his single fingered gesture and jumped from his car. The woman was still there, standing precariously close to the edge. She had her back to him He called out.

'Hello, are you okay. Do you need any help?'

She did not answer. He decided to approach her slowly
When he was within ten feet of her he raised his arms
in an attempt to attract her attention.

'Hello can I help', he shouted over the din of the
traffic.

There was no response. He could see her face now. It
was pale and wrinkled with age. Her dark eyes stared
blankly as if she was in some sort of trance.

'Hello.'

Still she did not react. He thought perhaps he could see
a tear trickle down her cheek and moved closer.
Suddenly the old lady raised her hands to her head and
screamed. To his horror, without looking she stepped
down from the kerb right into the path of an oncoming
truck. The violent screech of tyres assaulted Bill's
ears. A pungent smell of burning rubber filled the air.
He held his head at the sickening thud of impact. The
woman shot into the air, tossed like a rag doll thirty
metres down the road. He felt his stomach heave. Cars
braked and swerved and despite the din, Bill could
hear the dull thump of her body hit the tarmac. He
glanced at the deformed and twisted torso, a sea of
blood now flowing from it like an a bright red aura,
contrasting with the blackness of tarred surface upon
which she lay. Bill held his mouth and fought the
retching in his stomach. The truck driver, ashen faced,
climbed gingerly from his cab, momentarily dazed,
before summoning enough strength to walk towards
the bloodied mess.

CHAPTER NINE

Bill sat on a wooden chair in Pearse Street, Garda Station. Inspector O'Neill sat at the far side of his desk. It was a stuffy dark attic room, cramped and cluttered with files. A desk fan purred out welcome relief from the stifling heat, causing dust particles to swirl in the dry air, backlit by single shaft of light spilling through a small half open widow behind him. An angle poise lamp illuminated the lower half of O'Neill's face leaving his eyes darkened. Bill guessed he was in his late forties. He was bald and had the build of a wrestler. Bill could see his big hands illuminated in the pool of yellow tungsten light. He was holding a pen and flicking the ballpoint impatiently with his thumb. He could hear the snap of the spring as it engaged and disengaged repeatedly. O'Neill slapped the pen down upon the desk before him. He leant back on his chair and placed his hands behind his head.

'What in Christ's name were you playing at O' Malley, trying to get yourself a big scoop or what?'
Bill was surprised at the aggressive tone in O'Neill's voice.

'I was just trying to help her, for God sake, that's all.' '

'What made you think she needed help?'

'For fuck sake, she was standing in the middle of a roundabout on a busy motorway,' he snapped back.

'No need for bad language O'Malley.'
Bill was angry at being treated like criminal.

'She obviously managed to walk to the centre island, what made you think she couldn't walk back?

'She could have been disorientated, even dumped there for all you know, but hey, you don't really give a shit. To you she's just a statistic, nothing more.'

'No need for the theatrics, O'Malley.'

He tossed O'Neill an angry look.

'Hey, I was christened. I have a first name you know. It's Bill.'

'Okay Bill, what the fuck you were doing, driving on to the centre island of a roundabout? You could have got yourself, or worse still, innocent people killed. I have a good mind to rescind your driving license and put you behind bars.'

Bill craved a cigarette.

'The poor old dear looked traumatized. I felt she needed help.'

'What have we here, an expert in psychology?'

Bill shuffled in his chair. His voice was firm and controlled.

'No' but I'm lucky enough to have been brought up to respect people. If I think somebody needs help, then I'll do all in my power to help them.'

Outside, on a raised section of track a commuter train rumbled past causing the small window frame to vibrate. Bill could see the people crammed like sardines in the light green carriages as it trundled by and wished he was one of them.

'Very noble of you, O'Malley.'

'Bill. My name's Bill.'

O'Neill leant forward illuminating his face once more in the tungsten light. This time, he could see the cold blue of his eyes.

'Can you imagine the chaos there would be, if everyone starting sticking their noses into other people's business, just because they felt like it. How would you feel if some 'do-gooder' came up to you in the pub and told you; to go home because you've already had two beers', without even bothering his arse to find out if you were actually driving a car or not?'

A fly landed on the desk. O'Neill raised his hand. It flew away. Bill shook his head. It was like he was arguing with a stone wall.

'Why were you harassing her?'

Bill was now beginning to doubt O'Neill's sanity. 'What the fuck are you insinuating now' bellowed Bill.

'Language.'

O'Neill's face turned red and a dark blue vein bulged on his forehead. The fly landed once more. O' Neill's hand crashed down squashing it against a newspaper. He flicked it away with his finger.

'Why were you harassing her' he demanded?

Bill was not going to be intimidated. He roared back.

'I wasn't fucking harassing her.'

O'Neill raised his finger.

'Take it easy boy, or I'm warning you, you'll end up in the slammer!'

'Oh yeah!'

'Don't toy with me O'Malley!'

'I wasn't harassing her. You're the fucking harasser around here.'

O' Neill lifted the receiver.

'Do you want me to have you locked up?'

Bill backed off. O' Neill replaced the receiver. .

'Since when has trying to help someone, become harassment?'

'Did you know the woman?'

'I've told you a dozen times, I never saw her before in my life.'

'But you told me you work in current affairs?

'Was that a lie?

'No'

O'Neill lifted the 'Evening Herald' and opened it. He leafed through the pages and passed it over. Bill took the paper and looked at the open page. On it, much to his surprise was a photograph of the woman he had tried to help. O' Neill studied his reaction.

'How current does it have to be Bill? That was taken this morning at the 'Tribunal into Child Abuse'.

Bill read the sub text; '**Sister Agnes leaves the Tribunal after her acquittal**' Bill handed the paper back to O'Neill. He now understood the reasoning behind the questions and softened his tone.

'I swear I had no idea who she was. I've never covered any of the Tribunals.'

O'Neill gazed coldly at him as he folded the paper.

'Do you really expect me to believe that?'

'Believe what you want, it's the truth.'

'I'd expect somebody in 'current affairs' to be a little more informed than that.'

Bill was annoyed, he was being professionally ridiculed now, and O'Neill was rubbing his nose in it. He conceded.

'I know where you're coming from, I know what you're thinking, but you have to believe me when I say, I really had no idea who she was.'

Don't you think it's a bit of a coincidence that out of all of the people who drove by that roundabout today, the only person crazy enough to mount the kerb and attempt to talk to her was a reporter?'

'I told you I'm not a reporter, I'm a researcher.'

'Reporter, researcher, who cares, a media person was the last person to talk to her before she supposedly committed suicide.' She could have been running away from you for all we know.'

Bill shook his head.

'I didn't know who she was.'

O' Neill softened his tone. He leant back once more on his chair. For a moment neither man spoke. Bill became aware of the purring fan once more. Finally O'Neill spoke.

'Okay, you can go.'

Bill, relieved, took a deep intake of breath.

'But don't go anywhere without telling me. I might need to talk to you again in the next few days.'

Bill nodded relieved his ordeal had finally come to an end. O' Neill walked around his desk and approached him eyeballing him before he spoke.

'If I see or hear a word of this in the media before we inform the next of kin, or before an official statement is released, I'll have your arse in a sling. Do you understand?'

Bill didn't doubt his words

'Yes', he replied weakly.

O' Neill opened the door.

'In future, like a good man, stick to your own job, and let us get on with ours. Okay?

Bill didn't bother responding as he walked out into the bare timbered corridor. Floorboards squeaked under his weight as he headed down the back stairs towards the ground floor. A young attractive policewoman passed him on the stairwell. She smiled warmly restoring his faith in humanity. Shading his eyes he stepped out into the bright sunlight on Pearse Street and headed for his car. Despite a written note left on the dashboard explaining his predicament and whereabouts, his car had been clamped. 'Fucking Bastards' he bellowed. Amused 'passers-by' watched as he began kicking the wheel of his 'beetle' in frustration. 'Scumbags. 'Nothing but fucking scumbags.' It was now half-four and his day was well and truly ruined. He reached for his mobile and made a call.

Later in the sanctuary of his local pub 'The Harbour Bar' in Bray, Bill ordered himself a pint. It had been a fisherman's pub in years gone by with a bare flagstone floor and old stripped pine tables and chairs. The bar was small and full of old brique-a-brac hanging from the walls and ceiling. A large television mounted in the corner was a throwback to the exhilarating days of Jack Charlton and the Irish soccer team of the 'nineties' when the country was riding on a wave of euphoria having reached the quarter finals in its first appearance at the World Cup Finals in 1990. To be without a television in those heady days was commercial suicide. Many people accredit the Irish teams performance with the birth of the 'Celtic Tiger'. The Irish as a nation realized probably for the first time, that they could hold their own with the best in the world and began to believe in themselves. That summer of 1990, people, lived, ate, and of course drank soccer.

Bill regularly went for a quite pint after a day's work. He loved to relax and read the paper and enjoy a few pints before going home to make his supper. He opened the Evening Herald and studied the picture of Sister Agnes. He was still shaken from his ordeal, and could not get the horrific images out of his head. He lifted the pint to his parched lips and took a long satisfying swig. The six o clock news was commencing. Had she meant to kill herself, he wondered, or was she even aware of where she was?

If she had committed suicide, why? Why choose such a horrific end? An overdose of tablets seemed so painless in comparison. His attention was drawn to the television. A newscaster was reading the headlines.

Government to Pay Compensation to Victims. 'Now to our reporter Emer Curtin at the 'Child abuse Tribunal' Bill spun on the stool. Pictures were being relayed live. A female stood before the camera.

Reporter:

'There were mixed emotions here today, as a chapter was finally closed in Irish history. A chapter that was synonymous with all that was wrong with Irish society. A chapter, of terrifying abuse perpetrated by those who were trusted and considered 'pillars of Irish society' upon those who were most vulnerable and most in need of their protection. A chapter, where evil was swept under the carpet, and a 'blind eye' turned by those who could, and should have done something, to prevent this tragedy. Perhaps in this regard we are all guilty, to some degree. I have with me one of the leading campaigners of 'justice for the victims of child abuse'. This woman has fought tirelessly on behalf of the voiceless and the forgotten in our society. She herself joined the convent as a novice, but soon realized that she could not condone the abuse meted out to children and left, disillusioned. We know now, sadly too late, such abuse was rampant in the orphanages and industrial schools throughout the country'.

The camera pans to Claire.

Q. 'Claire Conlon how do you see the outcome of today's events?

A. 'I'm suffering mixed emotions. I feel happy that at last the victims will be compensated in some small way. Money was never the issue here. It was about justice, about a country holding up its hand and admitting finally, that it has done wrong. A country, that tried every trick in the book to suppress and intimidate the victims into silence, a country, that tried its living best, to break the support groups before they became a threat, a country that tried to cover up it's sinister past.

Q. How do you feel about the acquittals?

A. I think it was obvious from the start, that there was no hope of putting the guilty behind bars. The Church and the State are still bedfellows, each looking after their own interests. Whilst I am disappointed with this particular outcome, I have to say I am not in the least bit surprised. Real justice will never be achieved. How many helpless children died, under the most suspicious of circumstances, while in the care of these institutions? How many innocent souls lie in unmarked graves right across the length and breadth of this country, buried, under the cover of darkness, by faceless murderers?'

How many children lie forgotten, with neither a death certificate, nor a doctor's report, in their cold graves? What justice did they get today? I don't think the countless unmarked graves in Letterfrack, or Artane, or the numerous convents around the country, should ever be forgotten. It is up to the good, upstanding citizens of Ireland to make sure we never forget. Their memories should be enshrined in our hearts. We still need answers. We are not just talking 'abuse' here, we are talking 'death' and 'murder' at the hands of those, in whose care they were entrusted. This country will never fulfill its true potential until it has the courage and the backbone to admit to its own 'holocaust'. We owe 'the forgotten' at the very least, a memorial. I challenge you politicians out there, to stop hiding in the corridors of power, and fight for the justice and dignity they deserve. Before I finish, I would like to take this opportunity to thank 'Pat.'

''Pat' you have been my strength and inspiration. Today was for you.' The camera panned back to the reporter; 'On that poignant note, I hand you back to the studio'.

Bill turned away. He was struck by the passion and the venom of Claire's words. He took out his notebook and carefully wrote her name into it. As he sipped his pint, he pondered on her outrageous comments, 'Unmarked graves? Faceless murderers? He wondered could there possibly be any connection between this and the suicide he had witnessed earlier that day.

CHAPTER TEN

It was a glorious Saturday morning in Enniskerry. Bill drove through the quiet picturesque village past the monument in the square. The clock face on the tower read 10.15. Even at this relatively late hour, the streets were deserted save for one old lady out walking her dog. She was leaning forward as she slowly negotiated the steep hill. In her hand she held a newspaper and a litre of milk. Her dog ran ahead eagerly sniffing the lampposts and cocking his leg. Bill drove up to her and lowered the car window. He checked the address written in his notebook.

'Good morning. I'm looking for directions to Primrose Lodge?'

The old lady seemed glad to have the opportunity to stop and take a little breather. She walked towards the car and leant on the window.

'Is it the Yank, you're looking for' she enquired breathlessly?

'Eh…. Claire Conlon actually.'

'That's her all right.'

Bill smiled in amusement.

'Go down to the bottom of the hill and take a right turn. It's about a mile outside the village on the left hand side. It's just after the bridge you can't miss it.'

'Do you need a lift anywhere?

The old lady smiled.

'Does it show that much? I'm fine thank you I'm just home.'

Bill thanked her and drove back down the hill.

He had decided the previous evening he must talk to Claire. He didn't know if she would be at home, and if she was, would she even talk to him? Perhaps she could shed some light on yesterday's tragedy. Continuing his way along the small road skirting the river he spotted a fisherman standing knee high in the sparkling water. Bill stopped his car and stepped out. He leant against a moss-covered wall gazing down. The angler wore green waders a jacket and a hat. An odd shaped pipe hung from his mouth nearly resting on his chin. Behind him an old granite bridge spanned the river. It was ivy covered and dappled with what light had managed to penetrate the heavy foliage of the nearby trees. He was fly fishing, casting his line downstream, flicking it to and fro, in one flowing movement. The air smelt of honeysuckle and Bill filled his lungs. A little distance away a heron stood on rock scouring the flowing waters. Sensing the unwelcome intrusion, it lifted its wings tucked its head to its breast and lifted itself slowly into the air like some prehistoric creature, heading to a safer spot a little further downstream.

Bill observed the wily old angler, a solitary figure, in a backdrop of rich greens, pulling gently on his pipe through pursed lips; wafting little billows of blue grey smoke across his brown weather beaten face and out over the rim of his tartan tweed hat. He observed the spectacle with delight, privileged to witness at first hand this dying art. He watched fascinated, as the fine line, backlit by the morning sun drifted to and fro like some restless gossamer through the blue heavens. He listened intently to the silence, free of a single motor, or a distant voice, as pure now as it had been two thousand years ago. Yet, in that silence he could hear the ripple of the clear flowing water and the sporadic 'coo' of a wood pigeon in the sanctuary of a nearby wood and the ever present heart beat and subtle sighs of Mother Nature. A dark foreboding cloud drifted through his mind as he recalled the horrors of the previous day. Why had she done it, he wondered? Life can be so beautiful. Unable to make any sense of the tragedy, he brushed it from his mind and called down. to the fisherman.

'Lovely morning.'

The man acknowledged him without breaking his rhythm.

'Indeed it is,' he replied in a rich West Brit accent.

'Are they biting?'

'Not yet, but everything comes to those who wait.'

'I'm looking for 'Primrose Lodge,' Claire Conlon's place'

'Ah Claire.' 'Lovely Lady'…'I was'…

A trout broke the surface of the water. He stopped mid sentence, his facial expression suddenly serious. He lowered his voice.

'Did you see it?'

Bill nodded.

'I sure did. It was a beauty.'

The old boys face lit up.

'I reckon it was a two pounder, at least.'

'Was it a salmon' asked Bill, not wanting to sound an idiot?

The old man chuckled in disbelief.

'A two pound Salmon?'

Bill shrugged his shoulders, a blank expression on his face.

'Good Lord, it was a rainbow trout, the salmon around these parts can weigh up to fourteen pounds'. 'Of course, how silly of me,' said Bill unconvincingly.

Another trout rose. Bill caught a glimpse of the silver underbelly as it arched sideways, tail fin flapping, before it vanished back into the watery glaze. The old man steadied himself before whispering.

'Oh yes, Claire. Her house is the second on the left after you cross the bridge, you can't miss it.'
Bill gave him a friendly wave.

'Thank you. Good luck with the fishing.'

Not breaking his rhythm, the fisherman replied.

'You're welcome.'

Bill now stood outside Claire's home. It was hidden behind the wall of an old estate, an ornate metal plaque bearing the name Primrose Lodge was affixed to one of the pillars of the main gate. He stood looking in at the gravel driveway bordered with wonderful flowers leading up to an impressive house nestled beneath the shade of some copper beech trees. A metallic gold V.W. Golf was parked in the drive. He felt a little nervous. He hoped he wasn't calling too early or at an inopportune moment.

The old gate squeaked as he pushed it open and the wonderful smell of roses and fruit trees reached his nostrils as he strolled up the gravel path leading to the front door. It appeared to be a haven of tranquility. He could not find a bell so he tapped gently on the brass knocker. Inside, Clare sat at the kitchen table in her dressing gown and slippers drinking coffee and reading the 'Irish Times'. She was engrossed in an article on the events at the tribunal. She sighed at this untimely interruption. Whipping off her reading glasses, she wrapped her dressing gown tightly around her and headed reluctantly to the front door.

Outside Bill could hear a bolt being moved and a key turning in the lock. Claire popped her head around the half opened door.

'Good Morning, my name is Bill O' Malley.'
She spoke in warm soft tones.

'How can I help you,' she asked politely.
Bill was surprised. He had not noticed her American accent on the television, but then television and American accents were synonymous with each other.

'I saw your interview on the television last night and was fascinated. I'd love to talk a little about it if I may?

'Are you a reporter,', she enquired?
Bill did not want to lie.

'I do work for R.T.E. but I'm not a reporter, I'm a researcher and I'm here in a strictly private capacity.'
 She began to close the door.

'I'm sorry I have nothing to say. Now if you wouldn't mind excusing me?'

'Please just one moment. I need some answers.'

'I have nothing to say, please leave.'
Bill felt the moment slipping away. He was desperate.

'Does the name Sister Agnes mean anything to you?'
Claire half opened the door once more, her face betraying her anger.

'Of course it does, everybody knows she was one of the defendants at the tribunal. Is this your idea of a joke?'
He realized he had hit a raw nerve.

'I'm afraid I have some dreadful news.'

'What do you mean?'

'I'm sorry; I don't know if I should tell you this.'

'Is this about Sister Agnes' she enquired?
Bill nodded.

'Has something happened to her?'
 Claire watched as he struggled to find the right words. Eventually he blurted out.

68

'She's dead.'

'You must be mistaken.'

'I'm afraid not.'

'Yesterday afternoon I witnessed her commit suicide.'

Claire's face could no longer contain her shock.

'Suicide? What are you saying?'

'She stepped out in front of an oncoming truck at the Airport roundabout.'

Claire put her hands to her lips.

'How do you know it was her?'

'I recognized her from the photograph in last night's paper. It was her all right.'

'Could this be the fatality on the M1, announced on the radio this morning?'

'I presume so. They cannot release her name until they inform the next of kin.'

Claire opened the door.

'You better come in.'

CHAPTER ELEVEN

Sunlight poured in through the leaded windows spilling across the intricately woven patterns on the Persian rug. The room was large with thick oak beams supporting the low ceiling. The focal point of the room was a black marble fireplace, delicately carved, with an ornate copper canopy. Above the mantle piece, was a Victorian mahogany inlaid mirror. A matching pair of blue hand painted vases stood at either side. Each depicted a scene of rural life. Bill did not know a lot about antiques but suspected they might be French. A bookcase crammed with leather bound books stood to the right of the fireplace. A small table with a lighted tiffany lamp stood beside one of the burgundy red velvet chairs of the chesterfield suite. On the table lay an open book and some scribbled notes. A baby grand piano its lid closed and strewn with various documents and photos stood in the corner. Bill stood admiring the room.

'I'm sorry it's a bit of a mess at the moment' she shouted from the kitchen.

Bill smiled, thankful she couldn't see his flat.

'Make yourself at home I'll be with you in a couple of minutes.'

Some family photos hung on the wall. Bill wandered over to have a look. The first he presumed was a portrait of her parents. Noticing the speckled shell encased in the mahogany frame he wandered over and read the inscription;

The Chocolate Flamed Venus
Clifton 1963

On the far wall was the photo of Claire and Tim taken just before their engagement.

'Oh that was such a long time ago I'm afraid' said Claire, as she entered the room.

She had dressed and was carrying a silver tray with freshly brewed coffee and some fruit cake. She placed it on the coffee table.

'Milk and sugar,' she enquired?

'Two please and a little milk, thank you'.

Bill sat down on one side of the settee Claire on the other.

'I'm sorry if I was a bit abrupt at the door. I am very cautious of the media.'

She smiled as she continued;

'It's ironic, without the media we would never have gotten this far. It's such a powerful weapon, and it's imperative to our cause that we feed it only the right ammunition'.

'Thank you for allowing me to talk to you Miss Conlon.' I want to assure you once more I am not a journalist, and I am here strictly in a private capacity.'

'Please call me Claire'. Now how can I help' she enquired?

He stirred his coffee searching for an honest answer.

'The truth is I don't really know if you can. Perhaps you might be able to shed some light on a couple of things.'

'What for example?

He placed the spoon gently back on the saucer and looked in her eyes.

'Yesterday? What could possibly drive somebody to take their own life in such a hideous way, and why were you angry when I mentioned Sister Agnes's name?'

She sensed his bewilderment.

'Before I try to answer your questions, please tell me what happened, Mr. O' Malley?

There was urgency in her voice.

'Call me Bill.'

Her eyes scanned his face.

'What makes you think it was suicide, Bill,'

'I tried talking to her. She looked so lost, so alone on the centre island. I didn't know what to do, so I mounted the kerb in my car and slowly walked towards her. I called out, asking if she was okay but she didn't respond. It's hard to explain. It was as if I wasn't there, or she wasn't there. Then before I had a chance to stop her, she stepped off the kerb and straight into the path of an oncoming truck.'

Claire winced and lowered her head. For a moment neither one spoke. In the silence Bill could hear the tick of the grandfather clock in the hall. When Claire eventually lifted her head she again gazed into the empty fire place. Bill broke the silence.

'I'm sorry. I seem to make a habit of upsetting you.'

Taking a deep breath, she turned to him.

'It's not your fault. How were you to know?' '

Know what' he enquired softly.

A cloud crossed over the sun. The room darkened. Shadows snaked across the Persian carpet. She smiled weakly.

'To answer your first question, I have to say I honestly don't know. We all have our demons and regrets. Perhaps Sister Agnes had one too many.'

The grandfather clock struck eleven, its deep tones sounding uncannily like a death knell. Bill sipped his coffee and waited till it died away.

'And my other question?'

72

Claire looked him directly in the eye.

'To put it mildly, Sister Agnes and I were adversaries.'

'I see.'

She lifted the plate from the tray and offered him some cake.

'Please. Have some.'

He declined gracefully.

'I have to admit I watched your interview last night. It shocked and frightened me. Do you really think there are children lying in unmarked graves?'

Claire glanced out into the garden.

'Yes' she said, taking a shallow breath.

Bill waited for her to elaborate but she didn't.

'You thanked a Pat, for your inspiration last night. Who is Pat?

Claire's eyes moistened. For a moment she said nothing. Bill felt dreadful.

'I'm so sorry.'

The sunlight returned, creeping slowly back into the room brightening everything but the mood. Wiping a tear away, she turned and spoke.

'It's ok I'll be fine.

Shaking her head slowly she continued.

'It's ironic that you should ask me about Pat, especially after telling me the news about Sister Agnes.

'Forgive me, I don't understand.'

Claire held the cup between her hands as if trying to warm them from the chill she felt inside.

'If you have the time I'll try to explain?'

'I'm in no hurry,' he assured her.

Bill listened as she began to speak softly recalling her past.

CHAPTER TWELVE
(Ireland 1963)

'Tuesday, June 25th. 1963 was a special day in my
life. I was only eighteen. The whole country was
excited. John F. Kennedy the first Irish Catholic to
be elected president of The United States of
America had come to Ireland to visit the birthplace
of his Grandfather at Dunganstown. It was the first
time world attention had been focused on our little
nation and every man woman and child in the
country felt a sense of pride'
I watched a documentary on that very subject, last
week' added Bill.
Claire smiled.
   'I saw it too. It was good, but nothing could capture
   the euphoria of his visit.'
She continued.
   'My mother brought me on a special outing to New
   Ross to see him. It was less than twenty miles from
   where we lived, yet I was as excited as if we were
   about to embark on a mission to Mars. I stood in the
   crowd before the podium they had erected opposite
   the Albatross factory on the north side of the river.
   The anticipation of his arrival was electric. Finally
   we saw the cavalcade and the whole place erupted..
   Kennedy smiled and waved as he mounted the
   podium.'
   'It must have been amazing' said Bill, as he
   watched her face light up.
   'It was. I was less than thirty feet away from him.
   The first thing that struck me was his handsome
   face. He had the looks of a film star, with healthy

74

tanned skin, an infectious smile and large pearly white teeth. The crowd broke into spontaneous applause when he announced that had it not been for his grandfather emigrating, he too might have ended up working in Albatross.

'A fertilizer factory, wasn't it?'

'That's right. There was an outpouring of love for him which I have never witnessed since. This young man was returning home as the most powerful man in the World. Ireland was celebrating the return of its famous son. He had led the way and shown us what we all could achieve. To the citizens of this young nation, he was the epitome of all that was good about being Irish

'He must have been an inspiration to so many?'

'He was, believe me.'

Her expression changed.

'Ironically he was departing Ireland the same day I was leaving home. My mother, dressed in her Sunday best, stood with me by the side of the road outside our house waiting for the ten o' clock bus that would take me to Dublin and finally on to the convent which I was about to enter as an novice. I was so excited I could hardly contain myself. It was the beginning of a new chapter in my life. Each minute seem like an hour as I waited. Finally the bus arrived and I kissed my mother goodbye. She clutched a handkerchief tightly in her hand and wiped back her tears. I ran to the back of the bus and waved as it slowly pulled away. My poor mother stood crying and waving her hanky. I stood watching as she and everything I had ever known and held dear, gradually faded into the distance. My heart ached for her. I was gone. My father had died two years previously, and now she had lost her only child. I felt I was deserting her, leaving her to struggle on alone. I was confused and felt pangs of guilt rise inside me. It was a sacrifice we both made. Back then life seemed so full of sacrifice. I told myself it would be worth it in the end. I was giving my life to the service of God'.

'People had to make hard decisions back then' Bill added supportively.

She poured him some more coffee, and continued.

'The journey seemed to take forever. I spent that night in Westport. I chose a small hotel run by a German couple. It was the first time I had ever slept in a hotel and the first time I had ever seen a duvet.' She laughed at her own naivety, 'at first I thought it was a mistake and that they had forgotten to put some blankets on the bed. Imagine my embarrassment when I complained at reception I was mortified.'

Bill smiled.

'The next day I left early to complete my journey. It was a glorious summer morning. I sat by a window on the old bus as it wound its way along the mountain roads, trying to take in as much of this alien landscape as I could. 'Mayo has some spectacular scenery' he added.

'I remember my heart was bursting with joy. I felt a sense of serenity and strength inside me as if I had been touched by the hand of God.'

She lifted the coffee cup to her lips and took a drink.

Bill could sense the spirituality of the woman.

'Eventually the bus groaned to a halt outside the gates of the orphanage.

'I stood on the road as the conductor climbed up the ladder and lifted my suitcase from the roof. He pressed a half-crown into my palm and asked me to say a prayer for him. I told him he didn't have to   pay me I would gladly pray for him. He smiled warmly. 'Take it anyway Sister, as a good luck token. 'I thanked him. He wished me a happy life, as he climbed back on board. I stood rubbing the warm coin in my hand, my suitcase by my side, watching as the bus slowly pulled away. I listened as it faded further and further till eventually all I could hear was the bleating of a distant flock of sheep and the busy chatter of the birds nestled in the nearby hedgerows. Putting the coin carefully in my pocket I grabbed the suitcase and headed for the gates.'

'It had a wrought iron arch bearing the name St. Joseph's Orphanage above the main entrance. I looked up and read the words over and over. This was to be my home. This was where I would work and serve God, possibly till my dying day. I could see a potholed avenue shaded by chestnut trees, winding its way towards the main building. As I entered through the large iron gates I passed a quaint little gate lodge on my right. A cluttered clothes line sagging with nappies told me there were children living there. At the end of the avenue I got my first full view of Saint Josephs itself. It took my breath away. It was grey granite building, gothic-like in structure, standing alone, rising from its surroundings like some Transylvanian picture postcard. I stopped to take in the splendor of the place before I proceeded up to the main door.'

Claire turned to Bill.

'I'm sorry I'm probably boring you to death.'
'Please, don't stop, I'm fascinated.'

As she continued to relate her story Bill was transported by the magic of her words back in time. Back to 1963 and the orphanage.

CHAPTER THIRTEEN
(MAYO 1963)

The school bell rang out, piercing the still morning air, echoing down the valley, calling the reluctant pupils to their studies. Soon a chorus of children could be heard, calling out their 'five-times tables' their voices drifting through the tall open windows drifting out into the silence of the remote valleys and hillsides

Sister Claire stood by the blackboard. She was new to the orphanage, and brim full of the enthusiasm only one so naive, could possibly have. She held a cane in her hand, pointing to the tables she had written down. It was a large room with a high flaking ceiling. A dark wood stained wainscoting about four foot high encircled the room. Above, old maps and charts hung on the dull grey walls. The children all between the ages of six and ten sat in pairs in their school desks. They shouted out, 'five-threes are fifteen', 'five-fours are twenty', five-fives, and so on. Her class consisted of about fourteen young boys between the ages of seven and ten. Each head of hair was shorn tightly at the back and sides and full on top. They wore ill fitting jumpers frayed and torn at the elbows. Their short trousers were heavily patched. Some children wore their braces outside their jumpers making them look a little absurd. Their socks were darned and their boots and shoes had seen better days. Their little faces betrayed their utter boredom and indifference not only to maths, but to schooling in general. Claire had a wholesome young face, plain yet oddly pretty, with bright blue eyes. She seemed to genuinely enjoy

79

teaching the children, and despite her efforts to educate them, they seemed to like her. When they had finished she walked towards them .

'Who can tell me what six times five equals?'

There were no apparent takers amongst the children.

She pointed to a boy sitting at the front of the class. 'You 'Tommy, can you tell me what six times five equals?'

Tommy was big for his nine years, with a chubby cheeks and a red complexion. The children nicknamed him 'Tubby'. Slowly he stood up.

'I don't know Sister.'

'Why not Tommy?'

'We haven't learned our 'six times' tables yet Sister.'

'I see', she said, disappointedly.

'You may sit back down.'

She looked to the rest of the class. The children tried sheepishly to avoid eye contact.

'Is there any boy in class who can tell me what six times five equals?'

At first there was no reaction. Exasperation showed on her faced. Finally a hand rose at the back of the class.

'Ah Pat, can you tell me the answer?'

Pat stood up. He was small, eight years old, possibly the smallest in the class. His face was pale and freckled. His carrot red hair complimented his bright blue eyes.

'Six times five equals thirty, Sister.'

Her face beamed with delight.

'Very good Pat, will you explain to the rest of the class how you got this answer.'

'Six times five is the same as five times six, Sister. We have just learned that five sixes are thirty.'

'Excellent Pat, what a clever little boy you are.'

The other kids in the class turned towards him making faces and jeering, hoping he might laugh.

'Teacher's pet, whispers Joseph, as he sat back down.

'I'm just trying to help you dunces' whispered Pat through the side of his mouth.

Joseph was a year older than Pat and quite a bit taller. They hung around together all the time. Joseph was pale skinned and had a cow's lick in his hair. Unfortunately for him, his ears stuck out and turned bright red when he exerted himself even slightly. They were a constant source of amusement to the other children, and the butt of many a joke. Sister Claire addressed the class in a motherly way.

'Now let that be an example to you all. If a problem seems difficult don't panic, try to simplify it. We know for example that 'three-sevens are twenty-one', so if we need to know what seven times six is, we know it must be twice that, which is forty-two.

She smiled warmly at the children.

'It's that easy.'

Half the class stared back, dumbfounded by her logic.

'What in Jaysus, is she on about' whispered Joseph?

Pat plucked some wool from the sleeve of his gaudy green hand knitted jumper and rolled it into a ball.

'Must be some sort of rocket science. What's the score?'

'It's three one to me' said Joseph

'Tis not. Ya cheat.'

'Okay its two one to me.'

'That's better' whispered Pat, 'first to five wins.' Joseph carefully removed the two white ceramic inkwells and lay them on the desk. Pat placed the little wool ball on the bench. The rules were simple. Whoever managed to get the wool ball in the opponent's inkwell scored a goal. The two began to blow as discretely as possible. Their attention was drawn to the familiar squeak of the classroom door. They quickly curtailed their endeavors. Reverend Mother entered. She was a short stocky nun with a ruddy face and jowls of a bulldog. She wore thick bottle rimmed glasses that pinched her fleshy face making her eyes appear tiny and situated somewhere in the back of her head.

She walked with a slight limp causing her to roll like a boat on a rough sea. The kids called her Hopalong, behind her back of course. Though she was only in her early fifties, the children reckoned she must be 'at least a thousand. Quickly they sat up in their seats not wishing to incur her wrath. She hobbled her way to the top of the class and turned to face the children.

'Excuse me, Sister Claire.'

'Of course, Reverend Mother.'

Sister Claire retreated to the wall that held a tattered canvas map of Ireland. It hung like an ancient scroll on two timber poles and was made of some strange glossy canvas, cracked and broken with veins of antiquity. Curiously, the map contained no political border between north and south and the canvas was ripped on the side making the Shannon estuary look more like the Amazon delta. Hopalong held an envelope in her hands. Her face broke into a broad smile. The children gave a little sigh of relief.

'Well boys it's that time of year again', she said in her Derry accent. 'Tomorrow is Wednesday the 10th, the day we go on our annual outing.'

Excitedly, the children mumbled and shuffled in their seats. She dropped her smile and raised her voice.

'Quiet, while I am speaking.'

The children froze.

'As last year's trip to the beach was such a huge success, we have decided this time, to visit Clifden Bay for the day.'

The children's reactions were mixed.

'Shit not the beach again' whispered Joseph.

Pat covered his mouth with his hand and whispered,

'I told you so.'

Hopalong turned back to the class.

'As always, I expect you to be on your best behavior. Anybody, who steps out of line in any way, will have me or Sister Agnes to answer to. Those found guilty of misconduct will be made to peel potatoes during recreation for a whole week.

The children shuddered at the thought.

'Bollix to that' whispered Pat.

'One more thing' she added. We have received our summer sandals from our patrons, Coady & Sons, in Ballina.

She opened the envelope and withdrew a card. gesturing to Sister Claire.

'I would like each and every one of you to sign this 'Thank You Card'.'

Sister Claire took the card, and reached for a sheet of blotting paper. She slipped it inside the card and handed it to Tommy.

'When you're finished pass it on' she whispered.

Hopalong continued.

'Each of you will be issued with your new pair of sandals tomorrow morning, just before we leave for Clifden Bay. Sister Claire will make sure you all put your number on the inside. We don't want any squabbling as to who owns what, now do we?'

'No Reverend Mother' the children replied in unison.

Joseph received the card and the blotting paper from Stephen, the only black boy in the orphanage.

'Pass us your inkwell Golly, we don't have any ink in ours,' whispered Joseph.

Stephen carefully lifted the inkwell from its slot and passed it to Joseph who dipped his nib into the inkwell. The inkwell toppled and a large blob of black ink flowed onto the card.

'Oh shit,' he whispered, his face now white with fear.

Pat watched the ink flow down the card.

'Quick use the blotting paper,' he whispered.

Joseph stemmed the flow. He looked to Pat.

'Don't say a word.'

Each child signed the card with a Christian name followed by a number. Joseph nervously signed his 'Joseph 37'. Pat found a clean spot on the top corner and signed 'Pat 42'.

Though some children actually did have relations outside the orphanage and did know their family names, they were not allowed to use them and were identified within the system by a Christian name and a number. Pat had no idea what his real name was. He had never known his mother or father and had no idea if they were alive, or not.

Hopalong spoke. '

' You will also be receiving a new pair of white socks. I expect you all to look your very best. Don't forget that each and every one of you is an ambassador for St Joseph's.'

Sister Claire returned the card to Reverend Mother. She opened it. Her face reddened. She held the card up by the corner pointing to the ink stain.

'Who's responsible for this,' she demanded.

The children sat silently their heads bowed.

'Oh, so nobody did this, it was there all the time, was it?'

Sister Claire noted the anger in Reverend Mother's voice who spoke to the children in the front row

'Was it you Tommy,' she demanded?

'No Reverend Mother,' he replied nervously.

She looked to the next row.

'Was there a stain on that card when you got it Liam?'

'No Reverend Mother.'

She pointed to the next row.

'And you, Stephen?'

'No, Reverend Mother'.

Then she pointed to Joseph.

'And you, Joseph?'

Pat looked at Joseph. He was pale and trembling.

'No Reverend Mother.'

She pointed to the final row.

'And you, Sean?'

Sean stood up nervously.

'The stain was on the card when we got it Reverend Mother'

'That's interesting,' she said. It wasn't there according to Joseph when he got it, but it was there when you handed it to Sister Claire. How could that possibly happen?'

Sean shook his head.

'I don't know, Reverend Mother.'

She looked to Joseph and Pat, then to Sean and Kevin

'Now somebody's lying. Which one of you is it?'

Pat glanced quickly to Joseph whose eyes were fixed firmly on the desk in front of him. Hopalong took out her leather strap. Sister Claire looked upset.

'You have ten seconds to stand up whoever you are, or all four of you will be punished.'

Again Pat glanced at Joseph hoping he would spare the rest a beating. He whispered under his breath.

'We'll all get beaten if you don't stand up.'

Joseph didn't budge. Though Joseph was his friend, Pat did not like what he was doing. He knew it was an accident and that it could have happened to anyone in the class, but it hadn't, it had happened to Joseph and now he was going to let others be punished. Though Pat was annoyed, he would never squeal on a friend. Slowly Pat stood up. Joseph looked on terrified thinking Pat was about to betray him.

'I did it, Reverend Mother.'

The class turned to face Pat. Joseph lowered his head.

'At last we have the culprit, come up here to me you scurrilous little rat.'

Pat walked nervously to the top of the class. Hopalong removed her glasses, carefully folded them and placed them on the table behind her. Some of the children made rude faces and stuck out their tongues safe in the knowledge that without her glasses she was practically blind. Sister Claire gave them an admonishing look and they quickly stopped.

'It was an accident, Reverend Mother.'

She ignored his plea.

'Hold out your hand.'

The strap came crashing down. Pat winced in pain.

'This is for lying to me. I will not tolerate lies in St. Joseph's'.

The strap came crashing down once more. Pat blew on his red raw hand.

'Other hand,' she said angrily.

Joseph could not look. He winced as he heard the sound of the leather slapping against Pat hand. Again the leather came crashing down. Pat stood squeezing his palms tightly beneath his armpits trying to ease the pain.

'Let that be a lesson to you all, she said. I will not tolerate deceitfulness. Get back to your seat.'

Sister Claire looked visibly upset. Hopalong put her glasses back on.

'As I was saying before this little interruption, these sandals will have to last you all summer. I want you all to treat them with respect. They cost a lot of money, and as you well know, money doesn't grow on trees. She tapped the leather strap against her palm. 'If I see scratches or scuffmarks on them tomorrow evening when we get home, those guilty will be severely punished. Is that understood?'

'Yes Reverend Mother' replied the children..
'That's all I have to say. I want you all to a pray that tomorrow will be a beautiful day.'

The children's faces again filled with excitement. Sister Claire walked to the front of the class.

'Now children, show your appreciation to 'Reverend Mother.'

She began to clap gently. They quickly followed suit. Pat could not and did not clap. He winced in pain, holding his stinging hands tightly beneath his armpits. Joseph turned to him.

'Are you okay?' 'I'm sorry. I really am.'

Pat did not bother to respond. He was disappointed in Joseph and he let him know. Hopalong smiled accepting their applause, and left the room.

CHAPTER FOURTEEN

]
Children ran noisily around the schoolyard. It was an enclosed area at the back of the classrooms. On one side was a concrete bench that that ran the length of the wall, with a small galvanized shed at the end where the children sheltered when it rained. On the other side was a high wall with a crudely painted goal. Directly opposite the classroom windows were the field leading out to the farm. Some children were kicking an old deflated ball against the wall. Others sat on their hunkers playing marbles. Pat stood watching Joseph, Thomas, Liam, and Sean as they played marbles on a grill beneath an old drainpipe. The grill had about eight parallel grooves on which the marbles could roll freely. The children liked playing here. It was quick and contained. Marbles were won and lost in the blink of an eye. Thomas crouched low, his index finger hooked, his chubby face a study in concentration, his eyes wide in anticipation as he prepared to take his turn.

Joseph watched nervously as Thomas lined up his shot. Sister Claire sat alone at a desk in the teacher's room correcting the children's exercises. She could hear them playing outside. She closed the final copybook and tossed it on top of the others. She stood up, stretched her arms, and went to one of the open windows and watched the children playing. She was amused at how daft they could be running around like wild animals after the battered football, their faces red and sweating. She spotted the others huddled in the corner playing marbles.

'You never touched it,' said Joseph; grabbing his marble and sticking it quickly back into his pocket. Sister Claire withdrew slightly from the window not wishing to be seen.

'Hey, it's mine, I won it. Stop the messing, hand it over,' shouted Tommy.

Liam picked up his marble and wiped his nose in the sleeve of his jumper.

'That's it, I'm not playing with you'ze any more.'

'Give it to him Joseph, he won it' said Sean.

'Hand it over,' warned Tommy, grabbing Joseph by the scruff of his collar.

'Leave him alone,' shouted Pat.

Tommy sneered.

'Are you going to make me, you ginger dwarf?'

Pat jumped on Tommy's back and caught him by the throat. A quick elbow in the ribs sent Pat flying. He picked himself up holding a grazed knee. The sharp blow of a whistle made the children forgot their little fracas. They raced to the far wall. Sister Teresa entered the yard with a white galvanized bread tray in her hands. Sister Claire watched intrigued as she stepped into the centre of the yard, and placed the tray on the ground. Claire could see it was half full of sliced bread. The bread was cut into triangles. Each slice had a thin coating of jam. The children jostled on the concrete bench fighting for a place closest to the bin.

'Back's to the wall, the lot of you' she shouted.

The children straightened. She raised the whistle to her lips and gave a sharp blast. The children stampeded. Sister Teresa turned away and left them to it. Claire watched as the children pushed and shoved and fought each other to get to the bread. Though Thomas was not first to the tray he managed to fight his way through the scuffle tossing the smaller children aside. Pat was one of the unfortunate ones. Claire, saddened by the scene watched as the bigger children made off with several slices of bread. When Pat finally got to the tray there was nothing left. Some of the children actually laughed and waved the bread taunting him before stuffing it into their mouths. He turned and walked away hungry and despondent. As she watched her emotions swayed from disbelief to disgust. She hurried from the window.

Later, Pat stood alone by the metal gate that led to the farmyard. It was patched with chicken wire. Behind the gate were some pigs, ducks and hens. The children were running around as before. Sister Claire walked quietly along the perimeter of the yard. She spotted Pat standing by the gate, his back turned to the others and walked towards him. He did not hear her approach'

'Pat.'

He turned to see her standing there.

'Do you mind if I have a little chat with you?'

Pat wiped his face with his sleeve.

'But I've done nothing wrong Sister.'

She smiled softly.

'Nobody is accusing you of doing anything wrong', she assured him.

He did not feel like talking to anybody right now, especially to a nun. Joseph, Tommy and Liam stopped playing marbles and watched from afar.

'What has he done now,' inquired Tommy.

'He's probably getting a bollocking for spilling the ink' said Liam.

Joseph quickly changed the subject.

'Whose turn is it?'

Pat stood silently looking through the wire mesh, hoping perhaps she might go away.

'Do you like the farmyard animals,' she asked.

He nodded without replying. She stooped down to him.

'Has the cat got your tongue?'

He looked at her, confused.

'Do you not want to talk to me'?

'No Sister,' he said quietly.

She leant on the gate.

'What ugly creatures pigs are,' she laughed. Just look at the state of that one over there by the tree.'

A large pig furrowed the ground with its nose searching for food. Its ears flapped wildly as it did so. He looked across to the animal; it was covered from head to toe in mud.

'At least it's happy, Sister.'

She was surprised by his remark.

'And you seem so upset. What's the matter?'

'Nothing Sister.'

She looked into his little face.

'Are you sure? Why are you standing here all alone?'

'I don't know Sister.'

She put her hand on his shoulder.

'It's ok. I saw what happened.'

He looked askance at her, unsure as to exactly what she meant.

'Sorry, Sister?'

'I saw you at the bread bin. You didn't get any, did you?'

He lowered his head and said nothing.

'Well did you?' she pressed.

'No Sister, I didn't.'

'You must be hungry.'

Pat nodded.

Sister Claire stood up, took a brown paper bag from her pocket and stepped closer to him.

'Here it's for you, don't let the others see'.

She offered it to Pat. Hesitantly, he took the bag

'Go ahead open it.'

He opened the bag. Inside was a sandwich.

'Eat it. I made it for you.'

His little blue eyes opened wide as he took the sandwich from the bag.

'Its ham, I hope you like it.'

'Thank you Sister' he said, as he bit into the thickly cut sandwich.

She smiled and watched as he wolfed it down.

'Good God, you were hungry.'

He was too busy chewing to reply.

'Can I ask you a question?' Pat nodded.

'How long have you been here?'

He swallowed hard.

'About ten minutes, Sister.'

She laughed.

'No Pat, I mean how long have you been here at St. Joseph's.

'Oh. Always Sister.'

She felt saddened by his reply. He took another hearty bite.

'You mean you never lived in a house like other children?'

A piece of bread fell to the ground. Pat bent down and picked it up and was about to put it into his mouth when she stopped him.

'Don't eat that. It's dirty,' she said, holding out her hand. Reluctantly he placed it in her palm.

'You could get sick, or pick up some disease.'

The idea of being put in the sick ward appealed to him.

'So you've never been in a house before?'

'I don't even know what the inside of one looks like, Sister.'

She broke the bread into tiny pieces and threw it into the farmyard. The chickens and ducks hurried over and began pecking feverishly.

'The poor ducks, what chance do they stand with their round beaks' she said as an afterthought.

He knew only too well how they must have felt.

'Do you have any family?'

'I don't know Sister.'

'And you've never been in a family home?'

'Not that I can remember', he mumbled, biting more carefully into his sandwich.

'But surely you must have gone to a foster family at Christmas time?'

Pat stopped chewing. He looked towards the chickens pecking in the yard before him.

'No Sister.' I was never picked.'

'What do you mean' she asked, 'I don't understand?'

'Some boy's are lucky; they can go to their mothers or grannies. Others go to the same foster family each year. I never go anywhere.'

Claire looked down on the little lost soul standing beside her. She wanted to mother and protect him.

'But why,' she asked?

Once more he bit into the sandwich.

'I don't know Sister,' he said, struggling with the mouthful. 'I say my morning and night prayers every day'. 'I pray a foster family will take me out, but it never happens'. Sister Bernadette told me I must pray harder and that if I say a thousand 'Hail Mary's and a thousand 'Our Fathers' it will happen.

'Last year six of us were left in the orphanage at Christmas. Reverend Mother called for us all on Christmas Eve. We were told to wait in the hallway. There were four families in the drawing room looking to foster a child. We were brought in one by

93

one to meet them. We had to say a poem or sing a song and then leave the room. Myself, and Liam were the only two who were left behind in the orphanage for Christmas Day.'

'You were just unlucky,' she said sympathetically. He looked away, the chewing ceased.

'No Sister, is wasn't that.'

'What was it then,' she enquired?

'Have you heard me sing?'

'You can't sing I take it?'

'No Sister.'

'But you most know a poem?'

'I do Sister, but poems don't make people laugh.'

'Surely that's not a reason not to pick somebody'?

'There's another reason too sister.'

He pointed towards the pig snuffling his way around the tree. She did not understand.

'We were the ugliest.'

'Nonsense.'

'Liam has buckteeth, and I'm a skinny red head with freckles. Most people think red heads are always fighting.'

His words pierced her heart. Yet she understood in a strange way what he meant. Redheads were perceived to be temperamental and hot headed. Where this idea originated baffled her.

'Please don't ever say things like that. You are a wonderful little boy.'

Praise fell awkwardly on his ears. He held back tears.

'Nobody else seems to think so', he said softly.

The cackling of hens distracted him. Two had begun to fighting flapped their wings wildly and pecking at each other. The confrontation was short, and the vanquished quickly scampered away. She looked at his startled face and smiled.

'Do you think that's where the term comes from'
she asked softly?'
He looked up at her a blank expression on his face.
She smiled at his innocence.

'Henpecked'. 'Have you never heard the
expression?'
He was totally lost and shook his head.

'By the way, I saw what you did today.'
Again he looked confused.

'You weren't responsible for the stain on that card,
were you?
Pat looked to the chickens and said nothing. She poked
him playfully on the chest.

'Well? Are you going to tell me'
He looked into her warm eyes and shook his head
slowly.

'No Sister, I wasn't.'

'You're a very brave boy.'

'Or, very stupid, Sister'.
She laughed. He chewed on the crust. '

'I promise you, this Christmas you will go to a
foster home.'

'I don't think I'll ever be picked.'
Claire placed her hand on his shoulder.

'You will Pat. Believe me, you will.'
The bell rang. The children began to head inside. He
backed away from the gate.

'Thank you for the sandwich Sister' he said stuffing
the remainder into his mouth.

'You're welcome Pat. If you ever need to talk to
somebody I'm always here?'
He chewed hard.

'I don't want to be late for your class.'
She smiled at his sense of humour and walked towards
him.

'Here, I'll take the bag for you.'

He handed it to her. She rolled it into a ball and placed it in her pocket.

'If you ever feel as hungry again, just tell me. I might not be always able to get you a sandwich, but I'm sure I can get you something to keep the hunger pangs away.'

He smiled, then ran towards the classroom

CHAPTER FIFTEEN

Pat, like most of the children was overexcited and didn't sleep well that night. As he lay awake he hours tried to imagine what the school trip would be like and prayed for a sunny day. He recalled Sister Claire's kindness and Hopalong's cruelty He was disappointed with Joseph. Perhaps if he had owned up straight away, there would have been no punishment at all. Despite this Pat looked up to Joseph and treated him like the big brother he never had. They were bound together by the same unfortunate set of circumstances, two innocent children, caught in a hostile world.

Dawn was breaking and he lay wide awake in the stillness of the dormitory, gazing up at the imaginary friends he had discovered over the years, hidden in the many cracks running through the plastered ceiling above him. He was getting out, even if it was only for a day. He was getting away from the drudgery and the intimidation of the orphanage. He wondered about the world outside, a world he could not see. Though he loved learning about countries like Australia, France, and Africa, he knew absolutely nothing about the nearest village and the world just outside these walls. He placed his hands behind his head, resigned to the fact he could not sleep. Why he wondered did some boys and girls live out there all the time? Why couldn't he? He tried to visualize his mother's face. Did she too have freckles? He wondered why she had abandoned him. Was she still alive? Did he have a father, a sister or a brother? What had he done to deserve this? Why had God left him so alone in this great big world, yet so small and unable to fend for himself? He longed for the day when he would be bigger and older, when he could leave this place forever. The morning light intensified. From his bed he could see the grey skies slowly turn to a fiery ember red. Finally the first shafts of sunlight flooded in, lighting the dull interior and striking the dark stained dormitory door. From all appearances it was going to be a glorious day. His prayers had been answered. The door swung open. A bell rang out. Sister Agnes hurried through the dormitory, the bell swinging in her hand.

'Wake up. Wake up. We're running late' she called out in her heavy Cork accent.

The children, some groggy, some excited, tumbled from their beds.

'Mass is starting in ten minutes, don't be late.'

The little chapel was cold. Today the children were dressed in their green school blazers and their short grey pants. Pat knelt in the pew beside Joseph who whispered.

'This friggin blazer is way too small for me.'

'So is mine' whispered Pat. Don't forget we did get them last year.'

The nuns had a section of the chapel to themselves. It was up front near the altar on the right hand side and the only part of the church with central heating. They had cushions, while the children's bare knees had timber. Sister Agnes knelt at the back of the Chapel where she could keep an eye on things and sneak out for a quick cigarette. Fr. Dunn was celebrating mass as he always did on special occasions. He was a large man, tall with a balding head and stern face. His gold framed glasses sat awkwardly on a large bulbous nose betraying his love for whiskey. It came as no surprise to the children that the nuns sometimes referred to him as 'Rudolph' in their coded conversations.

'Ah Jaysus no, he's getting up on the pulpit,' whispered Joseph.

'Shite. We'll be here all friggin day.'

Father Dunn began his sermon. The congregation sat back down. Sister Agnes immediately bolted for the door and the pleasure of a quiet cigarette. Pat closed his ears and the diatribe began. Words of profundity, spewed from his mouth, half the time the children couldn't tell if he was still speaking English. So disjointed were his sermons that even the most pious and patient nuns succumbed. Poor Sister Bernadette had to be nudged gently by Sister Teresa when she began to snore loudly half-way through his sermon much to the amusement of the children. Eventually, to the relief of all present, he stepped down from the pulpit and continued with the mass.

Communion was a chance to eat. Pat never missed it. He often wondered if technically he could be classed as a cannibal, eating the body of Christ as he so regularly did. He loved the taste of the wafer. He would loosen it with his tongue from the roof of his mouth and savor it for as long as possible, getting as much pleasure from it as he could. Tubby, who served as an altar boy, had once told him that in the sacristy there was a huge box of these wafers waiting to become the body of Christ. He said he had once grabbed a handful and scoffed the lot and that it was one of the nicest things he had ever eaten.

That morning, breakfast seemed to take forever Perhaps it was the excitement of the day. Perhaps it was the children's eagerness to hop on the bus and get away. They sat excitedly waiting for their porridge and toast. As a special treat, on occasions like this, they also received a boiled egg. The refectory was large, and the only warm room the children were allowed into. It had two long pine tables running parallel in the centre of the room. The floor was covered in plain brown heavy duty linoleum. The smell of freshly baked bread wafted from the kitchen causing the children's tummies to rumble with hunger

. 'I wish they'd hurry up,' said 'Bugs' wiping his runny nose on the back of his hand.

'I could eat a horse,' whispered Tubby.

'You look like you just have' said Joseph. '

'Watch it, Big Ears.'

Pat sat quietly minding his own business. On the refectory wall was a print of Dali's 'Christ on the Cross'. Pat liked it. He didn't know why. Perhaps it was because it was painted from such an unusual angle. Perhaps it was meant to be God's perspective, looking down on his only son. It was a comfort to know that even Christ had somebody looking after him. He hoped God was now going to look down on them and gift them with a wonderful day. Finally when everything was ready, Sister Agnes stood in the centre of the room, said 'grace before meals' and the children tucked in.

After breakfast the children returned to class to collect their brand new sandals. Pat was handed a shoe box with the number '42' marked on it in red biro. He went back to his seat and opened the box. A pair of white knee-length socks lay beneath the lid on the crisp white tissue paper neatly folded over his sandals. The tissue crackled as he carefully lifted to one side and his eyes lit up. They were the most beautiful sandals he had ever seen in his young life. They were a vibrant red with a white rubber sole and white stitching. A shiny silver buckle was fastened at the side. On the inside of his sandals, at the heel, the number '42' was written in black indelible ink. Pat held them tightly never wanting to let them go. He lifted them to his nose smelling the newness of the leather. Joseph returned with his. He too was beaming with excitement.

'Look they're beautiful,' said Pat showing them to Joseph.

'I know. Frigging dynamite.'

'Right children,' said Sister Claire, 'Put on your new socks and sandals now. Leave your old socks and shoes neatly under your desk; we will collect them when we return.

The children quickly changed into their new socks and sandals.

'They're so light, I feel like I'm wearing nothing on my feet.

'Yeah, they're the dogs bollix,' said Joseph.

When they were ready Sister Claire led them in an orderly fashion out of the classroom.

An old blue battered bus stood forlornly outside the main door of St. Joseph's. The children filed their way out on to the gravelled drive and then on to the bus. They looked resplendent in their green blazers and grey trousers, with their spotless knee length white socks, and of course their brand new sandals. By now they were buzzing with excitement, and hardly able to contain themselves. 'Grab the back seat' whispered Joseph. When the children had boarded the nuns appeared at the main door. One by one they climbed on board. Finally Hopalong and Rudolph appeared. The children watched impatiently as they chatted and laughed before finally stepping on to the bus. When everybody was seated Sister Agnes stood up. She was the most hated of all the nuns in St. Joseph's and Hopalong's closest confidant.

She was tall, in her mid thirties, with a square face, soulless brown eyes, and thick knitted eyebrows. She had full lips and a broken nose. A chain smoker her fingers were brown and she stank of tobacco. She was cruel and mean to the children and had a violent temper. Often she beat them severely for the most trivial of things. The children feared her more than anybody or anything else in the whole world.

'Have we forgotten anybody,' she asked walking through the bus .

'12, 14, 16, 18, 20, 22, 23, all present and correct.'

She returned to the front and nodded to the driver. The old bus stuttered into life. The children cheered with excitement.

'We're off,' squealed Pat.

'They took their time,' said Joseph.

Clouds of blue smoke belched from beneath the shuddering coach, rising up past the windows as it slowly chugged its way down the avenue. The bus passed through the main gates and on to the public road. The children cheered loudly.

'Good riddance,' said Joseph.

Pat gazed back at the gates of the only world he knew with mixed emotions.

'Yeah good riddance.'

Sister Agnes sat behind Hopalong and Rudolph at the front of the bus.

'The children are a credit to you Reverend Mother,' said Father Dunn.

She smiled and turned to Sister Agnes

'Thanks in no small way, to Sister Agnes.'

'Nonsense,' said Sister Agnes coyly.

'Well all I can say then is both of you are doing a splendid job.'

The nuns exchanged a mutual glance of admiration. Sister Carmel and her constant companion Sister

102

Bernadette sat in the next row. They were the oldest nuns in the school, each having spent more than forty years there. Both held a large wooden rosary beads in their hands and were whispering the rosary. It seemed they were praying for a speedy end to this ordeal. Sister Claire sat alone but seemed as happy and excited as the children.

The children began to settle down for the journey ahead. Pat and Joseph only managed to get the second last row. They were leaning over the back of the seat talking to Sean and 'Bugs' who had managed to grab the back seat with Stephen and Kevin who sat together sneakily playing cards. Stephen had the unenviable distinction of being the only black boy at St. Joseph's, and was often at the receiving end of racist jibes. Seamus and Dermot were simply acting the eejit, as kids do. Tubby sat squashing poor Brian up against the window. Brian was just slightly taller than Pat. He was a thin blond boy with thick wire rimmed glasses. The more Brian objected the more he got squashed.

'That's typical of the nun's,' said Joseph. 'They bring us some place where there's nothing but sand and sea and not a sweet shop for miles. I've been saving the pocket money me granny sent me for this school trip and now I have nowhere to spend it.

'How much do you have,' enquired Sean.

'Never you mind,' snapped Joseph.

'I still have three and sixpence from my communion money,' said Bugs, his broad smile revealing his protruding teeth

'I'm not a bit surprised,' said Joseph, 'you're as tight as a duck's arse.'

' Shut it Big Ears,' warned Bugs.

'I don't know which is worse, your teeth or your disgusting snots,' jibed Joseph.

103

Bugs in anger swung out at Joseph clipping him on the side of the head.

'You bollix, you'll pay for that,' roared Joseph. 'Give over both of you,' snapped Tubby, 'if she catches us messing we'll be left in the bus all day.'

Pat pondered over Bug's words

'But that was over six months ago,' he said?

'It's not my fault I had nowhere to spend it.'

'He's right,' said Sean. 'How much do you have Pat?'

Pat turned to him, a weary expression on his face.

'You have to know everybody's business don't you? Does it matter how much I have, I can't spend it either'

Pat was hurting. His friends had somebody in the real world that cared enough to send them money. He had nobody, and there was nothing in his pockets.

'I hope it doesn't rain, if it does we're bunched,' mused Bugs.

'They'll make us sit in the bus if it does,' groaned Pat.

'How stupid is that,' said Joseph. 'They bring us to the seaside, miles from nowhere and the only bloody thing to do is swim, but we're not allowed.'

Pat contorted his face, and spoke in a high pitched voice, mimicking Sister Agnes.

'It's for your own good. We have your best interests at heart.'

The others laughed.

'Yeah. What a load of crap.'

'She's right. We probably would all drown if we got into the water' said Sean.

'You wouldn't' said Joseph.

'Why do you say that,' asked Bugs.?

'Cause shit floats.'

The others laughed.

'Joseph wouldn't drown even if his hands were tied behind his back' said Sean. '

'Why?' asked Pat.

'Cause he could paddle back to shore with those ears of his.'

The kids were in stitches.

'Watch it mutton head,' warned Joseph.

Pat tried to defuse the situation.

'I'll tell you why none of you can swim?'

The others looked to him for an explanation.

'Cause you're too dense.'

'Put a sock in it ya eejit.'

'This is stupid', moaned Joseph. 'Why didn't they bring us to the zoo or something like that?'

'Are you joking,' said Tubby 'they'd never pay for a bus trip to Dublin. Think of the petrol they would have to use.'

'Diesel you yobbo,' said 'Bugs'.

'At least in the zoo we could do something useful,' said Joseph.

'What's that,' asked 'Bugs'?

'Buy sweets and look at the poxy animals.'

Pat pointed to the front of the bus.

'We've got monkeys penguins even a Rudolph, sitting up there, what more do ya want?'

The children giggled uncontrollably.

Time passed slowly. Second passed like minutes, and minutes passed like days. The journey seemed to take an eternity. Children slept and dozed in the warm bus. Pat too slept, finally overwhelmed by his tiredness. Outside it was a glorious day, with hardly a cloud in the sky. They now passed through the bleak and beautiful landscape of Connemara. The old bus weaved its way slowly along the tiny coastal road, like some strange mechanical blue caterpillar. The grey-green Atlantic Ocean pounded the rugged coast below, smashing against the ancient cliffs, in an endless barrage of frothing waves, and glistening white spray. Those still awake sat spellbound, foreheads pressed against the window panes, gazing out at Clare Island and Inish Bofin, the last visible signs of Western Europe the next land fall being America.

'Wake up. Wake up Pat, we can see the sea.'
Joseph shook Pat vigorously. Slowly he opened his sleepy eyes. He was momentarily disorientated.

'Look the sea,' he cried excitedly.
 Pat squinted, in the searing bright light. '

'Oh, Yeah. Wow its magic isn't it?'
Soon, all on the bus were wide awake. 'Questions, like 'how much further' or 'are we nearly there yet' began to echo amongst the children.

'This journey just seems to go on forever and ever' moaned Bugs.

'I'd say we'll be there in about twenty minutes,' said Joseph, with all the aplomb of a seasoned traveler.

'Wha', another twenty minutes' repeated Sean incredulously.

'Christ, I'll have grown a beard by then,' moaned Pat.

CHAPTER SIXTEEN

The old bus creaked to a halt outside what could best be described as a glorified shed in the middle of nowhere. The building was painted in a pale blue gloss that sparkled in the sunlight. The doors and window frames were a bright pink. The sloping roof was corrugated and covered in red lead oxide paint. A blue plastic net full of brightly colored beach balls hung at one side of the entrance. On the other, a little red kite fluttered lightly in the breeze. Beneath it hung several brightly coloured buckets and spades. Above the door in shoddily painted black letters was the sign 'Tea Rooms'. On the gable wall, beside a poorly painted kettle were the words: 'Pot of tea 1/=' 'Pot of boiling Water' 6d.

The bus was now abuzz with excited children.

'I'm going to buy that kite' squealed Bugs.'

'It's mine. Hands off or you're dead meat' warned Joseph.

Bugs looked dejected. He was scared of Joseph, but tried hard to hide it.

'There's bound to be more than one'.

To Pat, this little shed was a magic kingdom, full of bright vibrant colours, a fantasy world, straight out of his dreams. Sister Agnes stood in the aisle her voice as gruff as ever.

'Sit back down the lot of you. If I catch any boy standing up before I give permission, he will remain on the bus all day. Is that clear?'

The children hastily took their places.

107

Father Dunn and Hopalong alighted first, followed by the other nuns. From the bus, the children could see them being greeted by a large fat red-haired woman in a dark blue flowery housecoat. She ushered them inside. Sister Agnes waited before calling the children by name. They left the bus in pairs. 'Line up outside' and wait for me' she ordered. Soon all the children were standing in a line beside the bus. 'Right Tommy, you lead them inside. If I see any pushing or shoving you'll get no lunch.' The children fought to contain their excitement as they entered.

Inside the 'Tea Rooms' things were scarcely better, the walls were nothing more than bare concrete blocks adorned with a few colorful posters of birds and animals, even the floor was bare concrete. The tables were covered in dull red Formica' chipped at the edges and placeed together in one long row for the children. There was a cup, saucer, and a plate, set out for each child. Along the length of each table was a wooden bench, painted in the same blue as the exterior. The children eagerly took their places. A smell of bacon and cabbage wafted through the room. Across from them, Father Dunn and the nuns sat at a circular table. It was covered in a white tablecloth. There was a knife and fork and spoon set at each place.

'Jaysus I'm starving,' whispered Tubby.

'What's new. You're always friggin starving,' said Stephen from the safety of the other side of the table.

The children sniggered.

'Watch it 'Gollywog,' warned Tommy.

'Smells bleeding great,', whispered Pat.

'Keep smelling,' said Joseph, 'that's about as much as you'll get.'

'What do ya mean?'

Father Dunn moved to the center of the room.

'Now let us all say our 'Grace before meals.' 'Bless us O Lord and these thy gifts.......'

The children bowed their heads in prayer muttering familiar words, their minds already elsewhere, 'through Christ Our Lord. Amen.'

They blessed themselves as he finished.

'I d like to say a little word,' continued Father Dunn Ah shite, I'm starving,' whispered Pat.

'Surely he's not going to start again,' Tubby agonized under his breath?

'If he does we'll end up getting supper not lunch,' moaned Joseph.

'Before we begin, I would like to emphasize once more, our debt of gratitude to Reverend Mother. I would like on behalf of all the school, to thank her for all she has done for you in the last year, for organizing this wonderful day and for the beautiful new sandals you all got this morning.'

Hopalong sat proudly at her table listening with the other nuns as Father Dunn heaped praises in her direction. She smiled broadly, an air of self importance emanating from her chubby face.

'Now children, I want you to give Reverend Mother a big round of applause

The children clapped loudly. Sister Agnes stood up and spoke briefly.

'Thank you Father Dunn. I would also like to remind you all to look after all your belongings. We don't want any torn clothes, nor do we want any scuff marks on your new sandals. Now could we have a big round of applause for Father Dunn.'

Father Dunn's face lit up like a harvest moon. The children clapped dutifully.

Across the room vegetable soup was being served to the nuns. The children sat impatiently waiting their turn their salivary glands working overtime. Tubby licked his lips, his stomach aching.

'Surely we must be getting soup too,' whispered Pat.

'Do you see a soup spoon in front of ya,' asked Joseph?

'No, I don't.' '

'Does that answer your question?'

'Ah Jaysus,' moaned Tubby.

When the nuns were catered for, the red-haired woman and her young female helper began to serve the children. In her hands she carried a large tray full of sandwiches. Her helper carried a large catering pot of tea.

'Ham or cheese,' she enquired in a flat culchie brogue.

The children's faces dropped in disappointment when they saw the sandwiches. Pat glanced at the nuns who were finishing off their soup. Sister Claire caught him looking. There was an awkward moment when their eyes met

'Ham please,' said Tubby, flatly.

The woman grabbed two triangles of bread and tossed them on his plate.

'And you,' she enquired of the next boy?

Joseph looked at Pat.

'What did I tell you?'

Pat didn't want to know. Soon the children were devouring their sandwich and drinking their tea like a pack of hungry wolves.

'Jaysus look at that,' whispered Tommy.

The nuns were now being served their main course. Bacon and cabbage and steaming boiled potatoes.

'Good Jaysus,' said Steven.

The other children eyed the food enviously.

'Is that it, is that all we're getting,' asked Tubby.

'What did you expect,' asked Joseph?

'A lump of meat wouldn't have gone astray,' said Pat.

'But ham is meat!'

'Oh yeah, and bread is cake,' muttered a disgruntled Tubby.

Later, to the children's surprise and delight they were served a helping of jelly and ice cream. Bugs looked to Pat.

'I'll give you three pence for it.'

'Piss off '.

'How about you, Big Ears?'

'A shilling, or nothing,' replied Joseph.

'A shilling? You could buy a block of ice cream for that!'

'Oh yeah. Go ahead then,' laughed Pat.

He shoveled the jelly and ice cream into his mouth. Liam quickly forgot the bartering and did likewise.

The red-haired woman returned with a tray full of small mineral bottles, half were red lemonade the rest orange. A wax straw protruded from each bottle neck. She plonked a bottle down in front of each child Pat was delighted when he got a bottle of orange. It had tiny bits in 'it so it had to be more filling' he told himself.

'Bollix I got the lemonade' said Joseph.

Pat quickly stuck the straw in his mouth and began to drink from the bottle. Half way through his drink Pat paused for breath.

'I have an idea' he said.

'Did it hurt', asked Bugs? '

Shut it, I'm not talking to you.'

'Well out with it then', said Joseph?

'Well you know the way they're warning us about our sandals getting marked?'

'Yeah.

'Well I know how we can stop that.'

'How? asked Sean, suddenly interested?

'It's simple. We won't wear them.'

'We have to wear them you gobshite', replied Tubby.

'Not on the beach, we don't.'

'He's right' said 'Golly, but what if somebody steals them?'

'I've thought of that.'

Pats little eyes lit up.

'They won't be able to steal them.'

'Why? asked Sean.

'Cause we'll hide them like the pirates hide their treasure.'

'We don't have a frigging treasure chest,' said Tubby.

'You're as thick as a plank, do you know that?'

'Watch it, or this plank will beat the shit out of you, carrot head!'

'Will you two just shut it, for Chris's sake', snapped Joseph.

When he gained their attention he turned to Pat.

'What do you mean like the pirates do'?

'We'll hide them'.

'Where?' asked Golly.

'In the sand. We'll bury them.'

''You're a friggin eejit, do ya know that' said Joseph.

The others joined in and began to make fun of Pat and his silly ideas. Though he was hurt, he tried not to show it and ignored their taunts concentrating on what remained of his bottle of orange.

CHAPTER SEVENTEEN

Clifden Bay was empty despite it being July and the height of summer. Tuesday afternoon's on remote Irish beaches always were. The children walked in double file, across the sand dunes towards the beach flanked by Sister Agnes and Sister Claire. Bugs held the red kite proudly in his hands, his face beaming. Joseph felt dejected but there was nothing he could do. He had learned a valuable lesson. Money was power. Though he wanted the kite, he couldn't afford it, Bugs could. Despite Joseph's empty threats it was Bugs who got the prize. As a consolation Joseph bought the yellow bucket and spade. Eventually the children beheld the mighty ocean and squealed with excitement.

Pat's jaw dropped when he saw the vastness of the beach that lay in front of them.

'Wow it goes on forever.'

'It's a big place all right,' said Joseph

'Jesus if we got lost here, we'd never be found again'.

'You're right.'

'Hey I have an idea, we could run away.'

Pat turned to Joseph. He wasn't sure if he was joking or not. He soon realized he wasn't.

'Don't be silly, where could we run to?'

'We could go to my Granny's place.'

'Where's that?'

'Skibbereen.'

Pat checked Sister Agnes was not within hearing distance.

'Where?'

'Have you gone deaf, I told you.' Skibbereen.'

'And you think I'm the feckin eejit?'

Joseph looked confused.

'I know where your granny lives, I'm asking you where Skibbereen is?'

'Oh' said Joseph 'it's in Cork.'

Pat eyes widened.

'Cork! Sure that's in the south of Ireland.'

'Yeah, so,' said Joseph

'So cop on.'

Joseph shrugged his shoulders and raised the bucket and spade.

'We could try digging our way to Australia.'

Pat laughed

'Or dig an escape tunnel when we get back to St. Joseph's'.

Soon the children were walking excitedly on the beach. To them it was another world, a world of sheer vastness, stretching out in all directions, a world so alien to that which they knew in the confines of the orphanage. They filled their lungs with the fresh salt sea air, and listened to the power of nature and watched the pounding waves break upon the shore. Sister Agnes blew a whistle. The convoy stopped.

'Right Children, this is where we will stay for the next three hours. I'm leaving Sister Claire in charge.'

Sister Claire looked surprised. The children reacted positively to this welcome news.

'Take off your blazers and give them to Sister Claire. She will look after them for you.'

The children were glad to be rid of their ill-fitting jackets in the searing heat.

'I want every one of you to be very careful and keep an eye on each other. We don't want any sunburn so keep yourselves covered up and I don't want anybody climbing up near the cliff face, is that understood?'

'Yes Sister.'

She cast a stern look along the line of children.

'Remember you are ambassadors for the orphanage, so we don't want any misconduct. Sister Claire will be reporting back to me. Any boy who tarnishes the good name of St. Joseph's, will have me to deal with. Is that understood?'

'Yes Sister.'

'Away with you all.'

The children scattered yelling and screaming and slapping their bums as they galloped away in all directions. Sister Claire smiled, in amusement.

'I'm returning to Reverend Mother' said Sister Agnes, 'she is not feeling very well, I think perhaps the heat is getting to her.'

'Poor Reverend Mother' said Sister Claire.

'I'll be back in three hours. Till then, you are in charge. Don't disappoint me.'

Sister Claire cast a cursory glance into the soulless brown eyes of Sister Agnes, but found little emotion in them. '

I won't Sister. I'll take good care of them.'

She watched as she headed back across the sand, her black veil flapping wildly in the breeze as she energetically climbed the crest of a dune and vanished from sight like some modern day Laurence of Arabia. Sister Claire was disappointed and a little angry that she had been left alone to mind twent-three children. She bit gently on her lip as she began to neatly fold the children's green blazers

By now Tubby was standing on top of one of the largest sand dunes. He was beating his chest like King Kong.

'I'm king of the castle,' he yelled.

The children took turns trying to dislodge him from his lofty position, with little success. Joseph tried his luck. He too was sent tumbling back down. Pat laughed

'What's so funny you little shite, see if you can do any better.'

Pat handed him back his bucket and spade.

'What's wrong with you, it's only a game?'

Joseph picked himself up and began dusting his clothes down.

'Christ my sandals are scratched already.'

'I warned you,' said Pat.

He looked at his own.

'Mine are starting to get scuffed too. That's it. I'm not getting in trouble with Sister Agnes.'

Pat unbuckled his sandals and removed his white socks.

'What are you doing' asked Joseph.

'I'm going to hide them in the sand like I said.'

'I thought you were joking.'

'I'm serious. I'm not getting the shit beaten out of me by that wan.'

Joseph watched as Pat slipped his socks over his sandals and walked away to hide them

. 'Hey wait, I'll hide mine with yours.'

The rest of the children watched what was going on, and followed them. Pat began to dig a hole in the sand with his hands.

'Here, let me do it. I have a spade.'

'You scoop with the bucket,' said Joseph'

'How will you find them again,' asked Stephen?

'Simple. We'll mark the spot with something. Anyway, the bus is directly opposite where we are

116

standing. If we can't find that then we must all be blind.'

'I still think you're frigging gobshites,' said Bugs.

'Look at your sandals, they're marked too.'

Bugs looked down. His face turned pale.

'Oh shit.'

Slowly one by one the children took off their sandals and socks and placed them in the hole.

'Look for a bit of drift wood, said Joseph we'll make a cross.'

Pat carefully filled over the sandals with bucketfuls of sand. The children tied two pieces of driftwood together with some reeds. It was a roughly made cross, but served their purpose perfectly.

Joseph stuck it carefully into the sand and then he shouted;

'Last one to touch the water is a gobshite.'

The children raced from the dunes screaming and laughing down towards the beach no longer worried about their sandals Behind them, the Nuns climbed into the old bus. It spluttered into life and slowly pulled away heading for afternoon tea in the gardens of 'The De Luxe Hotel' some ten miles further down the road. On the beach some of the children dabbled in the water. Others searched the rock pools for crabs and minnows placing them into an empty jam jar they had found. Pat and Joseph busied themselves building a sand-castle.

'Let's make the biggest castle ever', said Pat excitedly.

'With a bridge' blurted Joseph.

'Yes, and water all around.'

Soon they were lost in their endeavor working like a team of skilled architects, carefully tapping the bucket before lifting to reveal yet another perfectly formed portion of their kingdom. As they worked away they could feel the sun hot upon their backs.

'Jaysus I'm roasting,' said Pat.

'Me too, and we have 'nuttin' to cool us down, not even a drink of water We can't swim in case we drown, we can't take off our shirt in case we get sun burned. We might as well have gone to a sand pit somewhere in the arse-hole of Mayo.'

Pat laughed. He found it amusing when Joseph went off on one of his little tantrums.

'Still it's a beautiful day. I wish I could stay here forever' said Pat patting the perimeter of their castle with his palm.

'I'm sure it's not always as nice as this'.

Pat's face betrayed a tinge of sadness.

'Look' said Joseph, pointing to Sister Claire.

Pat turned his head.

'She's dead right. Can you imagine how warm it must be in those penguin clothes?'

Sister Claire, her hem raised, dabbled along the shore line.

'It's so weird to see a happy nun,' said Joseph.

'Yeah, she's different; she's not like the rest.'

'She's not a 'wagon' is that what you mean?

'I suppose' grinned Pat.

Sister Claire spotted the castle. Her face broke into a broad smile.

'That's absolutely beautiful boys.'

The children were chuffed.

'You can help us if you like Sister', said Pat.

Sister Claire laughed. 'It's been so long since I built a sandcastle, I don't think I would be able to anymore. Anyway you're doing great without me; it's far too   beautiful. I'd only mess it up on you.'

'Please Sister, we'll do the building and you can make it fancy.

Her blue eyes sparkled and she smiled warmly. Claire looked at Pat,

'How do you mean?

'You could put nice stones and shells on it for us.'

For a moment she stood hesitating like a child about to steal a sweet. She glanced around. The only stranger she could see on the beach was a man out walking his dog and was heading away from them towards the sand dunes. Enthusiastically she knelt down and began helping with the castle.

'Okay then, you build and I'll decorate the turrets.'

'What are turrets Sister,' asked a bewildered Joseph?

'Towers or battlements,' she said reaching for some shells.

'What are battlements' asked Pat.

They spent the best part of an hour working on their project. Pat was in Heaven. He looked out to the ocean, and watched the long narrow channel they had dug fill with water. It flowed slowly towards their castle and they watched in fascination as the moat began to fill. It was a magical moment, all their hard work and their architectural skills had been vindicated.

'It works' cried Joseph, jumping up and down. Sister Claire smiled; she could see the sheer joy in the children's eyes.

'It's beautiful isn't it,' she said softly. Some of the other children had gathered around. Some stood while others knelt in the sand.

'Did you know', said Sister Claire to the children, 'that the ocean that runs around this castle is the same ocean that washes the shores of New York and skirts the coasts of South America. It is the very same ocean that Columbus sailed before he discovered the New World.'

'Who's he Sister' asked Bugs?'

119

'I'll tell you all about him in history class, I promise.'

The children were fascinated. She continued.

'When he did discover America, this same ocean was used to transport black slaves from the West Coast of Africa to work in the cotton fields of the 'Mississippi Delta' and the 'Southern States' of America.'

The children were bamboozled.

'Where did you learn about that Sister,' asked Golly?

'He must be worried they're are going to come and take him too,' whispered Joseph.

She smiled at his question.

'I love to read. Did you know it was on this ocean that the Titanic sailed on her one and only voyage?'

'What happened to it Sister,' asked Brian?

'It sank and more than fifteen hundred people lost their lives.'

'You mean they drowned,' said Pat?

'Yuck' said Tubby, 'can you imagine all those bodies at the bottom of the sea.'

The children laughed. Sister Claire shook her head at the absurdity of a child's mind.

'And did you know it was built in Ireland.'

'Are we no good at building boats then,' asked Brian?

Pat was lost in thought. Here he was on the edge of this mighty ocean with Joseph and Sister Claire, building the biggest sand-castle this world had ever known. An inner peace overwhelm him, he felt this was where he belonged, not locked behind the gates of 'St Josephs'. He felt for the first time in his young life he was destined for better things. Perhaps one day he too would become an explorer of sorts and cross this ocean on his way to far off lands. A light breeze cooled his freckled face offering him respite from the suns warm rays. He looked up to the blue sky peppered with seagulls darting down, and listened to their strange human-like cries, as they swooped and soared above the craggy cliff face.

On the dunes, the man with his dog came upon the crude cross of driftwood. He picked it up, and broke its binding. His dog barked excitedly as continued on his way tossing both of the sticks as far as he could, ahead of him.

'Go. Fetch boy.

Back on the beach the castle was nearly finished. Sister Claire collected some final shells and placed them upon the turrets.

'That's a beautiful shell Sister,' said Pat pointing to the clam shell she was now embedding above the castle gate.

She picked it from the sand to have a closer look.

'It is, isn't it?

'They look like drops of chocolate' said Pat pointing to the little brown flecks on the shell. The children giggled.

Sister Claire laughed.

'Trust you to spot that.'

Carefully she replaced it above the entrance to the castle.

'There' she said, rubbing the sand from her hands, 'all done.'

It was a masterpiece, complete with turrets and towers, encircled by a water filled moat, adorned with beautiful shells of every shape size and colour. It was the biggest sandcastle ever built and Pat and Joseph were bursting with pride. If it wasn't the biggest, it was definitely the nicest. They had built the most beautiful castle ever to grace the shore line of the mighty Atlantic Ocean.

121

'Sister, can you help me now,' asked Bugs?'

'What's the matter Liam?'

'It's this kite. I can't fly it. It must be broken.'

Sister Claire took the kite in her hands and inspected it.

'No Liam, the kite seems fine, let's go and fly it.' The children followed eagerly as Sister Claire walked some distance down the beach. She noted the direction of the breeze then unwound some string, and asked Liam to move away with the kite. When he was sufficiently far away she shouted to him.

'Let Go.'

Bugs did as he was told. Sister Claire ran backwards pulling hard on the string. The little red kite fluttered and faltered before it slowly rose higher and higher. Sister Claire released more string. The children shouted with excitement as the kite swooped and turned above their heads. Soon it was soaring high on the sea breeze. She handed the string to Liam.

'Now Liam you can fly it'.

'Bugs face lit up. He wiped his nose. The 'two shilling and sixpence,' a small fortune, now seemed like money well spent. The children watched as the little red kite bobbed and weaved in the clear blue sky dancing to the timeless rhythms of the ocean.

'Can I have a go' asked Joseph?

'No' came the curt reply.

'Now now Liam, we have to learn to share,' said Sister Claire softly.

Bugs didn't want to share; he wanted his kite all to himself.

'Do I have to Sister,' he asked?

'You don't have to, nobody's forcing you. I think it would be a nice gesture, if you let each of the children have a little turn.'

'But that'll take forever Sister.'

122

'I'll make sure it won't and you will have loads of time to play with it by yourself.'

'Okay Sister,' he said reluctantly and handed the string to Joseph.

'Just little turns Joseph,' said Sister Claire. The other boys want to have a go too.'

For the next hour or so, the children were completely lost in their own world. They scoured the rocks searching for pirate treasures, they caught minnows in the empty jam jar, they played ball, and Blind Man's Buff, and flew Bugs kite. It was a world so wonderful so alien, Pat had completely forgotten about 'St. Joseph's'. Sister Claire had joined in whenever she could. She too was lost in another world. A quick glance at her watch brought her back to her senses.

'Oh my God. 'Is it that time already?'

She called to the children.

'Children we must hurry back. Sister Agnes will be here in fifteen minutes.'

Their faces dropped in disappointment, it was as if they were being plucked by some monster's hand from a magic kingdom, and tossed back into reality.

'We'll run and get our sandals', said Pat.

'What did you do with them' enquired Sister Claire?

'We hid them Sister' said Joseph proudly, 'to protect them from getting marked'.

'Where' she enquired.

'In the dunes Sister' said Pat.

She looked a little concerned.

'Don't worry, we marked the spot' added Tubby. Sister Claire smiled.

'What clever little boys you are. Right let's be on our way.

Reluctantly the children turned and headed towards the dunes. Pat cast a sad look back towards the sand castle. He knew he would never lay eyes on it again and now that the tide had turned it was in imminent danger. He ran to it, and carefully picked the pretty white chocolate stained shell Sister Claire had placed above the gate and stuck in his pocket before hurrying after the others.

The children searched frantically. They looked in vain for the driftwood cross, desperately trying to get their bearings.

'Where did we put them,' asked Tubby nervously?

'The cross has to be here,' said Pat confidently.

'Yes, but where is it,' asked Golly?

Pat was dumbfounded. There was no sign of it anywhere. Joseph tapped Pat on the shoulder and pointed.

'Look the bus is facing the other way'

'Oh no, they've moved the bus too.'

Tubby shouted to Pat.

'This is all your fault.'

Though Sister Claire was upset. she felt empathy towards Pat as she listened to him being vilified by his friends. She was aware that she too would be in trouble if they could not find the sandals. She knew in her heart the children's intentions had been good and that all they had wanted was to please Reverend Mother.

'We should have known better,' said Bugs.

'It's not his fault,' argued Golly, 'he didn't move the cross.'

Pat looked to Golly, thankful for his support. Golly shrugged his shoulders.

'We'll be killed,' said Tubby, his voice now trembling.

'Just stay calm and keep looking,' pleaded Sister Claire.

124

They searched frantically. Each child moved quickly up and down the dunes prodding the sand with bits of stick in the hope of finding the sandals.

'We did nothing wrong it's all his fault,' shouted Sean, his finger pointing directly at Pat.

Sister Claire began to worry. Time was running out.

'Now children please, no fighting.'

The sharp sound of a whistle drifted over the dunes.

'Oh God, its Sister Agnes', said Joseph.

Sister Claire closed her eyes and in exasperation. She turned to the children.

'Don't worry, I'll try to explain everything.'

The blood drained from Pat's freckled face. Below on the beach, unbeknown to him, their sand-castle had already crumbled to the advancing tide.

CHAPTER EIGHTEEN

The journey home had been one of deep
trepidation for all the children. They feared for their
lives. Pat sat alone, ostracized by his school mates.
Joseph sat in the back with Tubby and Bugs . Nobody
dared to speak to Pat, not even his friend Joseph, for
fear they too might somehow become 'guilty by
association'. Pat sat gazing out the window, his body
trembling. He felt lost and hopelessly alone. He had
been singled out by his so-called friends and chosen as
their 'sacrificial lamb'. It hurt him that Joseph should
behave in this way; he expected it of the others, but
not of him. Where was the collective responsibility, he
had buried his sandals and nobody else's, in the sand.
It wasn't as if he had put a gun to their heads. They had
their own free-will, they could have acted differently.
He valued friendship above everything, now he felt
hopelessly betrayed by all, especially the one he
trusted most.

They had spent an extra hour searching for the
sandals, and as a result everything was running late.
Sister Agnes berated Sister Claire while the children
searched in vain. She had called her 'a useless hussy
and good-for-nothing' and told her she didn't have the
qualities needed to become a nun. She rebuked her for
not having taken proper care of the children and their
possessions, and of having brought shame to 'St.
Joseph's'.

'You young wan's think you know it all. Never in
the history of our school has anything so shameful

occurred, and to make matters worse, it occurred in front of Father Dunn.'

Sister Claire sat alone, looking out at the fleeting landscape. She felt hurt and angry. The children were silent, most overcome by their exertions and the fresh sea-air; an odd whisper could still be heard above the groan of the old diesel engine as it struggled on the hilly terrain. Claire could see Father Dunn in the front seat beside Hopalong. His head bobbed forward and backwards as he struggled to keep himself awake. She had smelled the whiskey on his breath as he spoke incoherently whilst being helped on board the bus. Reverend Mother, embarrassed by his behavior, turned to talk to Sister Agnes. Claire watched as the two spoke quietly amongst themselves, and by the occasional glance towards her she knew she was a topic of their conversation. 'How' she wondered, 'had things gone so terribly wrong? Was it really her fault? Should she have paid more attention? She gave a weary sigh.

When the gates of St. Joseph's appeared, looming large and menacing in the twilight, Pat felt more alone than he ever had in his short life. He knew his hour had come. The inevitable could no longer be delayed. Tears ran down his cheeks. The bus pulled up outside the main door. Sister Agnes let the nuns alight before she turned to the children. 'Straight to the dormitory' there will be no supper for any of you.' Pat sensed the children's loathing of him as they began to leave. He dared not look in their direction. One by one the children alighted from the bus. They were a sorry sight in their green blazers, grey pants and bare feet. Pat cast a look at Father Dunne as he alighted. He sat there, arms folded, head resting on his chest, his face red and glowing as he snored loudly. When Pat alighted, Hopalong beckoned to him.

127

The other children walked across the sharp gravel in their bare feet, wincing in pain as they headed silently towards the main door.

'You. Go straight to my office. I'll deal with you in a moment.'

Pat trembled, knowing what was to come. Sister Agnes was arguing with the bus driver. He was pointing at his watch.

'I should have been finished three hours ago Sister.'

'You were hired by this school, and we'll decide when we are finished with your services, now be a good man and drive Father Dunn to the presbytery.'

'What about his car?'

Sister Agnes was losing her patience.

'The poor man is in no fit state to get behind the wheel of his car. He can collect it tomorrow, now be off with you like a good fellow.'

'I've often seen him in a worse state than this, behind the wheel.'

Sister Agnes had enough. She raised her voice.

'Just go, or you never get a day's work from this school again.'

The engine spurted into life and the bus pulled away. Hopalong turned to Sister Claire.

'I want to see you in my office also.'

It was a small cluttered room, smelling of must and polish. The walls were shelved and full of old books and official looking documents. Files lay untidily on the desk. A portrait of Pope John Paul XX111 hung on the wall. Reverend Mother took her place behind the desk half-hidden beneath a mountain of paper. Sister Claire and Pat stood in front of her. Sister Agnes entered without speaking and began pacing up and down behind the pair. Hopalong turned her attention to Pat.

128

'I don't know what sort of evil possessed you. How could you do such a stupid thing. You shamed not only yourself, but also St. Joseph's. What do you have to say for yourself?'

Pat sniffled, holding back tears, his eyes fixed firmly on the floor.

'I'm sorry Reverend Mother .I t was an accident.'

'Accidents don't happen, they are caused.'

She then turned to Sister Claire.

'Where were you when all this was going on?'

She spoke softly and succinctly.

'I was folding the children's blazers, Reverend Mother.'

'You were supposed to be looking after the children,' she snapped.

'With all due respect, Reverend Mother, I was left alone, to look after twenty-three children because Sister Agnes had to return to look after you. Perhaps somebody should have been sent to replace her.'

Though Pat was crying, he was amazed by Sister Claire's bravery. Reverend Mother cast an awkward glance to Sister Agnes whose guilt quickly turned to contempt.

'How dare you question how we run this school? This school was here long before you ever came, and it will be here long after you're gone.'

Sister Claire stood her ground.

'I would just like to say Reverend Mother, that I believe it was an accident. The children were afraid they might mark their sandals. Can't you see they were trying to protect, not lose them.'

'How would you know, you said you weren't there.

Sister Claire felt exasperated by this petty arguing.

'Perhaps both of you are lying to me?' .

Sister Claire stepped forward, her voice pleading for a little compassion.

129

'I'll take full responsibility for what happened today.'

Sister Agnes forced her way between the pair.

'Indeed you will,' she interjected, slapping her hand down on the desk before her.

'I will personally replace the sandals.'

Reverend Mother tossed an amused look in the direction of Sister Agnes.

'And pray tell me, how are you going to manage that? With your pocket money?'

Sister Agnes sneered, but Sister Claire stood firm.

'I have a loving mother; I will ask her for help.'

Sister Agnes turned to her. She stood so close, that Sister Claire could smell the stale tobacco on her breath.

'This is not a matter for your family. This is a matter between you, Reverend Mother, and this school. Reverend Mother shall decide how this debt is to be paid, not you.'

Hopalong stood up from behind her desk and walked slowly towards Pat.

'As for you young man, feel lucky that you are only getting six of the best, and a week's suspension from class. You shall clean the grounds during school hours.'

A trickle could be heard on the bare floor boards. Pat had wet himself. He stood lost, ashamed, and bare footed in a little pool of his own pee. A mild smell of urine filled the air. Sister Agnes rushed to him and slapped him hard across the face.

'You horrid, creature, you'll pay for this.'

Sister Claire quickly stepped between the pair.

'For God's sake Sister, that's no way to treat a child.'

Hopalong cast a stern look in Sister Claire's direction.

'How dare you.'

Sister Claire pleaded with her.

'Have forgiveness, Reverend Mother, he's only a child, he didn't mean any harm.'

'How dare you question our authority or how we run this school. I'm in charge here and my decision is final.'

She turned to Pat, her voice cold and heartless.

'When you have cleaned up that disgusting little mess, and Sister Agnes has finished with you, I want you to go to the landing and pray all night before the statue of the Blessed Virgin for forgiveness.'

Sister Agnes brushed Sister Claire to one side. Pat's lip quivered. Sister Claire pleaded with Reverend Mother yet again on his behalf.

'This is cruelty.'

'This child needs to be taught a lesson,' snarled Sister Agnes.

Hopalong turned to Sister Claire, her fleshy jowls red with rage.

'I warned you not to question my authority.'

Sister Agnes produced a cane. Sister Claire lowered her head and shut her eyes.

'Hold out your hand you ruffian,' she growled, grasping Pat's wrist.

Sister Claire could hear the whacks of the cane and the whimpers of pain as she gave him 'six of the best. Sister Claire began to cry.

'And the other hand,' yelled Sister Agnes, as she proceeded to strike out with the cane.

'That will teach you,' she said lowering the cane.

Pat sobbed uncontrollably, his hands squeezed tightly beneath his armpits. Reverend Mother tossed a newspaper on to the floor.

'Now clean up your mess, you horrid child.'

'I'll do it,' said Sister Claire, you've put him through enough for one night.'

'How dare you speak like that in front of Reverend Mother,' snapped Sister Agnes.

Hopalong cast a cold glance at Sister Claire.

'You will remain up and take over Sister Theresa's duties not just for tonight, but for the entire week. I expect you in class at nine o' clock in the morning as usual. Use your time wisely and pray for a little contriteness.

CHAPTER NINETEEN

Reverend Mother's thick glasses lay on her bedside locker beneath the dim light of her bedside lamp. She lay in her brass bed propped up by two large pillows. Her face devoid of spectacles, was unrecognizable in the white nightcap she wore. It was buttoned so tightly, it exaggerating the number of fleshy folds beneath her chin. She was awake and staring blankly at the darkened corners of the room. She appeared agitated and a little uneasy. Finally she spoke.

'Do you think I was too hard on the little fellow?'

A voice from the bathroom answered. There was no mistaking the thick Cork accent.

'He deserved what he got,' said Sister Agnes

'He's an unfortunate little fellow really. He always seems to be getting into trouble.'

'How come none of the others are so unfortunate?'

Reverend Mother yawned. It had been a tiring day.

'What do you mean,' she enquired.

'You call him unfortunate because he gets into trouble. The real reason he is unfortunate, is because he causes trouble, and then gets found out.'

'Perhaps you're right, but I don't think he intentionally tried to lose the sandals.'

The flush of a toilet could be heard.

'Well he did,' said Sister Agnes The embarrassment of it all, and to make matters worse Father Dunn was there to witness it.'

Reverend Mother smiled.

'I wouldn't worry too much about him, he was that drunk he couldn't see in front of his nose,. That man is a raving alcoholic. He's not fit to wear the collar

133

and he's getting worse by the day; something should be done about it.'

She placed her hand over her mouth stifling yet another yawn. The sound of tap water could be heard.

'Like what?'

'Perhaps I should write to the Bishop and inform him of the problem.'

'Fat lot of good it would do writing to the Bishop. He has enough problems of his own to sort out.'

'Don't believe all you hear, I'm sure half of it is just malicious gossip.'

Reverend Mother listened to the gurgle of water emptying down the drain.

'The man needs help,' said Sister Agnes. 'Had he been awake he would have driven back to the Presbytery and killed himself or worse still, some poor innocent soul .'

Reverend Mother knew her words were true, but felt there was nothing she could do to change things. The bathroom door opened and a shaft of light flooded into the bedroom. Reverend Mother shaded her eyes. Sister Agnes stood in a nightdress. She quickly switched out the bathroom light and crawled under the sheets. Reverend Mother fumbled with the bedside lamp. The room fell into darkness,

'Your feet are freezing,' she protested.'

'It's those cold tiles in the bathroom, you should get a little rug for yourself.'

'I must,' she said, sliding lower down into the bed. Sister Agnes rested her head on Reverend Mother's shoulder.

'Do you think I was too harsh on Sister Claire?'

'She got what she deserved. She let you down, she let the school down and she let the children down.'

'Maybe it was asking a bit much of her to look after the children all by herself.'

134

'Nonsense it would not have happened if you or I were looking after them.'

Reverend Mother leaned across and kissed Sister Agnes gently on the forehead whispering softly,

'I don't know what I'd do without you?

Sister Agnes laughed.

'You'd find someone new.'

'Don't be silly, you might, but not me.'

CHAPTER TWENTY

Pat stood sobbing uncontrollably, blowing hard on his red raw hands. He stood on the landing at the top of the stairwell. He was barefoot and alone. It was dark and he was frightened. Before him was the statue of the Blessed Virgin. A strong smell of wax polish filled the air. His cold wet trousers stuck uncomfortably to his thin legs and the only morsel of comfort came from the single nightlight at the base of the statue and what little moon-light managed to filter through the tall stained glass window to his left. He looked up at the Virgins face flickering in the candle light, and prayed for strength. Though she was looking down, watching over him, he felt little comfort. The grandfather clock on the stairwell struck eleven. He jumped, frightened out of his wits and prayed louder to the Virgin Mary, hoping to filter out the strange and spooky noises all around. The clock struck twelve, and still he stood shivering at the base of the statue. By one o' clock he lay exhausted, in a foetal position on the cold linoleum floor, his teeth chattering in fretful sleep. A shadow crossed the landing. Two hands reached down, and raised his head placing a pillow underneath. Carefully a blanket was placed over him.

Beams of light began to filter through the stained glass window. Pat opened his eyes nervously and looked to the clock ticking in the corner of the stairwell. It was half-past four. Slowly he lifted the blanket and stood up. He could feel the cold linoleum beneath his bare feet. Images flashed back of the beach, the seagulls, the red kite, the blue sky, and the sandals. He blew on his tender hands warming them. He looked around as if searching for something. In the corner, in a dark alcove, he spotted the old electric polisher. Beside it lay an extension cable. Quietly he crept along the landing and retrieved the cable. Looking up to the Blessed Virgin he said a little prayer and carefully tied one end of the cable to the banister. He stood shivering and gazing down for what seemed an eternity. Placing his hand in his pocket he produced the sea-shell and rubbed it gently between his fingers. He could feel the subtle texture of the outer shell contrast with smoothness of the inner. Admiring its intricate shape he raised it to his ear. Once more he could hear the mighty ocean.

Memories came flooding back. He could feel once more the warm sun upon his skin and the gentle breeze upon his face. He could see the happiness on Sister Claire's face as she worked on the turrets. Joseph was there too, smiling proudly, watching the water filling the moat. . Those were the most beautiful feelings he had ever experienced. It was Heaven. He longed to go back there. Trembling, he tied the cable around his neck. Now, he was going to.

'No. Pat no!'
Sister Claire rushed along the corridor. He turned confused, ashamed and embarrassed, towards her. She grabbed him tightly in her arms. Her voice quivered.

'Oh my God, Pat. Oh my God!'
Quickly her trembling hands unwound the flex from around his neck.

'You silly boy, what were you thinking of?'
Her voice was strained with emotion. She shook him forcefully.

'What in God's name has gotten into you?'

He could not look her in the eye and lowered his head. She softened.

'Why' Pat? 'Why would you want to do such a horrible thing?'

Pat's mind was awash with confusion. He felt cheated, like a child caught in the act of stealing from an orchard, with all the associated guilt, yet deprived of ever having tasted of the fruit. He felt he had failed once more, and no matter how much he tried he would never get it right.

'Don't move,' she warned him, as she picked up the cable and replaced it by the polisher. When she returned she bent down and hugged him tightly.

'You poor little mite.'

A feeling of warmth and protection engulfed him. For the first time in his young life he experienced the warmth of an embrace. Tears flowed freely down his cheeks. All his pent-up emotions gushed to the surface as he sobbed uncontrollably.

'Promise me you'll never do that again.'

She loosened her grip. He did not answer. She took him by the shoulders and shook him gently.

'You have to promise me,' she said in an animated whisper, 'do you hear, you have to promise me.'

Pat raised his head. He could see the anguish on her young face.

'Please don't tell Sister Agnes'.

She smiled painfully.

'It'll be our little secret Pat, just between you and me. Nobody else need ever know. I promise you I won't say a word to anybody.'

'Here'

She handed him her handkerchief.

'You need to wipe your face and blow your nose. Don't be afraid, I can wash it later'

138

He lightly touched the spotless white linen against his face.

'Go ahead,' she encouraged him.

He wiped his eyes and blew his nose, folded the hanky and handed it back to her. She placed it in her pocket.

'You have to promise me that you will never attempt anything like that again, is that understood?'
He sniffled and nodded his head.

'I promise Sister.'

'Good boy. Wait there.'

She folded the blanket, grabbed the pillow that lay on the landing floor.

'I have to get this back to my room before the others get up. Will you be okay for a moment?'

Pat nodded.

He was alone once more, shaking like a leaf and looking down through the banisters into the main hall. A shaft of sunlight lit the interior casting blue and red hues from the stained glass window on the ornate plume patterned tiles below. It seemed different, almost beautiful. He never thought he could think such a thing of St Josephs. Now that the building lay silent and lifeless it had lost its menace. It was just four walls nothing more. A squeak on the corridor sent his trepidations racing back. She had returned. In her hand she carried some fresh clothes.

She handed them to Pat.

'I found these in the laundry room
. Pat began to undress.

'Not now, later.'

'We can get you something to eat in the kitchen. Would you like that?'

Pat nodded.

'You must be starving , follow me' she whispered.

Pat had never been to the kitchen of the orphanage. It was out of bounds to all except the nuns. Quietly Sister Claire led him down the dark corridor and through the large wooden door. The table was covered in loaves of freshly baked brown bread. A wonderful smell wafted through the room. Pat's stomach rumbled.

'Baked it all myself,' she said proudly.

'Smells great!'

'We have the kitchen all to ourselves for a least another hour,' she whispered.

'Take off those wet clothes. I'm just going out to the yard to gather some eggs. I'll be back in a second.'

He watched as she pulled the bolts on the kitchen door and walked out into the farmyard. He quickly changed into the fresh clothes. A chicken cackled by the crack in the kitchen door. Shafts of light filtered through casting the bird's strange elongated shadow on the dull grey flagstones. Everything seemed alien to him. An old radio, its dial illuminated perched on a shelf by the door. He listened to the strange accent;

'This is the B.B.C weather forecast at 05.00 hours. He could hear him talk in strange staccato sentences about Mizzen Head, Carnsore Point and the Irish Sea' Though he knew the man speaking English, to him it may as well have been double Dutch.

He moved to the large Victorian range to warm himself. It was like an altar, the centre piece of the kitchen. A large black kettle steamed on the hob. A ginger bushy tailed cat slept in a cardboard box by the side of the oven. He raised his palms and watched the timber logs crackle and blaze in the fire grate throwing out welcome heat to his hands and legs. Even the flagstones beneath his bare feet were warm and

140

inviting. Above him a wooden rack, draped with an assortment of towels, hung on ropes attached to the ceiling. Large black pots of every shape and size were stacked on shelves near the large metal sink that stood in front of the large curtain-less window. From where he stood, Pat could look out on the surrounding country-side. He could see the distant hills daubed in the red glow of morning light. Although he knew these places to see from afar he had as much knowledge of them and as little chance of walking there, as he had of walking on the moon. A rooster crowed noisily in the yard. Pat was terrified it might wake the other nuns. Trouble, was the last thing he needed right now. He wondered what possessed a rooster to crow at dawn. Had they a built -in clock? His attention was drawn to a large pine dresser full of ornately patterned china plates carefully arranged in symmetrical rows. Matching china cups hung from hooks in a neat line like decorated soldiers in a pageant. He was distracted by the sound of Sister Claire's footsteps as she returned.

'I've some lovely fresh ones'

She smiled, holding out a basket full of large brown eggs for Pat to see. His hunger was insatiable, when she placed some strips of bacon and some sausages on the frying pan. He had never seen food being cooked before. The smell was wonderful. He stood and watched as she broke some eggs and basted them in the lard. His mouth watered. She placed some large odd-looking gloves on her hands and opened the oven door. He could feel the heat envelope him. A wonderful smell wafted past his nostrils as she pulled a tray of freshly baked brown bread from the oven. He watched as she quickly tossed the bread from the tray on to wire meshes for cooling.

'You should try it when it's hot' she smiled.

She cut a thick slice of bread from one of the loaves, covered it in butter and placed in on a plate on the table.

'There, sit down and tastse that.'

Pat sat and took the warm bread in his hands.

'Thank you Sister.'

He could see the lump of butter melting as he raised it to his mouth. It was heavenly.

'Not bad eh,' said Sister Claire, who herself was biting into a fresh slice.

She placed a fry in front of him. Soon both were seated at the large table enjoying, what was to Pat, nothing less than a feast. He ate till he could eat no more. She smiled at him.

'You have a wonderful appetite for such a small boy,' she remarked.

'It was so good I couldn't stop.'

She checked the clock.

'We better get a move on. I'll send your clothes to the laundry.'

She bent down and tossed them into a wicker basket.

'Thanks for everything Sister.'

She smiled warmly

'It was my pleasure.'

'Thank you for trying to help me yesterday.'

She was no longer smiling.

'I only did what any decent soul would have done.'

'You stood up for me, and now you are in trouble.'

'I stood up for my principles, if that means I get into trouble so be it. I would do the same for any other child.'

Pat knew she would, that she really had the children's best interests at heart. She moved towards him.

'I have to ask a question,' she said, her voice now deadly serious. Pat looked into her eyes. She picked her words carefully.

142

'Why did you that, on the landing?'

Pat lowered his head before he spoke.

'I don't know Sister,' he said softly.

She looked concerned.

'You must know? People don't do things like that without a reason?'

She waited for his reply.

'I don't know Sister, maybe it's because of who I am.'

'What do you mean Pat?'

'Well I always end up in trouble, no matter how hard I try.'

'Yesterday was not your fault. I accept you might have come up with the idea of burying the sandals, but you can't be the only one responsible for losing them. I think perhaps your class let you down.'

She paused a moment before making eye contact.

'I think perhaps your friend Joseph let you down'. His eyes moistened. She had broached on something painful. The cat rose from its box, arched its back, stretched slowly, and meowed by the door. Sister Claire pulled the latch, chickens came running, the cat peered out hesitating before darting sideways across the yard.

'Can I ask another question?'

Pat nodded silently. She closed the door gently.

'What made you stand up when Reverend Mother asked who stained the Thank You Card.

'We were all going to be slapped Sister, so I thought it better one of us gets slapped than all four.' '

'That's because, Joseph didn't own up. Why were you prepared to take the punishment for something you didn't do? Would he have done the same for you?'

Though Pat knew in his heart, the answer to her question, he looked into her blue enquiring eyes and replied,

'I don't know, Sister.'

She spoke cautiously now, aware of his vulnerability.

'Friends should help one another; look after each other, be there when you need them most. I want to be your friend Pat, can I?'

Pat looked up.

'Yes Sister.'

A smile crossed his face

'You already are my friend.'

'Pat, remember what I said; if you have a problem, any problem, please come to me and I will try to sort it out for you. Do you understand?'

'Yes Sister.'

'Real friends don't break promises, so I need you to promise me you will never attempt anything like that again'. Do you promise?

'Yes Sister.'

She glanced at the clock on the wall.

'Right we better get you back upstairs before the rest of the nuns get up'.

Sister Claire quickly led him up the back stairs to the landing. Though he was tired, Pat felt good. He had eaten a wonderful breakfast, and his little tummy felt like it was about to burst. The despair he had felt earlier that morning seemed to have vanished like a bad dream. He stood once more in front of the statue of the Blessed Virgin. Sister Claire patted him gently on the head.

'Remember our promise?'

Pat nodded.

'Give me your little finger.'

Pat raised his hand unsure as to what she meant. She took his little finger and interlocked it with hers.

'Pinkie promise.'

Pat smiled.

'Pinkie promise.'

'I better get back to work, before the others arrive.' She winked at him, and headed quickly down the stairs.

CHAPTER TWENTY ONE

When Sister Claire left, Pat no longer felt alone. He stood looking at the statue of the Virgin at her kind face gazing down at him, and her welcoming arms. He had never given it much thought before, but now he knew the significance of welcoming arms. He felt strong, stronger than he had ever felt before. He was surprised when he noticed the Virgin too was in her bare feet. Yet despite this, she had managed to pin the Serpent's head beneath her. It was a triumph of good over evil, a triumph of timidity over aggression, a triumph of courage over all.

The clock struck seven. Pat no longer jumped, but gazed calmly in its direction. Soon footsteps could be heard on the stairs. It was Sister Agnes, her voice as gruff as ever.

'Get up to the dormitory. Mass is in ten minutes, don't be late.'

When Pat entered the dormitory the others were dressing. They turned away half-ashamed, half-embarrassed to make eye contact with him. He walked slowly to his bed, his head held high. Joseph turned to him.

'Are you Okay?'

Pat stood for some moments not knowing what to say. Was this his friend? Did he really care? He doubted it. Where was Joseph when he needed him? Where were his so-called friends when he stood alone to face the wrath of Sister Agnes and Hopalong, or when he stood all night upon the landing, frightened and alone in the darkness? Did they know that by their actions each and every one of them had put him there? He wondered would they have even cared if he had jumped? How many of them he wondered, had lost a moment's sleep thinking about him? He already knew the answers. He probably knew them all along. He had a best friend now, someone who showed him kindness and respect. Sadly that person was not in this dormitory. He turned away not bothering to reply.

Sister Claire stood at the blackboard her ruler pointing to the 'six-times' tables. She looked tired and dishevelled. The children monotonously rhymed off 'six-threes are eighteen, six-fours are...etc. The sky was dark and overcast and the morning seem to carry the sombre mood felt by all. Rain pelted against the window panes. She looked to Pat's empty seat and to the black skies outside. No longer able to concentrate she ceased. The children carried on briefly before they too stopped. Slowly she walked towards them.

'I want to apologize to you all for what happened yesterday. It was as much my fault, as it was anybody's. I'm the adult, I was in charge and I let you down.'

The children looked perplexed. She bit her lip trying to remain in control.

'We were having such a nice day, and such a wonderful time. Then I went and ruined it all for everybody.'

Tubby raised his hand to speak. She nodded to him. 'Yes Thomas?'

'It wasn't your fault Sister, it was Pat's.

A chorus filled the room.

'Yes Sister it was Pat's fault.'

Her eyes moistened.

'Tommy' she asked, 'who put your sandals in that sand dune?'

147

Tubby hesitated, then blurted out.

'I put them there Sister, but he covered them up.'

'It was his idea in the first place' interjected Joseph.

'Please stand up Joseph,' she said, a look of utter disappointment on her face.

'Yesterday, when I asked where the sandals were, you replied.

'We hid them Sister. They were your very words. 'We hid them. Now you tell me it was Pat alone who hid the sandals in the dunes.

Joseph, sensing her growing frustration, backtracked

'No, we all did,' he replied awkwardly, 'but we wouldn't have, if it hadn't been for him.'

The other children voiced their agreement. She bit her lip harder till she could taste blood on the inside of her mouth.

'Was he responsible for the ink stain on the card, Joseph?'

Joseph blushed.

'And did he deserve the punishment he got?'

The children turned to face him.

For a moment there was total silence as they awaited his answer.

'Yes Sister,' he said, unable to hold her gaze.

'I see,' she said bitterly disappointed.

'You may sit back down.'

Joseph sunk slowly back into his seat. For some time she remained silent before eventually speaking.

'I want you to study your tables silently for a moment. I'll ask you them, in a little while.'

She walked through the class, past Pat's empty seat towards the front window. Stopping she looked out at the pouring rain. Pat stood alone on the avenue with a sweeping brush in his hand, his shirt sticking to his back, his red hair matted and hanging limply over his forehead. He was busy sweeping the loose gravel from the sides back on to the centre of the avenue. He did not see her watching. A car drove up the avenue, splashed through a puddle soaking Pat some more. Father Dunn was collecting his car. She glimpsed his unconcerned face sitting in the passenger seat as the wipers washed the teeming rain away and observed as he quickly changed cars and drove away, passing Pat as if he wasn't there. She sucked subconsciously on her lip tasting the blood, overwhelmed by her sense of helplessness. The children turned and stole a peek as she dropped her head in her hands and began to cry.

CHAPTER TWENTY-TWO

It was a dreadful week for Sister Claire. By Wednesday she was physically and mentally exhausted. She had managed to get some sleep by going to her room after supper for a few hours before she commenced the night work at ten. She usually got back to bed at about five in the morning and slept till six-thirty. Tonight her body ached so much she decided to have a bath before she retired to bed. She tidied up the last of the kitchen utensils and placed the bread neatly in a row on the metal racks before she turned out the light and headed up the back stairs.

The bathroom was basic. It was nothing more than a converted bedroom with an old bath with decorative caste iron feet standing in the middle of the floor. Sister Claire quietly closed the door. There was no means of locking it, not that she cared too much at five o'clock in the morning. The naked bulb hanging from the ceiling was not just the only source of light but also the only source of heat in the room. The walls were green and dull. There were no curtains on the large solitary window just plastic contact sheeting diffusing the dull morning light. White tile patterned linoleum adorned the floor.Steam rose from the large bathtub as it quickly began to fill. A single black chair stood in the corner near an old disused radiator. Placing a towel on the chair she slowly began to undress.

For some time she lay motionless in the warm invigorating water. She could feel the heat soothing her tired muscles and relieving her aching bones. She looked so different, like any young teenage girl, once free of the habit that concealed her shapely figure and made her look so androgynous. Slowly she lowered her head beneath the water and began to wash her hair. Her firm breasts broke the surface as she did so. Despite her badly shorn blonde hair she looked beautiful as she emerged from the water and swept it off her face. To her horror when she opened her eyes somebody was standing observing her. For a moment she didn't recognize Sister Agnes. She held two cups of tea in her hands. She looked much younger without her veil and her curly black hair softened the harder features of her face, making her oddly attractive.

'I couldn't sleep' she said gently.

Sister Claire sat upright trying desperately to conceal her nakedness.

'So I went to make a cup of tea. When I heard the bath running, I decided to make a cup for you too.

Sister Claire smiled weakly.

'Thank you Sister.

Sister Agnes reached out with a cup. Sister Claire not wanting to remove her arms from her breasts nodded to the chair.

'You can leave it there Sister, I'll have it later.'

Sister Agnes smiled and placed the cup carefully on the chair and walked back over to the bath.

'It looks so good.'

Sister Claire felt uneasy and vulnerable as she stood looking down on her.

'It is good,' she said weakly. '

I feel like jumping in' she chuckled, sipping from her cup.

Sister Claire shuddered inwardly at the thought and smiled nervously.

'I'm afraid there's no room,' she joked.

Sister Agnes then ran a finger through the water. 'Water is such a beautiful thing. Without it there could be no life. Everything depends on it.'

'I suppose so. I hadn't really given it much thought.'

'It is used in the bible to symbolize purity, and a cleansing of the soul. Even Christ was baptized in it'.

She lifted her fingers from the water and shook her hand.

'The Romans were a very clever lot; they knew the value of it too. They built baths wherever they could. They knew there was no better way to relax than to soak in a bath and wash your cares away.

She sat on the side of the tub.

'I hope you don't mind me sitting here?'

Sister Claire did mind, but she was not about to say so.

'That's okay,' she said in a non convincing tone.

` She began to rub her arms with the soap hoping perhaps Sister Agnes might take the hint and leave, but to her growing discomfort she sat there unconcerned sipping her tea.

'You know I nearly drowned once.'

'Oh.' said Sister Claire, hoping to avoid a drawn out conversation.

Sister Agnes gazed into her cup recalling the event.

'I was eight years old. Mary and I were inseparable. We used to spend our summers walking the hills or playing by the stream that ran through the farm. We would spend hours by the pond trying to catch minnows in jam jars. One day I overreached and fell in. I couldn't swim. Mary tried to grab me but couldn't. I splashed and splashed but it was no use. Resigned, I gave up and let the water take me. I

152

remember looking up at the shiny mirrored surface above. Strangely everything seemed so peaceful. I was not afraid. There was a beautiful calmness down there. I could hear little bells chiming in my head calling me.'

Sister Claire listened curious as to where this might lead.

'Images of my short life began to flash before my eyes. Tranquility began to overcome me. I felt a sense of inner peace. I did not struggle. Then out of nowhere a hand grabbed me by the hair and pulled me kicking and screaming to the surface'.

'Was it Mary?'

Sister Agnes shook her head, her eyes began to moisten.

'Oh how I wish, he had let me drown.'

'You don't mean that.

'Oh I do' she said in a quivering voice.

She had never seen Sister Agnes betray emotion before and was uncertain how to respond.

'Who saved you?'

Sister Agnes winced and focused her soulless eyes on the ceiling.

'It was my Uncle. My uncle Bill.

She stood up as if trying to obliterate the memory from her mind. Sister Claire watched as she placed the cup upon the window ledge.

'Here give me that soap I'll wash your back for you.'

Sister Claire protested.

'I'm fine Sister really I am.'

'Nonsense girl, I insist, you're not an octopus. Nobody can scrub their own back. I think it's a design flaw. God must have been having a bad day.'

Though Sister Claire tried to resist Sister Agnes held out her hand.

'Good girl, give it here.'

Reluctantly she handed over the soap covered her breasts and leant forward.

Dawn was breaking and light began to filter in through the opaque glass. She sat there uneasily as Sister Agnes tenderly rubbed her pale soft skin. Sister Claire was surprised at the gentleness of her touch. Just as she was beginning to relax Sister Agnes stood up and handed back the soap.

'There you go. All done,' she smiled. Picking up her cup, she headed for the door.

'Drink your tea before it gets cold and get some sleep.'

'I will sister'

'Goodnight then' she said closing the door gently behind her.

Sister Claire lay back in the tub perplexed and relieved.

CHAPTER TWENTY- THREE

The following day was glorious. The rain clouds had vanished and the sun beat warmly down from a clear blue sky. Pat delighted in the fact he was not stuck inside the stuffy old classroom. He could hear the children rhyming out their seven-times tables through the large open windows. He was working again on the avenue, this time weeding a large flowerbed set in the middle of a lawn a little way down from the main building, with shirtsleeves rolled and kneeling on an old Hessian sack to shield his knees. He wore Noel's leather gloves to protect his hands. Though they were much too big for him he didn't care. They saved him from the dreaded thorns and nettles he was weeding.

Noel was the handyman, at St. Joseph's. Work was scarce in rural Mayo, so he had to take what work he could find. Though he was overworked and underpaid he lived rent free with his wife Molly in the gate lodge, at the entrance to the school. They had two children a boy Cormac aged three, and a six-week old baby girl, Emer. Though the lodge was tiny and in poor repair it was sufficient for their present needs and they were contented. There was the added bonus of not having to buy the vegetables or fruit he grew on the farm and that made up in no small way for his poor wages. He was a handsome young man in his early thirties with a kind face and receding brown hair. Though Noel did not like Pat getting into trouble, he was glad of any help he got around the farm.

Pat hummed quietly as he worked. He enjoyed the outdoors. It made him feel good; it gave him a sense of freedom. He loved the fact he was unsupervised and hadn't got some nun's beady eyes watching his every move. The rattle of the milk lorry distracted him as it made its way up the avenue. It came to a stop beside him. Miko stepped out from behind the wheel. He was wearing his customary white coat and cap. He was a small jolly man in his fifties. The peaked cap covered his bald head but not the long bushy sideburns sticking from the sides of his rotund face, framing his button nose and dancing green eyes, reminding Pat of an oversized leprechaun.

'God bless the work,' he said warmly.

Pat stood up to greet him.

'Good morning Miko.'

'How are you today Pat?'

'Fine thanks.'

'You poor thing, you didn't look too fine yesterday in the pelting rain. Did they not give you a jacket to wear?'

'They did, but I didn't want to get it wet, in case Sister Agnes gave me another hiding.'

'She must be a right auld bitch,' said Miko.

'You have no idea,' said Pat.

'Where's Noel,' he enquired. Have you taken over as the head gardener now?' '

I wish,' said Pat with a smile. 'I'm out here for the week.'

Miko cast him a sideways glance and raised a bushy eyebrow.

'Oh I see. A form of punishment is it?'

Pat nodded.

'Ah well, boys will be boys,' he said philosophically. '

156

Noel's gone into town to get a new wheelbarrow'
said Pat.

'Jaysus that fella has a great time, off
gallivanting, leading the high life, while you're
stuck here to do the dirty work.'

Pat smirked.

'I'm happy to do it.'

He glanced towards the large grey structure of St.
Joseph's.

'Can you imagine been stuck in there, on a day like
this?

'Now that you mention it, I can see you're better off
out here all right', said Miko, lifting his cap and
scratching his bald head.

'Noel said he wouldn't be too long. He's left about
an hour ago so he should be back shortly.

'Ah it's not that important. I'll catch him again.'

'Do you want me to give him a message for ya?

Miko tousled Pat red hair.

'No it's fine thanks. You look after yourself do ya
hear and try to keep out of trouble.'

'I will' said Pat.

He went to the truck and returned with a bottle of
milk.

'Here drink this I'm sure it's thirsty work.'

Pat's eyes lit up as he handed him the bottle.

'Thanks Miko.'

'Your welcome son, save the bottle for me. I'll
collect it tomorrow.'

Pat stood watching the little lorry rattle its way
towards the orphanage and vanish around the side of
the building. He peeled back the foil cap, and took a
long satisfying gulp of the thick cream at the top of the
bottle. Wiping his mouth he placed the bottle in the
shade of a laurel bush. Miko was gone when Noel
arrived back from town. Pat watched as he parked his

157

Morris Traveller outside the gate lodge and walked proudly up the avenue pushing the brand new wheelbarrow.

'Well what do you think,' he called out.

 Pat ran towards him.

'Looks great,' he said casting a critical eye over it.

'Did they not have another colour?

Noel laughed.

'They told me I had three choices I could choose any one of them, provided it was black.'

Noel patted the side of the barrow.

'Hop in,' he said.

Pat climbed into the barrow.

'Well what do ya think,' asked Noel running and swerving the barrow along the avenue.

 Pat held on tightly.

'You're trying to kill me,' he squealed excitedly.

When they were opposite the flower bed Noel set the barrow down and Pat jumped out.

´That was a great laugh' he enthused. 'Oh by the way, Miko was looking for ya.'

Noel rolled the barrow on to the lawn stopping by the bundle of weeds Pat had pulled.

'What did he want?'

'He said it wasn't important that he'd see you again.'

Pat looked up at Noel, his small freckled nose twitching as he gazed into the harsh bright light.

'He gave me a bottle of milk.'

'Did he now?'

'Yes.'

'Ah that man's the salt of the earth, you could trust him with your life, he'd never let you down.'

 Noel glanced at the flowerbed.

'Christ you're doing great work altogether.'

'Thanks' said Pat.

158

He grabbed the bottle of milk and offering Noel a swig.

> 'No thanks lad, but you had better drink it before it gets too warm.'

Noel watched in amusement at the milk trickling down Pat's chin as he attempted to drink from the wide necked bottle.

'You're a good kid; I'll miss you when you're back in class.'

> 'I'll miss you too,' said Pat pausing for breath 'if it wasn't for Sister Claire, I don't think I could stand it here anymore.'

Noel picked up the leather gloves and placed them on his hands. He bent down and began to toss the weeds into the barrow.

'You like Sister Claire?'

Pat took another swig of milk and wiped his mouth. 'She's good. She gave me her pillow and covered me with a blanket the night I spent on the landing. She even stood up for me against Hopalong and Sister Agnes.'

'Hopalong?'

'Oh that's just a name we call Reverend Mother.'

'Ya better not let her hear you calling her that, or you'll be murdered stone dead.

He tossed some more weed into the barrow.

'So Sister Claire stood up for ya did she?'

'Yeah and now she has to work at night in the kitchen for a whole week.'

Noel stopped what he was doing and shook his head in despair.

'You mean to tell me they have her working night and day for a week?'

Pat nodded and finished the remains of the milk. He wiped his mouth with his sleeve.

'Yeah, she has to bake the bread at night.'

'God love her,' said Noel, pulling on a thorn bush. 'She's great'

Pat's eyed widened.

'She's not afraid of them, and she made me the biggest breakfast I've ever seen, and she told me she wanted to be my friend.'

Noel continued loading the barrow.

'She sounds like a lovely person. You're very lucky to have a friend like her.'

Pat placed the empty bottle on the grass.

'Will you be my friend too' he enquired hesitantly?

Noel tossed the last clump of weeds into the barrow and patted him reassuringly on the back.

'Of course I'll be your friend'.

'No really Noel, will you?'

Noel smiled and went to pick up the barrow.

'Can I do that Noel?'

'If you want to' he said stepping back.

'Where are we going' enquired Pat

'Follow me mate', he said walking towards the farm.

CHAPTER TWENTY- FOUR

The strains of Liszt's Hungarian Rhapsody emanated from the kitchen radio. It was one o' clock in the morning and Sister Claire was busy kneading dough. Logs crackled brightly in the fire grate and the old range glowed, making the kitchen uncomfortably warm. Even the cat had vacated its cozy bed in favor of the cool night air. Sister Claire had removed her outer garments, party to protect them and partly because of the heat. Without the veil and wimple she looked like a child, and though her face was clear and fresh the signs of exhaustion were showing in the darkness around her tired blue eyes. She stood wearily by the table in her sleeveless white bodice and large blue flowery wrap-around apron. Carefully she began to place the dough on to the various greased trays she had laid out in front of her. When she had finished she began placing the trays in the oven. Sister Agnes stood at the kitchen door wearing a dark green dressing gown, her short dark hair wet and curly from her recent bath. She stood for some time drying her hair and observing Sister Claire. Unaware of her presence Sister Claire continued to place the bread trays into the oven.

'Good night Sister.'
Sister Claire jumped.
'I'm sorry I didn't mean to startle you. Perhaps I should have knocked'.
'It's quiet all right it's my own fault' she blurted, patting her chest and pointing to the radio.

'I didn't hear you come in.'

'You look so different without your veil, Sister Claire.'

'Don't we all' she replied uncomfortably.

'I was surprised by how young and pretty you looked last night.'

'You looked younger too' she said, placing some more trays in the oven.

Sister Agnes voice was soft and warm, and it made Sister Claire feel decidedly uncomfortable.

'But tonight my child, you look tired and weary.'

'Well I have to admit I am a little tired Sister.'

'The combination of night duty and classroom must be exhausting.'

Sister Claire laughed weakly.

'So I've discovered' she said closing the oven door. She had never heard Sister Agnes speak in such a caring way. Had she misread the woman? Perhaps she had a heart after all?

'You need some sleep.'

Sister Agnes moved closer and took Sister Claire's face gently in her hands.

'You're too young and pretty to have bags under your eyes.'

Sister Claire turned away and busied herself collecting the remnants of dough from the work top. Sister Agnes moved close behind her effectively pinning her between herself and the tabletop. Sister Claire, though uncomfortable, tried not to show it.

'Here, let me ease your aching muscles.'

'I'm fine Sister, really I am.'

'Nonsense my dear it will do you good' she insisted and began to slowly massage Sister Claire's shoulders.

'You're all knotted up. You need to learn to relax.'

Sister Claire could feel her fingers working on her aching back.

'Perhaps you're right Sister,' she said still rolling the leftover dough.

'I mean really relax, stop what you're doing for the moment. Let yourself loosen up, let go.'

Sister Claire stopped and tried to relax a little.

'That's much better, good girl.'

'You do that very well Sister.'

Such was the soothing sensation to Sister Claire's aching muscles she involuntarily arched her back and raised her head.

'Does that make you feel any better?

'Yes it does Sister,' she said moaning slightly, as her weary muscles reacted to the stimulation.

Before she realized it, Sister Agnes had gently slipped her hands inside the sleeveless bodice and began to caress her firm young breasts. For a moment Sister Claire stood confused and breathless. Nobody had ever touched her there before. She liked the sensation, how it made her tingle all over. Ripples of pleasure began to wash over her, running up and down her body like tiny electric shocks.

Sister Agnes kissed her softly on the back of the neck and whispered in her ear.

'You need rest; let me take you to my room. Nobody need ever know. I'll come back down here and finish up and you can have a good night's sleep.' Sister Claire struggled with the physical pleasure she felt. Sister Agnes kissed her on the neck once more and whispered softly; 'If you want, I can speak with Reverend Mother and get her to rescind the rest of night work?'

Pulling Sister Agnes's hands from her breasts she struggled to break free. Sister Agnes refused to let her go and in despair Sister Claire turned and hit her

163

across the face smearing her cheek with dough. Sister Agnes fell backwards. '

'You bloody bitch, you'll pay for this', she said wiping the dough from her face with a tea towel. Sister Claire fled the kitchen.

'Mark my words you'll pay for this.'

CHAPTER TWENTY-FIVE

It was a scorcher. Pat was once more working on the avenue. This time he was trimming the hedge with a pair of garden shears. He heard the unmistakable sound of the milk lorry as it came rattling up the avenue. Pat stepped to one side and waved as Miko passed him by on his delivery to the school. He grabbed the shears and began working once more. It was hard work. When Noel trimmed the hedge it looked so easy. Pat found it hard to hold the shears never mind cut the hedge. He wished he was grown-up and had a job like Miko's. He loved the idea of being out and about meeting people and seeing different places. Miko, he reckoned must be one of the best known men in the whole country. On his way back Miko stopped the lorry and walked over to Pat.

'Where the hell is he now?'

'He's gone back down to the gate lodge. He said he wouldn't be long.'

Pat handed over the empty bottle.

'Thanks Miko.

Miko placed the bottle in one of the empties crates, and grabbed a full one. He handed it to Pat.

'There you go lad. You need to keep your energy up.'

Pat shook his head.

'No thanks Miko, I can't take it.'

'Why not' he asked, scratching his sideburns in bewilderment?

'You'll get in trouble.'

Miko's green eyes twinkled.

'Don't you worry your little head about me. Have you ever heard of breakage?'

Pat looked at him blankly.

'I thought as much. You see every milkman is allowed to lose the odd bottle or two. It's part of the job.'

'You mean you don't have to pay for it?'

'Not a penny.'

He held out the bottle once more.

'Go on lad, take it.'

Pat took the bottle. Miko winked.

'Thanks Miko, you're a star.'

'Do you know what, you're very close.'

Pat looked confused. Miko face lit up

'The wife says I'm wired to the moon.'

He chuckled heartily at his own joke much to Pat's amusement.

'Thanks again' said Pat, sporting a broad smile on his freckled face.

'Good luck son.'

Miko climbed into his truck and drove off down the avenue towards the gate lodge. Pat lifted the red foil cap and began to drink. Soon his attention was drawn to the sound of footsteps. A woman in a white cardigan and blue dress was walking down the avenue towards him, backlit by the morning sun. Pat quickly hid the milk from view and began to clip the hedge once more. He could see she carried a suitcase in her hand. As she neared Pat noticed her cropped blond hair. At first he did not recognize her and continued clipping the hedge. She stopped beside him.

'Hello Pat.' He immediately recognized her voice and looked disbelievingly.

'Sister Claire?'

She smiled weakly, her face drawn and tormented. 'Yes it's me. Do I look so different without my habit?'

'Why are you dressed like that, Sister?'

She hesitated a moment and looked down the avenue, searching for the right words, but there were none.

'I'm leaving.'

Pat could not believe his ears and dropped the shears from his hands.

'Leaving the school?'

She nodded, and lowered her eyes.

'For how long,' he asked.

'For good, Pat.'

'But why, you're the best nun we've ever had.' Tears welled in his eyes.

'You promised you'd be my friend.'

Sister Claire looked away, not knowing how to answer.

'The hedge looks lovely; you're doing a great job.' Pat was not listening. He was trying to absorb this catastrophic news.

'Why sister?' She pointed to the half-hidden milk bottle.

'That was nice of Miko.'

'Yes,' said Pat, still waiting for her reply. She looked down at him. In the three days since she had seen him the freckles on his face appeared to have multiplied from exposure to the sunlight. He appeared so sad, so utterly lost. Her heart ached. She was terrified he might try something drastic, that he might harm himself in some way.

'I'll remember you every night in my prayers Will you pray for me?'

Pat lowered his head.

'Yes Sister,' he muttered.

'Every night, promise?'

'Yes Sister.'

She dropped the suitcase and got down on her hunkers and held his hands in hers.

' I'll write to you every week. Will you write back?' To Pat her words sounded so final he could only manage a nod. She took him in her arms and hugged him tightly. Her eyes welled with tears. Pat began to sob.

***

From her vantage point on the convent landing, Reverend Mother watched through the net curtains, Sister Agnes by her side.

'I'll be sad to see her go,' she said.

'The children liked her, and she obviously has a special bond with young Pat. He'll miss her terribly.'

Sister Agnes scoffed at her remarks.

'Had I not stepped in, there would have been no bread this morning. That young hussy was prepared to let the children go hungry.'

'What happened exactly' asked Reverend Mother turning from the window?

'When I entered the kitchen to make a cup of tea she attacked me verbally then physically. I tried to calm her down, but she was like a wild animal and stormed out the door. Good riddance I say.'

What were you doing up so late?'

'I couldn't sleep.'

'Why didn't you come to my room,' asked Reverend Mother? '

I was going to, but first I wanted to make us a cup of tea.'

Reverend Mother looked back out through the net curtain.

'I would never have thought that of her, she seem so gentle and loving, especially to little Pat.'

168

'There can be no favoritism shown to children in this school. Anyway, she was too hot headed too insubordinate. She would never have made the grade.'

Reverend Mother shook her head gently.

'She is headstrong, I'll grant you that, but that in itself is not a bad thing if harnessed properly. I tried to reason with her this morning. I begged her to stay.

'You what?'

'Then I asked her why she insisted in leaving so suddenly.'

Sister Agnes glanced nervously towards Reverend Mother.

'But she wouldn't say. I asked if it was because of the excessive workload I gave her. She said the work had nothing to do with it. I even offered her an apology.'

'An apology.'

'You, apologized to her?'

'Yes, I asked her to forgive me.'

'And what did she say?'

'She told me she accepted the apology, but was leaving anyway. She said she could not condone the way this school was being run.'

'Cheeky slut, who does she think she is?'

Reverend Mother appeared shocked at this verbal outburst.

'She said some of the Nuns in this school are in the wrong institution.'

Sister Agnes turned her face away.

'Did she name any?'

'No I asked her to elaborate, but she wouldn't.'

Sister Agnes breathed a sigh of relief.

'Do you think perhaps, she was talking about us?'

Sister Agnes reached for reverend Mother's hand.

'Of course not. Nobody knows about us. She's just a troublemaker She's was evil. Good riddance I say.'

Reverend Mother had seen enough and walked away. Sister Agnes lifted the net curtain and stole one last look.

***

Pat's world was crumbling once more. A tide of emotion was washing his hopes away, leaving him bereft and dazed. The one friend he trusted most was leaving him. He stood in her warm embrace not wanting to let go. Sister Claire wiped the tears from her eyes and put on a brave face.

'Maybe you could spend Christmas at my house. Would you like that?'

Pat nodded, too emotional for words. She smiled through her tears trying to lighten the situation.

'I promise, I'll take you out this Christmas. You can spend the holidays at my mother's house. You'll like that. We'll have lots of fun. There will be loads of things to do. We could even stop off in Dublin for a day if you like.'

Pat's face broke into a half-smile. She pinched him playfully on the cheek.

'That's it. That's what I want to see.'

The tone of her voice changed and she spoke softly.

'Remember our little secret?'

Pat lowered his eyes and nodded.

'Promise me you'll never attempt anything like that again, no matter how bad things get.'

He did not reply and she shook him gently by the shoulders.

'Pat look at me, I want you to promise.'

'I promise, Sister.'

She offered him her little finger.

'Pinkie promise.

Pat smiled through his tears as they interlocked their little fingers.

'Pinkie promise.'

She stood up biting on her lip

'Goodbye Pat, I'll miss you.'

'Goodbye Sister Claire.'

She smiled.

'From now on, you can call me 'Claire'.

Pat felt awkward, it sounded so strange.

'Goodbye Claire.'

He watched, emotions churning as Claire picked up her suitcase and headed down the avenue towards the main gate. She had only gone a few yards when he ran after her.

'Sister. Sister.'

Claire dropped her suitcase and turned towards him.

'Yes Pat,' she said wiping her eyes.

He put his hand into his pocket and pulled out the shell.

'I want you to have this.'

'What is it,' she asked.

'It's for you,' he said, placing it in her palm.

She looked down at the shell; her voice cracking with emotion.

'It's the speckled shell from the beach, the one you said looked like chocolate. You kept it?'

'I took it, but now I don't want it.'

'Why not,' she asked.

'I don't want to listen to it anymore'

'But the sound of the ocean is beautiful.'

'I'll get sad and lonely if I listen to it now.'

Claire's heart was aching.

'I'll mind it for you. Whenever I see its chocolate speckles I think of your little freckled face. We can listen to the ocean together when you come to stay with us at Christmas.'

Pat nodded and wiped his nose with his sleeve.

'Goodbye Sister.'

'Goodbye Pat.'

He turned and ran away. She closed her eyes, emotionally drained and physically shattered.

Miko and Noel walked out of the gate lodge just as Claire was passing. Noel spotted Claire and rushed to help her with her suitcase.

'Sister Claire, what's the matter, why are you dressed like that? Why are you carrying a suitcase?

He noticed how upset she was as he took it from her

'Come inside, I'll make you a cup of tea.'

'Thanks Noel, but I must get going, I don't want to miss the train.'

'What happened,' he asked?

Tears began welling up again.

'I tried Noel, really I tried.'

Miko moved towards them.

'I can drop you to the station Sister, it's on my way, he said helpfully.'

'That would be so kind of you.'

'It's my pleasure, Sister.' Here let me take your things.'

Miko took the suitcase and went to make some space on the back of the lorry.

'Maybe you'll feel differently in a day or two' said Noel supportively. '

I don't think so. I know I don't belong here anymore.'

'But you were the best teacher the children ever had. They all loved you.'

She placed her hand on his arm.

'It's nice of you to say so Noel. I miss them already.'

Noel rubbed his unshaven face with his hand.

'Poor Pat is going to miss you terribly. He never stops talking about you.'

She lowered her head and sobbed.

'I feel so guilty. Please keep an eye on him for me. The poor mite's so vulnerable. I know he likes and trusts you. Help him if you can.' 'He's a good child. 'Of course I will'

Claire glanced away.

'You know it's not the children who are the problem, it's the adults.'

He sensed the irony in her voice.

'You've uncovered some rotten apples?

Claire did not answer, she didn't have to. He looked her in the eyes.

'I think I know who they are.

Her silence spoke multitudes. '

'It only takes one rotten apple to destroy the barrel.' Claire sighed and nodded her head. Noel patted her gently on the arm.

'Maybe you are doing the right thing, getting out now.'

Claire smiled weakly, thankful for his support.

'I'm not proud of what I'm doing, but I'm in no position to remove the bad apples myself, perhaps on the outside I can bring it to the attention of others?'

'I'm ready whenever you are Sister,' said Miko climbing down from the back of the milk lorry.

Claire shook Noel's hand and thanked him.

'I'll be off then. Please keep an eye on Pat, especially for the next week or so.'

'I promise, I will.'

Noel helped Claire up into the cab of the lorry. The engine spluttered into life, and the bottles rattled in their crates as they drove out the gates of St Josephs. Claire turned and took a final look through the rear

173

window of the cab. Noel stood waving. In the distance she could see the Pat standing alone in the middle of the avenue. He seem so tiny, so alone, and so lost.

CHAPTER TWENTY- SIX
(Enniskerry 2005)

Bill listened to her story, studying the woman who sat before him. The sun streamed into the room and reflected off the silver tray on the coffee table casting light into the darkest corner of the room. He could see pain still etched on Claire's face. As she wiped her eyes he felt she was reawaking the ghosts of her past.

'I'm sorry,' he said quietly, 'I didn't mean to cause upset.'

She placed her coffee cup back on the tray, and gave a brave smile.

'I'm crying because I'm angry. I'm angry with myself for having left him there all alone'.

Bill tried to console her.

'He wasn't alone; he had Noel and the other children.'

His words soothed her.

'I suppose,' she said wearily. 'Would you care for some fresh coffee?'

Bill shook his head.

'Thank you Claire, I'm fine. May I ask, is that the same shell I see hanging on the wall?'

She stood up, carefully removed the glass case and handed it to Bill.

'It's beautiful' he said 'I've never seen one like it before.'

'Nor I. I discovered later that this particular shell is normally only found in the Indian and Pacific Oceans.'

'So how did it get here?'

'God only knows' she replied,

'I put it down to one of life's little mysteries.'

'I can see why it reminded Pat, of chocolate, said Bill.'

'The irony is, I later discovered this particular shell is called a 'Chocolate Flamed Venus'.

'What a beautiful name, what an incredible coincidence.'

'Later I had it framed and the inscription added with the place and year it was found.'

Bill handed the case back to Claire.

'What a treasured memento.'

She thanked him and went to hang it on the wall.

'It's too nice to be indoors, let me show you my garden and my sanctuary.'

The smell of roses wafted through the fresh clean air as Claire led Bill down a little rustic path towards the river. The only sounds he could hear were those of nature. He could hear the twitter of sparrows and chirp of finches above the murmur of the Dargle river, and the occasional buzz of a passing bee.

'It's beautiful here. I'd give anything for a house and garden like this'.

Claire thanked him.

'I was lucky. I heard about it before it went on the market. I think I might not have been able to afford it had it gone to auction.'

'Do you still have a home in New York?'

Claire stopped by a rustic trellis adorned with pink roses. She cupped a rose and inhaled its fragrance.

'Yes' as a matter of fact I do. It's strange' she said releasing the rose 'I love New York, but I don't think I could ever live there again.'

She walked towards an old white Victorian garden seat and sat down, inviting Bill to join her.

'It's from St. Joseph's' she said running her hand lovingly along the freshly painted beams.

176

'Pardon?'

'This seat is from the orphanage. I had it restored. It used to stand on the front lawn. I managed to salvage it.'

Bill looked a little surprised.

'So you did go back to the orphanage?'

'A couple of times.'

'To meet Pat', he enquired?

She shook her head gently and looked away. He sensed her unease. Eventually she spoke.

'I'm glad you called. It's good to talk about it and get it off my chest. I've had to bottle it up for so long, it was beginning to poison me.'

'Where is Pat now?'

She took a deep breath and continued her story.

CHAPTER TWENTY-SEVEN
(Orphanage 1963)

The next few weeks were the hardest in Pat's young life. Now that Sister Claire was gone, he had accepted that he had no true friends in class. Noel had now become his most trusted friend but Noel was busy doing his chores and he rarely got to see him. He had accepted Joseph for what he was, a schoolmate, just like the rest, nothing more. He was somebody whose company he kept only because he was there, not because he wanted to. Joseph in fairness had tried hard to recapture what they once had, but he never could own up to his own weaknesses, or rise to a simple apology. Three weeks had gone by since Claire had left. There was still no letter. It seemed that Pat had been let down once more. This time by Claire, somebody he had considered his best friend in the whole world. He was disillusioned, disheartened, and in despair. A promise to a friend was sacred. If Claire could not keep her promise, then why should he. Pinkie promise, or not.

Every day he woke hoping for a letter from Claire. He stood morning after morning waiting in the corridor outside Sister Agnes's room with the other children. They too were waiting in anticipation for post from family or friends. Sister Agnes would come to the door and call out the names of the lucky children who had received post that day. One morning she went to Pat and asked;

'Why do you waste your time standing here, you have no family or friends, who could possibly want to write to you?'

The other children laughed at him, but he did not care. Each time he went he was turned away, empty-handed, shattered, and disappointed. Had it all been just a hoax? Was this Claire's way of softening her goodbye, and easing the pain of parting? Had her words been hollow and meaningless? He felt betrayed. She was gone. He was out of sight, and obviously out of mind. In the following weeks Pat retreated into his own little world. He distanced himself from his school friends. At night he lay awake in the dormitory too upset and lonely to sleep. In the daytime he was tired and lethargic. He could not concentrate; every little thing seemed to irritate him. In class, it was no different. He had lost all interest and spent most of his time daydreaming, lost in his lonely prison. One day as he gazed out through the tall windows of the classroom, watching storm clouds gather overhead he heard his name.

'Pat. I asked you a question.'

He looked confused as he stood up. '

' Sorry Sister, I didn't hear the question'

'You'll have to concentrate or I'll have to report you to Sister Agnes.'

It was Sister Josephine the replacement nun at the orphanage. She was in her early twenties; small, stocky, round-faced and she wore dark horn-rimmed glasses. She was rubbing out the 'twelve-times' tables with a duster.

'You didn't hear my question because you weren't listening.'

The class laughed. Pat showed no reaction.

'I asked you what twelve times nine equals?'

Pat paused momentarily.

'Ninety-six.'

Sister Josephine looked disappointed.

'If you'd paid some attention, you might stand a chance of getting it right.

Several hands rose in the class.

'Me, Sister.'

'I know, Sister.'

She pointed to one of the children.

'You, Joseph', what do twelve-nines equal.

Joseph stood up.

'One hundred and eight, Sister.'

Pat sat slowly back down in his seat. He could see a smugness written all over Joseph's face but couldn't have cared less.

The following day Noel was cutting the lawn. It was a dull cloudy day. Noel had his shirtsleeves rolled up as he busied himself with the push mower. Tommy the postman, a tall thin man in his late fifties came laboring his way along the avenue on his push bike.

'Ah the man himself,' he said, wheezing badly.

'I've got a letter for you.'

'How are you keeping Tommy?

'I'm knackered, if you must know,' he said panting heavily 'I think you must be raising the slope on the avenue?'

Noel stopped what he was doing, glad of a little rest.

'Fat chance,' he laughed, 'I've enough to be doing.'

'It must be sismic then!'

'Or you're growing older. It's been like that since the ice age.'

Tommy gave him a doubting look.

'Look on the bright side; it's down hill on the way out.'

That seemed little comfort to Tommy.

180

'Any more hills like this, and I'll be on me way out.'

He climbed awkwardly off his bike, slipped on his reading glasses, and sifted through his bag of letters.

'Ah here we are. It's addressed to a Mr. Noel Cummins, The Gate Lodge. St Joseph's Orphanage, Moyross. Co. Mayo.

'That's me! Another bloody bill I suppose?'

'No I don't think so. It looks like a woman's handwriting.'

Noel took the letter in his hand and studied it.

'Could there be a little lady on the side' enquired Tommy cheekily.

'You must be joking; I have enough on my plate with a wife and two kids.'

Noel opened the letter. Inside was another envelope addressed to Master Pat Deegan. He quickly read the note.

'Dear Noel,

I have written several letters to Pat and have received no reply. I am worried that perhaps something might have happened to him, or that he is not receiving my correspondence. I would be obliged if you would give him this letter for me. I trust you and your family are well. Thank you,

Claire Conlon.

p.s. My address is on the back of Pat's letter.

'I hope it's not bad news Noel?

'No. No. It's fine. Maybe you can help?'

'Of course, what is it', asked Tommy?

Noel stepped closer.

'I'm just curious to know, if you have delivered any letters to a 'Master, Pat Deegan, in the last month?

'Indeed I have' said Tommy, without a moment's

181

hesitation. 'I must have delivered over half a dozen'.

Noel looked a little surprised by his statement.

'What makes you so sure?'

'That's easy; it's the same name as the mother-in-law.'

'What are you talking about?'

'Her name is Patricia, we call her Pat for short'.

'Are you certain about that', enquired Noel, his face flushed in anger.

'I'm positive.'

'Thanks. You've been a great help.'

'Well I'm off; I've still got loads to do. Thank Jaysus it's downhill after this delivery. '

I'll be seeing you.' Noel folded Pat's letter and put it carefully in his shirt pocket.

'Yeah Tommy, take care.

Later that day Pat was sitting forlornly on his hunkers watching the others play ball when Noel entered the school yard.

'Hi Pat, can I join you a moment?'

Pat was delighted to see Noel. He loved the feeling of importance talking with a real man gave him.

'Yeah, of course.'

Noel sat down beside him and leaned back against the school wall.

'How are you?'

'I'm fed up', answered Pat glumly.

Noel pulled his legs away just in the nick of time, as the children thundered blindly by, in pursuit of the old tattered ball.

'Jesus, you could get killed here,' laughed Noel.

Pat smiled weakly.

'You still miss Sister Claire?'

'I don't want to talk about her,' he said in a sad voice.

'Why?'

'She's like the rest of them.'

'I thought you said she was nice?'

'I've changed my mind. She lied to me, said she'd write but she never did.'

The old ball smacked against the wall just above Pat's head.

'Watch it Bugsy, he shouted angrily.

'Watch it yourself, 'carrot head.'

Noel tapped him on the shoulder.

'Pat, I have something to tell you. She did write. She wrote lots of letters but none of them were given to you.'

Pat turned his head sharply.

'How do you know that?'

'She wrote to me.'

Pat's mood changed to one of excitement.

'She did. What did she say?'

The school bell rang. The children stopped what they were doing and formed a queue by the door. Noel took a quick glance around, pulled the letter from his pocket and handed it to Pat.

'Here. This is for you.'

Pat's face lit up and he sprung excitedly to his feet.

'Don't let anybody see it or it might be taken from you.'

He folded the letter and stuck it deep into his trouser pocket.

'I won't Noel, thanks very much.'

Noel stood and watched as he joined the others and headed back into class.

Once seated, Pat couldn't wait to read the letter. Sister Josephine was busy writing English words on the blackboard. Carefully he pulled the letter from his pocket and looked at the address:

Master Patrick Deegan, St. Joseph's Orphanage, Moyross, Co. Mayo.

For a moment his heart sank. He thought there had been a mix up. Then he realized it was correctly addressed. He was Patrick Deegan. He did have a family name. Where did Claire get this information he wondered? Perhaps she got it when she was applying to foster him for Christmas. 'Deegan.' 'Patrick Deegan?' He wasn't so sure about the sound of it, but it made him happy to know somewhere there was a cousin or an aunt he could contact when he was older who could tell him about his mother and father. He wondered if Deegan was his mother's name or his father's.

'Hey I'm Patrick Deegan,' he whispered.

'Look.'

Joseph looked at him as if he had two heads.

'What are you on about?'

'My name is Patrick Deegan, look.'

He showed the envelope to Joseph.

'Where did you get that from?'

'It's from Sister Claire' he said proudly.

'She's wrote me lots of letters but Sister Agnes has kept them all.'

'How do you know that?'

Noel the gardener told me.'

'How would he know?'

'He asked the postman, and he should know.'

Joseph let Pat's words sink in before adding,

'She's some bloody bitch that wan.

Pat opened the letter. Inside was an orange ten shilling note. Pat's little heart pounded with delight. Joseph watched in envy.

'Jaysus, she sent you a ten bob note as well' he whispered in disbelief.

Pat eyes danced in their sockets. For the first time in his life he had money, his very own money. He held it beneath the desk staring at the lady's face printed on the front, and reading over and over again the words 'Ten Shillings'. It was a fortune, an absolute fortune. Joseph watched as he carefully folded the money and placed it into his trouser pocket before he began to read the letter beneath the desk. Sister Josephine spotted him.

'Pat, I'm warning you for the last time, pay attention. It was not the first time she had warned him that day and now her patience was wearing thin. Quickly Pat stuck the letter back into his pocket and sat upright. Sister Josephine adjusted her horn rimmed glasses on the bridge of her nose.

'Right' she said. I want you to take out your English Spelling books.'

The children lifted the lid of their desks and took out their books. She sat down in front of the class.

'Before we begin I am going to ask you a few spellings. Who can spell Wednesday? Tubby raised his hand. 'Right Tommy, off you go.'

'W E N S DA Y', he spelled slowly.

Sister Josephine spoke encouragingly.

'A very good try Tommy, but I'm afraid you're wrong.'

Other hands in the class rose to answer.

'You ,Joseph.'

Joseph stood up. Pat was too happy and excited to even notice.

' W E H N S D A Y'

Sister Josephine smiled.

'Hard luck, Joseph good try.'

'D-E-E-G-A-N.' Pat was spelling his name over and over in his head. She noticed him sitting there with the smile upon his face.

'Pat if you find it so funny, you spell it.'
He involuntarily stood up. The children waited in anticipation.

'Spell what,' he asked Joseph under his breath? 'Wednesday' whispered Joseph.

'W E D N E S D A Y'
Sister Josephine looked over the rim of her glasses
. 'Very good' she said surprised. Well done.'
Pat sat back down again. Sister Josephine went to the black board and wrote WEDNESDAY in large letter on the board.

'Sometime's there are silent letters in words. In this case the 'D' in Wednesday is silent.' She underlined the D. Most of the children were by now totally disinterested. Sister Josephine wiped the board clean again. Pat watched the minuscule chalk dust particles caught in the sunlight float through the air like a miniature chalk galaxy. He wondered how chalk could float in air. He wondered why it didn't fall. Then he wondered what held the planets. The Sun was huge, and he reckoned it must weigh at least a couple of tons, yet it sat there in the middle of space held up by nothing. He knew the earth had some excuse, something to do with the sun pulling us around in circles but if the sun wasn't there, would the earth fall? If it did fall where would it fall to? The bottom? The bottom of what? He chewed on the end of his pencil wondering. Looking out the window he could see the clouds above. How could they possibly float? Everybody knew they were full of water and every so often it would bucket down. He knew how heavy a bucket of water was and reckoned there must be hundreds of buckets up there floating around like the sun for no apparent reason. Nobody not even the nuns knew what kept them there

He wonder what happened to the red sandals, had they ever been found, and if they had, he hoped it was by children playing in the dunes. Maybe they were still there, buried beneath the sand forever. He knew the sandcastle was gone, washed away without a trace, but maybe the sandals were still there. He vowed when he was older he would return to the spot and see if he could find any trace of them. If he had learned anything, it was, life was unpredictable. He had given up on Sister Claire and had shut her from his life, yet when things were at their worst, she had found him again, despite the obstacles. Sister Josephine slapped her hands. Once more the chalk dust rose into the air, but this time he no longer questioned it. She turned to the class.

'Now I want you to write a two-page essay for me. Has anybody got an idea for a subject?'

'Golly' raised his hand.

'Yes Stephen?

'My best friend Sister.'

'He'll probably write about a monkey' whispered Joseph.

Pat ignored his remark.

'That's a great suggestion Stephen. Right, I want you all to write an essay on My Best Friend. Remember if it's not neatly written, I'll make you write it all over again.'

The children raised their eyes to the heavens.

Sister Josephine clapped her hands once more.

'I have an idea. We will have a prize for the best essay.'

Suddenly the children became interested.

'What will the prize be Sister' asked Joseph?

'I haven't decided yet. Maybe Sister Agnes can be the adjudicator; she might even help us decide what the prize should be.'

The children were not unimpressed..

CHAPTER TWENTY- EIGHT

Every day after class the children were sent to the "workshop". It was an outhouse with a galvanized roof and large iron framed windows on one side. The inside consisted of a long narrow area with several workbenches running down the sides. Each allocated workstation had a small timber box fixed to the back of the bench with some rudimentary tools, long-nosed pliers, an awl, a wire cutters and a large spool on wire. Battered biscuit tins full of brightly coloured beads were spread evenly around the room. The windows were frosted and on the far side of the room the light was poor. The children worked for up to three hours a day making rosary beads, scapulars, and St. Brigid's crosses.

The importance of such work was instilled into the children. Without such endeavours, there would be no money to cloth and feed them. In reality it was a commercial adventure using child labour, a way for the convent to make extra money. The orphanage already received payment from the state for each child incarcerated in the institution. Each child was assigned a specific task. Hopalong was in charge of this venture. For hours on end the children would stand often in the cold and damp, with insufficient light and heat churning out their wares. Pat stood thinking about Sister Claire's letter. He felt guilty he had doubted her.

She was his friend. She had proved that beyond doubt. He now believed she would indeed foster him next Christmas. As he stood by his workstation threading beads and bending the stiff strands of wire with his long-nosed pliers, he received a firm blow to the back of his head. He winced in pain.

'How many 'Hail Mary's' are there in a decade,' 'asked Hopalong picking up the rosary beads he was making.

'Ten, Reverend Mother.'

She handed them back to him

'How many do you have?'

Pat began to count under his breath.

'Louder boy, I want the rest of the boys to hear.'

He raised his voice, 'seven, eight, nine, ten, eleven, twelve, thirteen, fourteen.'

'Well, well, have you discovered a new religion, Pat?' The children giggled

'I suppose you'll have us praying at the twenty five station of the cross, before we know it?'

Now they roared laughing. Another blow to the back of the head made him duck for cover.

'Now sort that out' she barked.

'One more mistake like that and you'll have Sister Agnes to deal with.'

Hard as he tried he could not concentrate. The excitement of the last twenty-four hours had been too much for him. He had discovered his family name; he had his very own ten shilling note and he had received a letter from Claire. He tried to visualize her mother, what she looked like, and her home, and what the inside of a house felt like. Christmas with friends must be wonderful he reckoned, not just because of presents and the turkey but because of the people themselves. He was excited that for the first time he was going to spend Christmas like a normal child. In that split second he decided he would write his essay about Claire. She was his best friend. It would be his little tribute to her, his way of saying 'thank you. Later that evening, before 'lights out' Pat put Claire's letter under his pillow. When Sister Bernadette had momentarily left the dormitory, he opened it and read it over and over again.

> The Gables,
> Ratheen Lane
>   Kiltealy.
>   3-9-'63

'Dear Pat,

I am at my wits end. I have written many letters but you do not reply. I hope you are okay. and in good spirits. I miss all the children, and in a funny way, I miss the orphanage, and you, of course. I hope things are a little easier since I left. I keep your shell by my bedside. Sometime I switch off the light and place it to my ear and let the sound of the ocean fill my head.

Pat's face broke into a smile.

I've told my mother all about you. She can't wait to meet you. She has been in contact with the local parish priest looking for references so she can foster you for Christmas. I will write you a long letter when I know you have received this one. Try and stay out of trouble especially with Sister Agnes. Please write back soon. I wait every day for the postman to arrive, hoping he has news from you. Remember our promise.

Your best friend Claire,

p.s. The money is from my mother. She wanted you to have it.

Pat closed the letter. His little face was radiant. He held it in his hand and passed it under his nose smelling the paper. Sister Bernadette returned and the dormitory fell into darkness.

***

The following day a young missionary visited the school. Sister Josephine was writing Irish Poetry on the blackboard when the door gave its familiar squeak and in walked Hopalong with this strange looking man. She introduced him to the class.

'This is Father O'Grady. He works with the 'black babies' in Nairobi, in Africa. He has kindly given up his free time to come here and have a little chat with you all'.

The children were delighted, anything was better than Irish class.

'Imagine that, living with lions and tigers,' whispered Pat.'

Joseph leant forward. He tapped 'Golly' on the shoulder.

'He's come to take you home.'

'Golly' ignored Joseph's snide remark. Pat shook his head in disgust.

'What did ya say that for, what has he ever done on you?'

Hopalong raised her hands.

'Quiet, the lot of you, or I'll give you all a hundred lines.'

The children settled.

'I'm leaving Father O'Grady in charge. He's going to give you a little talk about his work as a missionary.

'What's a missionary,' asked Pat?

'An oddball like him,' whispered Joseph.

'I expect you to behave yourselves,' said Hopalong Sister Josephine and I will be back in about a half an hour.'

Pat observed the missionary. He was a young man in his early thirties with a black beard a tanned face and a head of wiry hair parted at the side. He noticed his strange brown habit and the large hood hanging at the shoulders. It was half dress half a coat. He looked like no other priest he had ever seen in his life. Father Dunn and the other priests always wore a black suit with a white collar; this man wore white cord knotted around his waist and hanging to one side. From the cord hung the largest wooden rosary beads Pat had ever seen.

'Jaysus, imagine trying to bend the wire for those beads,' he whispered.'

The missionary grabbed a chair from behind the desk and placed in the centre of the floor in front of the children. Instead of sitting the normal way, he sat on the back of the chair and placed his feet on the seat. Pat noticed his toes protruded from his ugly brown sandals.

'Right children, I have come here today to have a quick chat with you about the missions.'

He spoke in a strange Scottish accent.

'Hands up those of you who know where Nairobi is?

Golly' raised his hand. The priest pointed to him.

'In Africa, Father.'

'I'm not surprised he knew that' whispered Joseph.

'Yes you're right, it is in Africa, but can anybody tell me where exactly in Africa it is?'

None of the children seemed to know.

'Have any of you heard of Kenya?

The children shook their heads.

'Kenya is on the east coast of Africa. It received its independence from England only this year. Next year President Kenyatta hopes to form the new republic. Can anybody tell me anything about Kenya?'

192

Bugs raised his hand. Father O'Grady pointed to him.

'There are elephants and snakes, and man eating tigers and lions there.'

The class broke into laughter. Father O' Grady put his finger to his lips. The chuckles abated.

'That's true too, but what is really important about Kenya and many other countries in Africa, is that the word of God is still only reaching them now. My job is to spread the word of the Lord. That is what I do in Africa, I have a mission, and my mission is to convert as many people as possible to the way of the Lord. That is why they call us missionaries. We have being going out into the world for centuries preaching the word of the Lord. Without Missionaries the word of God would never come to these poor people. Every year we need new young people to help in our quest. That is why I am speaking to you now. Maybe someday, you too will be a missionary doing the work of God. In ten years time you could be the one sitting up here, travelling to strange lands, seeing all the tigers, lions, and elephants. Would you like that?'

The children were excited at the idea and nodded enthusiastically.

'I'll be handing out information after this little chat and if any of you would like to become a missionary just tell Reverend Mother and she will fill in the necessary forms for you. Has anybody got any questions?'

Joseph raised his hand.

'Yes my child?'

'Is it true that the black babies who die without being baptized go to Hell, Father'?

'What a wonderful question, let me explain.'

He shuffled on the chair before speaking.

193

'All children are born with 'original sin' on their souls. It is the sin of their parents that they have to carry with them into this life.'

Though Pat didn't understand, he thought this a little unfair on the poor babies.

'It is only through the sacrament of Baptism that these poor unfortunate children can be cleansed of their sin'.

Pat raised his hand. '

Yes what is it'?

'But you said father that it was the sin of the parents, not the children. Why don't the parents not the children have the sin on their souls?'

'God knows best my child.'

He tried to explain.

'Those children who die before they are baptized in the Catholic Faith go to 'Limbo'. It is not horrible like Hell but it is someplace where they will never experience the love of God.'

It suddenly occurred to Pat, it wasn't just life that was unfair, even in death injustice seemed to follow people to the grave. Later the Missionary spoke about the dangers of sin. He told the children to close their eyes and not to open them till he said so. When all the children had done what he asked he began;

'I want you to imagine you are in total darkness. `You cannot see a single thing. You realize you are trapped and cannot move. There is so little space you cannot even turn, or raise a hand or foot. You are terrified, lost, and alone.'

Pat peered through his half-open eyelashes, watching the expression on the missionary's face become more menacing as he spoke. He raised his voice, his face contorting.

'You shout and scream but nobody can hear you.'

The children eyelashes twitched as they fought to

194

keep their eyes closed. He lowered his voice again and continued;

'You begin to feel your feet getting warm, but you don't know why. Now they are beginning to get a little hot and uncomfortable you try to move them but you can't bend your knees to lift your feet. The pain is becoming unbearable, you scream out but it is useless, there is nobody there to help you. Then you begin to get a strange smell.'

Pat tapped Joseph on the leg. Joseph lowered his head and peered across at Pat. They both grinned at the absurdity of it all. Again he raised his voice.

'It's the smell of burning flesh, your flesh. You look down and realize beneath your feet is glowing red. Your skin is sticking to the floor and your toes sizzle like sausages on a pan. You realize you are locked in a metal box.'

The children, frightened by his words began to open their eyes nervously.

'Shut your eyes, I'll tell you when to open them', he roared.

The children reluctantly did as they were told.

He continued.

'Slowly you notice the glow rising up the metal walls. It has reached your knees. You scream and scream.'

Pat glanced at Joseph, he was no longer giggling. The missionary's voice began to build and build. '

It climbs higher and higher. Your backside begins to burn. You scream out no longer able to bear the pain. Now your back is burning and your hair bursts into flames. His voice had now reached a crescendo

Eyes fluttered nervously. Pat glanced at Joseph's shocked face. He paused for a moment letting his words sink in. The children began to open their eyes nervously.

'Shut your eyes'. 'This' he said manically, 'is what happens if you die with a mortal sin on your soul'.

'Now open your eyes. Open your eyes to the evil of the Devil'.

The children quickly opened their eyes.

'Yes, it is up to each and every one of you to open your eyes and follow God's commandments'.

He cast his eye around the room.

'And where do we go if we die with a mortal sin on our souls?'

Tubby raised his hand.

'To Hell, Father.'

'That's right my child, Hell.'

He raised his finger and pointed to them all

. 'Remember Hell is not for a minute or an hour. Hell is for eternity.'

Pat looked at Joseph. Both were frightened and lost for words.

'Is it worth it I ask you. Is it worth risking such an end because of sin. Sin is the work of the Devil and he who sins works for the Devil. When you grow up and leave here, remember my words.'.

By this stage you could have heard a pin drop.

'Did you know it is a mortal sin to miss mass on Sundays? If you should die with that sin on your soul, then you too, will burn in that metal casket for eternity. Think about it. One hour, once a week is all God asks of you. He loves each and every one of you and it's only right you should show him love in return.'

The children were relieved to hear the squeak of the classroom door heralding the return of Hopalong, Sister Josephine and thankfully a semblance of normality. Father O'Grady proceeded to hand out leaflets to each and every child.

'Should any of you feel you would like to become a missionary, just put your name on the back of this form and hand it to Reverend Mother.

'Right' said Hopalong

'I would like you all to put your hand together for Father O'Grady and thank him for giving you his time this morning.'

The class dutifully clapped long and loud.

'He's scary,' said Pat, beneath his breath.

'He scared the shit out of me', whispered Joseph, 'I never want to die.'

Pat's face grew pale as he pondered on what would have happened to him if Sister Claire had not stopped him on the landing. He would now be burning in Hell. She had not only saved his life, but also his soul from eternal damnation. The Missionary's words had scared and traumatized the children. For several weeks after his visit, the children flocked to Father Dunn in the confessional, to cleanse their souls of even the most venial of sins.

CHAPTER TWENTY- NINE

Pat knocked nervously on the door.

'Come in,' said Sister Agnes.

He opened the heavy varnished door and walked inside. It was a small dark room void of direct sunlight. Outside, Pat could see the granite walls and stained glass windows of the church. A narrow passageway separated the two buildings. A bluish haze of tobacco smoke lingered in the air making the room smell stale and noxious. Sister Agnes was seated behind her desk. She held an ornate china cup in her hands sipping tea. She gestured Pat to approach. The desk was cluttered with open books and copies. A brown bakelite ashtray overflowing with cigarette ends was perched precariously on top of a well- thumbed prayer book.

Pat stood and waited, not knowing what this visit was all about. From her demeanor, he felt decidedly uncomfortable. She placed the cup back on its saucer, leant forward and rummaged through the copy books in front of her. Finally she pulled his from the pile.

'What is this supposed to be', she said, holding it up by the dog-eared corners?

Pat wasn't sure he understood the question, and did not reply.

'I'm asking you a question, and I want an answer.'

'It's my exercise copy, Sister,' said Pat nervously.

'I know it's your copy book, you cheeky brat. I want to know what this is.'

She opened the copy book and pointed to his essay

. 'It's my English essay from last week, Sister.'
She looked spitefully towards him.

'And what was the subject of this essay?'

'My Best Friend, Sister' he replied.

'And, who did you write about?'

'Sister Claire'.

Sister Agnes stood up, slowly moving from behind her desk.

'Firstly, let me inform you, she is no longer Sister Claire. She is no longer a servant of God. She has left this order, and all I can say is good riddance. She is a nasty evil person who has lost her way.'

Pat stood motionless watching Sister Agnes as she poured out her condemnation. She continued;

'She should get down on her knees and beg God for forgiveness. I do not want to see, or hear her name mentioned in this school again. Is that understood?

Pat averted his eyes to the floor. Sister Agnes caught him by the hair and lifted his head. The stale smell of tobacco nearly made him retch.

'Am I making myself clear?'

'Yes, Sister.'

She let him go.

'Secondly, how can you call this woman your friend? She abandoned not only you, but this entire school. She is a gutless greedy traitor, who cares only for herself. She doesn't care about this school or any of you children. She hasn't even bothered to write you a single letter, or send a parcel since the day she left. I'd hardly call that a friendship, would you?'

Pat felt aggrieved; he wanted to stand up for Claire.

'She's still my best friend.'

'Don't be silly. Young boys don't have women as their best friends.'

'But I do,' said Pat.

Sister Agnes was taken aback by his pluckiness.

'Why doesn't she act like a friend? Why hasn't she written to you? That's not too much to ask now is it?'

Pat's courage rose. He lifted his head and looked her straight in the eyes. Before he could stop himself he blurted out; '

'She is my friend. She did send me letters, but you kept them from me.'

Sister Agnes was shocked and appalled by his effrontery. She lost control and grabbed him by the scruff of the neck.

'How dare you speak to me like that,' she yelled.
'They were my letters; you had no right to…'

Before he could utter another word Sister Agnes's hand came crashing down across his face. He fell to the floor holding his cheek.

'You brazen bastard,' she roared, 'nobody speaks to me like that.'

She dragged him along the floor kicking him wildly.

'I won't tolerate insubordination, do you hear me?'
Pat didn't know what the word meant but he could hazard a good guess

'An education is wasted on the likes of you. For your punishment I'm sending you out to work on the farm for the rest of the week is that understood?'
'Now get up, you troublemaker.'

Pat picked himself gingerly off the floor. His eye was swollen and his face bruised. Realizing what she had done, she panicked.

'Are you okay my child?

Pat nodded and placed his hand over his stinging eye. Quickly she reverted to her aggressive tone.

'You better not mention a word of this. If anybody asks you what happened, tell them you fell, do you understand?'

Opening the door, she grabbed him by the hair and tossed him out into the corridor.

'Now get out of my sight before I do something I might regret.'

CHAPTER THIRTY

It was a warm September day. Noel was working in the old walled garden that supplied the fruit and vegetables for the nun's table. He stood on a wooden ladder precariously perched against one of the apple trees. He held a white enamel bucket in his hand. The old gate that led into the garden squeaked nosily. Noel turned to see Pat enter, and called out.

'Ah Master Deegan, to what do we owe the pleasure?'

It was strange to hear somebody call him by his surname. He felt it sounded much nicer than it looked. He wandered across the orchard towards Noel who assumed an upper-crust English accent.

'And what crimes have you committed today Master Deegan,?'

His expression changed when he noticed Pat's black eye. He climbed down from the ladder.

'Ah Jesus no. What happened to your face?'

Pat did not answer. Noel did not need to be told.

'Are you okay?'

Pat tried to smile but his face hurt.

'I'm fine thanks'.

'How long is your sentence this time?'

'A week.'

Noel whistled in mock horror.

'Good God, what did you do, kill one of the nuns?'

He tapped him lightly on the shoulder and pointed to an upturned apple box.

'Listen you just take it easy for a day or two.'

202

'I'm here to help Noel. I'm fine, really I am.'
Noel patted him on the head.

'Are you sure? It must have been one hell of a serious crime.'

'It was over my essay.'

'They did that to you because of an essay?'
Pat nodded.

'Have they gone mad, or what?'

'I think Sister Agnes has, if you ask me.'

'Oh, her again?'
Noel gently rolled the apples from the bucket into the wheelbarrow. Pat noticed the base was covered in crumpled old newspapers.

'Why the newspapers' he asked?

'It's to stop the apples bruising. A bruised apple will go bad. And one bad apple can ?

'I know,' interrupted Pat, 'one bad apple can rot the barrel.'

'Yeah, something like that.'
The irony of the statement was not lost on Noel.

'I'll be harvesting the apples all this week; you check that none of them are bruised, if they are, just put them to one side. You can keep as many of those as you like.'
Pat's face lit up.

'Really?
Noel knelt down on his hunkers.

'It's a perk of the job. Be careful though not to let the nuns see them. We don't want any more 'shiners' on that face of yours.'
He clipped him gently on the chin as he examined the eye. '

'You look like you've just gone fifteen rounds with Sonny Liston.

'Who's he?'

'He's only the biggest, scariest, boxer in the world.'

'At least, if I had fought him I would have been allowed to hit back.'

Noel stood up, amused.

'I don't think Liston will lose too much sleep on that count.'

He plucked an apple from the tree and handed it to Pat.

'Here. You need to build your strength up.'

Noel sat at the base of an apple tree and pulled out a packet of cigarettes.

'Time for a break, sit down and eat your apple.'

Pat watched as Noel lit the cigarette and inhaled deeply. A cloud of grey blue smoke billowed from his mouth as he slowly exhaled.

'Are they nice?'

'Cigarettes you mean?

'Yeah.'

'Smoking is a disgusting habit, you don't want to know.'

'Why do you smoke then?'

'I suppose it relaxes me, I don't know, I never really thought about it.'

'Can I see the packet?'

Noel pulled on the cigarette before tossing the packet across to Pat who was sitting opposite him. Pat studied the packet. His eye was drawn to a bearded sailor in a blue uniform. He was encircled by a life-buoy with the words 'Players Navy Cut'. He noticed the letters 'HERO' on the sailor's hat. A ship at full mast was leaving the harbour behind him. It was about to embark on an adventure across the high seas. He wished he could sail far away and leave this place behind. He slid the packet open and smelled the tobacco.

'Smells nice.'

'Would you like to try' he asked, offering his cigarette?

'Could I' he beamed?

Noel stood up and went over to Pat.

'You can have one drag but you must promise me you'll inhale it properly.'

'I will, I promise I will.'

Noel handed the cigarette to Pat. He put it to his lips and sucked hard. A strange nauseating feeling crept over his whole body. His face turned white. He coughed and wretched and his head spun. Noel grabbed the cigarette back from him.

'Let that be a lesson to you, smoking is a horrible disgusting habit, don't ever start.'

'I won't' coughed Pat.

'You'll be okay in a minute, just sit back and take some deep breaths.'

Pat groaned and rested against the tree. Slowly the colour began to return to his cheeks.

'Would you like another drag?'

Pat practically got sick at the thought.

'No,' he said shaking his head, 'I think I'm going to die.'

Noel laughed, sat back down and continued his smoke. Pat watched in bewilderment.

'Why did she do it,' asked Noel his voice now serious?

'My eye, you mean?'

'Yes. Why did she hit you?'

Pat munched gingerly on his apple.

'Because of my essay'.

Noel licked his lips, spitting loose tobacco from his mouth

'But what did you write in your essay?

'We were asked to write an essay on 'our best friend' so I wrote about Sister Claire.'

205

Noel listened intently.

'She gave you a black eye because of that?'

Pat bit into the apple.

'She started calling 'Sister Claire' bad things. She
`said she wasn't my friend and that she didn't care
about the school or the children. Then she said that
Sister Claire couldn't be my friend, because she
never wrote to me. I told Sister Agnes she had
written but that she had kept those letters from me.'

Noel sighed and ran his fingers through his hair.

'You shouldn't have told her anything.'

'She just went crazy and slapped me in the face'. I
fell on the floor and she began to drag and kick me,
then she said I had to work on the farm for a week.

Noel stubbed the butt against the bark of the tree and
went over to Pat, his voice gentle but firm.

'You have to promise you'll never mention
anything about a letter from Sister Claire again or
how you managed to get hold of it. The less they
know about this the better. Do you understand? It's
really important, for both of us.'

Pat nodded innocently.

'Good boy.'

He reached inside his pocket and pulled out a letter.

'It's for you, it arrived yesterday.' Pat eyes lit up.

'Thanks Noel, I'll save it for later,'

He carefully folded the letter and placed it deep into
his pocket.

'Right young man if you're feeling well enough you
can start picking up all the apples lying on the
ground and put them into that box over there.'

CHAPTER THIRTY- ONE

It was Sunday. The early morning light crept into the dormitory. The children slept soundly. Pat was awake, wide awake. His bruised eye had darkened to a greenish color. He lay in his bed happily munching an apple and re-reading the letter from Claire:

Dear Pat,

Thanks for your letter. I was so thrilled when I received it. I was worried when I heard nothing from you, I thought something might be wrong. I should have known Sister Agnes would have something to do with this. I was in Dublin on Saturday. It's such a busy place. Cars were flying up and down the streets, honking their horns at the poor horses and carts still surviving the mayhem. I climbed up Nelsons Pillar and nearly died of exhaustion on the hundreds of steps leading to the top. Oh Pat, it was worth it.. What a view. I could see for miles in all directions. I thought of you and wished you were with me. I know how much you would have loved it. When you get your Christmas holidays I'll take you there on a day trip. We'll have such fun, walking around the city and looking at the brightly-lit shop windows. I'll bring you to the Museum and to the Art Gallery if you like. We can even go for a spin on the top of a double-decker bus.

Pats expression changed.

I know it's difficult for you Pat, and I know they must be giving you a hard time, but don't let them upset you or make you do something silly. Perhaps they still are angry and blame you for losing the Sandals. I know it wasn't your fault, and you weren't to blame, it was just an unfortunate accident. Thank you for honouring me with your essay, but please, for your sake don't mention my name to Sister Agnes. I'll explain things when you're are a little older. Try to be a good boy and ignore their taunts. Just think about it, only fourteen weeks till Christmas. I've told my mother all about you and she's looking forward so much to meeting you. She has even started to paint the spare room already. She's crazy.

Oh, my mother's cat had kittens, and we've decided to keep the ginger one. Guess what we named him? 'Paddy.' I hope you don't mind.

I better go now, keep your chin up. Remember me in your prayers.

Your Friend
Claire

P.S. Don't forget our 'pinkie promise.'

Carefully Pat folded the letter and placed it under his mattress.

Sunday, was the children's favourite day. Everybody had a chance to sleep on that little bit longer. They did not have to rise until eight-thirty. There were no classes as such, just a study period in the morning and afternoon. In study they were allowed to borrow books from the library. Pat loved reading. It was his means of escape, his chance to lose himself in a different world. The one thing every child hated about Sunday was the compulsory shower. The shower room was always cold, even in the middle of summer it was just slightly above freezing. The heating never seemed to work and in winter, taking a shower, was like crossing Antartica in your birthday suit. In the late fifties a large storage area had been crudely converted into a shower room. The walls were tiled and four

208

metal shower heads erected heads two feet apart. There were no partitions. Privacy was something the children never had, and perhaps never missed. The waste water flowed down a single drain beneath their feet which often clogged forcing the children to stand in up to two inches of cold water. There were strict rules when showering. Play acting of any kind was strictly forbidden. Children had to stand in the cold corridor wrapped only in a small towel and wait their turn. It was crucial to get to the head of the line. Those unfortunate enough to be last, usually had to suffer the agony of the coldest shower. The old boiler had never been designed to produce the output of hot water necessary, so there were often angry exchanges between the children as they jostled for the best possible positions.

Sister Bernadette sat on a chair in the hall by the shower room door. She held out her walking stick and used it as a barrier to the room. Each group was given about three minutes to shower, before she would call the next group in. Pat's group was next in line. The children danced on their toes trying to avoid the cold linoleum beneath their feet.

'This reminds me of the day he lost the red sandals' whispered Joseph to Tubby, who suppressed a laugh.

Though Pat heard the remark, he said nothing.

'Next four' shouted Sister Bernadette in a shrill voice.

The four dropped their towels on the wooden bench and headed reluctantly for the showers. Golly's dark skin made the others look positively white and anemic. He gasped as he stood under the cold water.

'Jaysus' the water is freezing already.'

'What's new,' said Pat, getting on with it.

'The friggin boiler must be bollixed again', said Tubby. His large frame shivered uncontrollably as he tried to avoid the spray of cold water. Joseph held his hand under the spray and winced. Pat began to wash his hair with some soap. His eye hurt when he tried to hold it shut. He wasn't sure which was worse, the pain he suffered shutting his eye, or the stinging sensation of suds. Tubby quivered like a beached whale as he too stood underneath the cold spray. Joseph stood outside the water spray and reached in to wet his hair with his hands to make it appear that he too had showered. Golly gave him a pathetic glance.

'Your one sad bastard, do you know that?'

'Shut your face nig-nog.'.

'If that's the way you wash, then it's my nose I'll need to shut.'

'What's that supposed to mean?'

Golly ignored him. Pat turned to Joseph.

'Leave him alone'.

Joseph raised his fist. '

'Do you want another black eye?'

Now it was Pat's turn to ignore him. Joseph turned his attention back to 'Golly'.

'Hey I'm talking to you, jungle boy, what was that supposed to mean?'

'Ah quit it Joseph' said Tubby, trying to calm things down.

'Everybody needs to wash. You'll feel much better after it.'

'A big fat smelly lump like you definitely will.'

'Flap those big ears of yours and piss off.'

Make me!'

Pat stopped washing his hair. He looked to Joseph pleadingly.

'Will you just shut up and wash yourself.'

'Why should I. I'm not dirty like the rest of you.'

'You're no different to the rest of us' said Golly.

'That's funny coming from you.'

'Just have a wash.'

'Well well, if it isn't the Golly Wog telling me what to do. I have a good mind to give you a black eye too, but the trouble is nobody would see it.'

He laughed, expecting the others to join in. Golly continued to wash himself. Joseph eyed him with contempt.

'Why do you bother,' he asked?

'When I wash I'm spotless. If you wash yourself all day long you'd still be as black as the ace of spades?'

Pat was angry.

'Cut it out.'

.Joseph grabbed Pat by the hair.

'Shut up 'Carrot head I'm not talking to you'

Golly grabbed Joseph forcing him to let Pat go. Before Joseph had time to react, Golly hit him solidly in the stomach. All his pent up anger and frustration was focused in that one punch. Joseph doubled up and fell onto the floor. He lay under the cold spray in a pool of soapy water holding his tummy and moaning. Pat looked at him lying there without feeling any pity. In fact, if he felt anything at all, it was contempt.

'I'm sorry I know he's your friend', said Golly 'but he had it coming to him.'

'Thanks' said. Pat.

Outside, Sister Bernadette could be heard calling the next four children. Soon the next unfortunates arrived. Bugs was amongst them. He looked in confusion at Joseph, lying in the water and turned to Pat, Golly and Tubby who were busy drying themselves and behaving as if nothing at all had happened.

'What's wrong with him?'

211

Drying his hair with his towel Pat answered.

'He slipped on the soap and twisted his ankle.'

'Then why is he holding his stomach?'

Golly smiled at Pat. Joseph picked himself slowly up from the floor, and went to fetch his towel.

CHAPTER THIRTY- TWO

After their showers the children returned to the dormitory to put on their Sunday clothes. Sister Agnes entered the dormitory accompanied by Sister Bernadette who held a folder in her hand. She sat herself down at the little table by the dormitory door opened the book and carefully unscrewed the top of her black fountain pen. The children knew what was coming. Sister Agnes spoke.

'Line up at the end of your beds right away!'
The children, caught in various stages of undress did as they were told. Sister Agnes walked along the aisle of the dormitory.

'I want you all to open your mouths wide. Each boy is to check the teeth of the boy next to him. If you can see any bad teeth you are to raise your hand. I'll make spot checks, any boy who fails to report a bad tooth will get 'six of the best' for his troubles.'

Pat looked momentarily towards Joseph then turned away to face Tubby who stood on his opposite side. Joseph was seething with anger. In that instant Pat knew their friendship was dead but rather than feeling sad, he felt relieved. Their comradeship had crumbled like their sand-castle on the beach in Clifton Bay.

'Right' said Sister Agnes, 'begin your inspection'. Pat walked over to Tubby. '

'Don't put up your hand,' whispered Pat.

Tubby looked decidedly nervous. The color had drained from his fleshy cheeks, and Pat wondered about the wisdom of his choice.

'What if she does a spot check,' whispered Tubby?

'She better not.'

Pat tried to reassure him.

'She's trying to scare us, that's all. You don't want to be sent to the 'Butcher O'Brien' do you?'

Tubby shook his head. His wide eyes peered over his fat cheeks as he looked down at Pat and opened his mouth for Pat to inspect

'Then say nothing.'

Pat stood on his tippy toes.

'Will ya bend down, I'm supposed to be checking for holes in your teeth not snots up your nose.

Tubby stooped down.

'Jaysus, you do have two bad teeth in the back,' Tubby's eyes widened.

'So have you,' he whispered, 'but don't put up your hand' he implored.

'I won't if you don't.'

Several boys looked on in horror, as their opposite number raised their hand. Sister Agnes smiled, and then barked out an order.

'All those boys with bad teeth, report to Sister Bernadette she'll take your names.'

Pat and Tubby stood watching nervously as seven children were marched up to Sister Bernadette's table. Golly was among them. Sister Agnes cast an eye over the remaining boys.

'Joseph, who did you check?

'Liam Sister'.

'Come here Liam.

Pat watched as Bugs walked nervously towards Sister Agnes.

'Open wide.'

Bugs opened his mouth.

'Well well, what have we here,' she asked.

Pat glanced across at Joseph. He appeared edgy.

'Go join the others she said, raising her voice and pointing to Sister Bernadette.

She then pulled out her leather strap and went to Joseph and grabbed his hand.

'If you don't hold it steady, I'll give you another six' she barked.

Pat could see the panic on Joseph's face.

'Let that,' (whack) 'be a lesson,'…(whack)….'to all of you,'….(whack).

She grabbed his other hand and gritted he teeth.

'I will not, (whack) tolerate, (whack) deceit' (whack).

Joseph squeezed his stinging hands and clasped them tightly underneath his armpits, tears rolling down his cheeks. Pat felt sorry for him. She turned to the others.

'Tommy who did you check' she asked abrasively?

'Pat, Sister,' answered a visibly petrified Tubby.

'Come over here Pat, and let me check your teeth.'

Pat did as he was told.

'Open wide.'

The stench of the stale tobacco on her breath repulsed him.

'Well well. So you couldn't see any bad teeth Tommy?'

'No Sister,' he answered nervously.

'So you weren't trying to be being deceitful then, were you?'

'No sister.'

'Well then it's conclusive, you're going blind Tommy. Did you know that?

The children laughed timidly, finding the whole scenario anything but funny.

'No sister.'

'Now come over here Tommy and let me check your teeth.'

Tubby dressed only in his underpants and string vest walked slowly over. His entire body trembled with fear. Sister Agnes inspected Tubby's teeth.

'What a coincidence,' she said sarcastically.

'We have two blind boys trying to inspect each other, can you credit that?'

The children again laughed nervously. She grabbed Pat by the hand.

'I'll teach you, you trouble- maker.'

Pat now became the focus of her anger. As she proceeded to deliver 'six of the best' she became demonic, like something possessed, something alien, her black robes flaying wildly as she raised the strap high above her head bringing it crashing down with every ounce of her strength upon his outstretched hand. The children squirmed as each blow reverberated around the dormitory. Sister Bernadette, visibly upset, had to look away. The pain made Pat want to scream at the top of his lungs but would not allow himself to do so. He stood blowing hard upon his stinging hands. He was happy that at least that he had not given her the satisfaction of a single tear.

'Let that be a lesson you little cur,' she snarled, her face glowing from her exertions.

She turned to Tubby who was already crying. This time the blows were masked by Tubby's squeals of pain. Golly looked to Pat who despite his pain managed a wink. Golly smiled. It was a defining moment in both their young lives. It was the moment they realized that together they were stronger; together they could support and help one another through the testing times ahead.

Pat stood at the table in front of Sister Bernadette. Behind him Tubby cried like a baby. Sister Agnes

216

stood close by, observing procedures. When Sister Bernadette finished writing Bugs entry, she raised her head. A look of concern crossed her brow.

'I meant to ask you earlier child, what happened to your face?'

Pat cast a quick glance towards Sister Agnes. He did not know whether he should lie or tell the truth. The murderous look she gave him left him in no doubt.

'I was working in the orchard Sister, picking apples with Noel and I fell from the tree'.

Sister Bernadette seemed concerned. She spoke in her shrill voice.

'You must be more careful, you could have lost an eye.'

She turned to Sister Agnes and shook her head.

'He seems to be such an unfortunate little fellow.'

'Perhaps Sister, he brings misfortune upon himself?'

Soon the children were dressed and ready for mass. Sister Agnes watched as they made their way out the dormitory door and down the large wooden stairs. Sister Bernadette leaning heavily on her walking stick followed gingerly behind. The thunderous sound of feet could be heard pounding the landing below. When everybody had left, she turned and headed straight for Pat's bed.

Kneeling down, she opened the little stained locker by his bedside and rummaged through his few possessions. Behind an old jumper she found four apples. She placed them on the bed and continued her search. To her surprise, she found nothing else apart from a few chestnuts and a couple of marbles. She lifted the mattress. Beneath it, in a neatly folded brown paper bag she found what she was looking for. She sat on the bed and opened the bag. As she pulled the letters out, a ten shilling note fell to the floor. She bent

217

down, picked it up, and put it in her pocket. Sitting down she began to read.

CHAPTER THIRTY-THREE

In the sleepy village of Kiltealy on the foothills of Mount Leinster, villagers busied themselves for another dull and uneventful day. Claire stood at the kitchen sink in her mother's small bungalow, washing up the breakfast things and gazing out the window at the tranquil scene. She loved it here. She cherished those childhood memories this place held for her. She realized now how wonderful it had been, compared to the lives of the children in the orphanage. Hers had been a childhood of love, freedom and adventure. She looked up to the peak of Mount Leinster, recalling the day her mother and father brought herself and her school friend Peggy for a Sunday drive to the very top in her father's old Morris Minor. So steep was the road in places he had to use first gear and still the car stalled. Even the handbrake couldn't stop the car from rolling backwards. She remembered her mother panicking but her father pressed hard on the foot brake and the car gradually came to a halt. Once stationary she opened the door and quickly jumped out, demanding the girls do likewise. Despite her pleas, the girls sat in the back revelling in the excitement. Her father pulled on the starter, stuck the car in gear, revved the engine fiercely and crawled past his wife, who had begun to walk on ahead. The children waved through the windows as they passed. The image of her standing white faced with fear, in her light blue coat and bright red polka dot headscarf flapping wildly in the wind, was forever etched in her memory.

Claire's father was a quiet pleasant man. He was seventy eight, when he passed away. Since his death and Claire's departure, her Mother had been living alone. It was with a mixture of disappointment and delight she welcomed Claire home from the orphanage. Despite her strong Catholic beliefs, she was always supportive of her daughter.

Claire's day-dreaming was interrupted when she heard the key turn in the lock. The hall door opened and her Mother entered. She had just returned from the local village shop with some groceries.

'There's a letter here for you' she shouted breathlessly, as she unbuttoned her coat and hung it on the wall hooks in the hall.

Claire wiped her hands in the tea towel. Her mother entered the kitchen tossing the newspaper and a loaf of bread on the table. She handed the letter to Claire and watched as a smile grew on her daughters face.

'It's from Pat.'

She opened the letter excitedly.

'Well go on, read it, what does he say?'

Claire read the letter aloud.

Dear Claire,

Thank you for your letter, I was so happy. Thank your mother for the money too. I read your letter over and over again… It's hard to believe that in a couple of months I'll be at your house and spending Christmas with you. The idea of spending some time with nice people is so exciting, I can't wait. I'm looking forward to getting on a double-decker bus and seeing Dublin City. Things here are getting harder since you left. I hate this place, and I hate Sister Agnes. She really is a bad person, not like you.

When I feel upset and lonely, I think of you and it helps me to be strong. I want to be strong because you want me to be strong. I pray for you and your mother every night.

Thank you for being my best friend.

Pat.

P.S. Don't worry I haven't forgotten our Pinkie Promise.

Claire wiped the tears from her eyes. Her mother tapped her on the shoulder.

'What's a 'Pinkie Promise?'

Claire's face saddened.

'It's just a special promise' she said forlornly.

She could not fool her Mother.

'There's something you are not telling me.'

Claire sat down at the kitchen table.

' I'll stick the kettle on and we'll have a nice cup of tea and a chat.'

'That would be great.'

Her mother listened as Claire related her story.

'Oh my God, the poor child.'

'I feel so guilty. Perhaps I should have stayed.'

CHAPTER THIRTY- FOUR

Sister Agnes kicked the door to her office open, dragging Pat behind her by the ear.

'Get in there right now you sneaky brat.'
She tossed him across the room and slammed the door shut behind her.

'Well. What do you have to say for yourself ?'
Pat had never seen her quite so angry. He was scared and trembling

'Nothing ,Sister,' he said weakly. 'Nothing.'
She walked over to him.

'You have bitten the hand that feeds you. You have stolen apples from St. Joseph's, the same convent that clothes, feeds, and educates you. You are nothing but a thieving scoundrel, and you have nothing to say?'
Pat lifted his head.

'I didn't steal them, Sister, Noel said if they were bruised I could have them.'

'They are the property of this school, not Noel's.'
'I'm sorry Sister, I was hungry.'

'Do you think that you have some God-given right to special treatment at this school'
'No Sister, I'm sorry.'

'You're sorry?'
She repeated herself.

'You're sorry? You bloody well will be when I'm finished with you.'

She reached into her habit and pulled out the brown paper bag.

'And what is this?'

She opened the bag and spilled the contents on to the floor. Pat recognized the letters immediately. He was horrified his few private possessions had been plundered, yet he was too scared to reply. He could tell from the way the pages were scattered all across the floor his letters had been read.

'How did you get these letters,' she demanded.

Pat was afraid to look at her. She caught his chin and roughly lifted his swollen face, causing his eye to sting.

'I'll ask you once again. Who gave them to you?

Pat began to sob. He could not answer.

'Where did you get that money?'

'Sister Claire's mother sent it to me?'

'What have I told you? This woman is no longer a nun. Don't you dare sully this school with her name. The ten shillings will go towards replacing the sandals lost as a result of your outrageous behaviour.'

She bent down, scooped up the letters and began to tear them into little pieces. Pat watched them fall to the floor, closing his eyes in resignation.

'I warned you I didn't want to see or hear her name mentioned in this school again. Yet you defied my authority and corresponded with her against my wishes.'

She pointed to the scraps of paper littering the floor. 'Pick them up, and throw them in the wastepaper basket.'

Pat knelt down and gathered the tiny fragments. He stood up and dropped them into the waste-paper basket, They fell away like his hopes and dreams.

'You seem to think that 'rules' are for other boy's, and that they don't apply to you. This very morning you lied about Thomas's teeth.'

Leaning back she disturbed the ashtray, toppling it from her desk, spilling ash and cigarette ends all over the floor but she was too angry to notice.

'I want to know who's helping you. How did you get these letters?'

Pat had never been so scared in his life.

'You'd better answer me, or I swear to God......'

Pat, unable to help himself, wet the floor. Sister Agnes walked to the corner of the room and picked up a sally rod. It was long and thin like a whip. Pat rushed for the door. Sister Agnes grabbed him before he made good his escape and flung him back across the room.

'Don't you dare try that again,' she warned.

Pat watched as she turned the key in the door and put it in her pocket.

'Well my boy it's about time you were taught a lesson you'll not forget.'

CHAPTER THIRTY-FIVE

It was a chilly October morning. An old flat bed truck was parked outside the gate lodge. On the back was an old pine dresser, a cot, a gas cooker some beds and mattresses. They were interspersed with tea chests and cardboard boxes of every shape and size. Noel's 'Morris Traveler' was filled with bedding and kitchen utensils. In his arms Noel carried a radio and placed it carefully on the back of his car. Two removal men carried a table from the cottage and placed it on the truck, then began tying down the load with a tarpaulin and some long ropes. Noel's wife Molly sat in the car sobbing, while breastfeeding her baby Emma. Their son Cormac, oblivious to what was going on played with his toy truck on a patch of gravel by the front gate. Sister Agnes observed the scene from an upstairs window of the convent. She watched as the last few pots and pans were placed into the back of Noel's car and a smile of satisfaction crossed her lips when Noel pulled the cottage door shut and closed the garden gate.

Pat having again been expelled from class was weeding the avenue. Guilt-ridden and broken-hearted, he stood watching the scene from the shelter of some laurel bushes. Tears streamed down his face. He felt like a traitor, ashamed of having betrayed his friend. Noel spotted him as he cast a final glance around the place and despite his predicament, managed a smile and a wave, but Pat was too upset to wave back. Through his tears he watched Noel sit into the car. The

225

starting motor on the old truck groaned, the engine spluttered, belching blue smoke before firing and slowly moving off, followed closely Noel's 'Morris Traveler'. Not since that morning on the landing had Pat felt so desperate, so low, so useless and so utterly alone.

CHAPTER THIRTY- SIX

The day was dull and dreary. Claire sat in the kitchen with her mother drinking tea. Outside it was raining heavily and the view of Mount Leinster was lost beneath the low clouds and the condensation trickling down the window pane. An oil heater stinking of paraffin glowed in the corner, drying some tea towels on a stool placed in front of it. Both mother and daughter were in a subdued mood. Claire's mother pulled on a cigarette. She exhaled deeply and the grey blue smoke rose towards the naked bulb above the table.

'Maybe you should ring the convent,' she said eventually.

Claire looked anxiously at her.

'I know something's wrong. I can feel it.'

'That's all the more reason you should ring,' her mother said, as she flicked her ash into the empty cigarette packet in front of her.

'I haven't had a single word in four weeks.'

She sipped her tea and pondered on the situation.

'If I do ring, I might end up getting Pat into more trouble and that's the last thing he needs right now. Sister Agnes will use any excuse to make life difficult for him.'

Claire's mother picked up the tea pot with its green knitted cozy and offered Claire another drop of tea.

'You could talk to Reverend Mother. Sister Agnes doesn't have to know.'

Claire despaired.

'Those two are as thick as thieves.'

'Why does Sister Agnes despise Pat so much? What's he ever done on her?'

Claire stirred her tea, broke a whole grain biscuit in half and put it in her mouth. She hesitated before she spoke.

'We never got on, Sister Agnes and I. She didn't like the way I spoke my mind. She knew Pat and I had a special bond. I think she's trying to use him to get at me.'

Claire's mother stubbed out her cigarette, stood up and threw the packet into the bin.

'Poor child.'

She sat back down.

'There's something I've been meaning to ask you.'

Her expression changed. Claire recognized that face, she had seen it so often over the years.

'Come on mammy, tell me, what's bothering you'

'Perhaps it's none of my business, but I was wondering, if you had given any thought to what you might do, now that you've left the convent?

Claire sipped from the cup and placed it back on the saucer. She knew her answer might hurt.

'I'm thinking about America.'

'So, you'll be leaving then?'

Claire looked into her mother's sad blue eyes.

'What future does this country hold for me, mammy?'

'At least you'd be amongst your own' she said forlornly.

'To do what, join the dole queues?' Her mother sighed in acknowledgement.

She went to her coat hanging on the back of the kitchen door and pulled out a new packet of cigarettes.

'I know things are bad at the moment, but they'll get better. You'll have this house when I'm gone; you're a bright girl, I know you'll be alright.'

'I don't just want to get by, mammy; I want to do something with my life.'

Claire watched her mother light another cigarette. She took the spent match and placed it under her nose. As a child she had loved the smell of sulphur.

'You're smoking too much.'

For the first time Claire noticed the change in her mother. The strong vibrant woman she once knew seemed to have lost her zest for life. The woman she now beheld looked frail and vulnerable.

'You wouldn't deny your poor mother one of her few remaining pleasures' she said wearily.

Claire rolled the matchstick between her fingers.

'I'm just asking you to be careful that's all.

'Why. What do have I to live for,?

'I know you miss daddy terribly, but you're still a young woman, with lots of living to do.'

Claire tried to lift her mood.

'You could come and visit me in the States; we might even hitch you up with a rich cowboy.'

Her mother smiled and pulled on her cigarette.

'There are enough cowboys in the village of Kiltealy, than there are in the whole of America.'

Claire laughed.

'But none of them are rich. When Christmas is over and Pat has gone back to St. Joseph's I'll be heading off.'

Her mother lifted the cup to her lips.

'I might not like what you're doing Claire, but you know you'll always have my full support.'

Claire reached across the table and gently took her mother's hand.

'I'm aware of that mammy. I don't know what I'd do without you.'

CHAPTER THIRTY-SEVEN

Life in the orphanage had become unbearable. Pat lost himself in his schoolwork. He became more and more introverted. Joseph and he hardly spoke to one another anymore. Pat had built up a relationship with Stephen and they had become firm friends. Stephen was nothing like Joseph. He was quiet and unassuming. He wasn't a great talker but when he did talk he made sense.. The nun's openly criticized his mother for being a woman of low morals. The idea of an unmarried Irish girl engaging in pre marital sex was taboo, doubly so, when the man happened to be foreign and black. Pat admired how Stephen ignored the nun's taunts, and outbursts Despite the hurtful comments he had to endure about the color of skin, he refused to let it get him down. Stephen chose to laugh about it.

'If you are born with black skin, you better make sure it's thick too' he would say.

He was a strong boy both mentally and physically and knew how to look after himself having learned the wisdom of speaking at the right moments.

The dull grey morning mirrored Pats mood. The day he had been dreading had arrived. The dentist, butcher O'Brien as he was known, was visiting the school. The unfortunate children who had been selected were sent to see him. Pat sat in the corridor waiting his turn. Only four boys remained on the bench. 'Bugs' was next in line. He sat on his hands in silent prayer. Pat sat next to him, then Stephen and finally Sean. Pat tried desperately to take his mind off the impending visit. He looked at the old black and white pictures hanging on the opposite wall. They were of past pupils, who had the misfortune of attending St. Joseph's. He wondered where they were now. Had they managed to survive? Were they normal people and did they adjust to life outside? He wondered where he would be and what he would be doing, twenty years from now. The door opened and Tubby, in a state of collapse, with a bloodied handkerchief held to his mouth, was carried down the corridor by two strong male assistants in blood splattered white coats.

'Next boy' shouted O'Brien from within.
'Bugs' stood up and entered nervously. The others watched as the door closed behind him.

'Jaysus Christ it's a torture chamber they have in there,'said Stephen nervously?

'Stop,' said Pat.' 'It's bad enough as it is, don't 'make it any worse.'

'How can it get any worse for Christ sake,' asked a terrorized Sean?

A scream echoed through the corridor quickly followed by wailing.

'Sound like they're killing Bugs,' laughed Sean nervously.

Pat looked at Sean.

'The laugh will be on the other side of your face when they are finished with you.'

The butchers assistants returned.

'I'm never going to eat jam again, as long as I live,' said Stephen.

'Can I take your helping at breakfast then 'Golly', asked Sean?

Stephen realized the implications of such a rash statement. The door opened and 'Bugs' exited. He was ashen faced and held a wad of cotton wool to his mouth.

'Next,' hollered O'Brien.

Pat managed to get a quick glimpse around as he entered. The school desks had been stacked around the walls, making an open space in the middle of the room. He could see a strange looking chair and a big bright light above it.

'Sit down,' bellowed O'Brien.

Pat now got a good look at it. It looked like an executioner's chair complete with straps.

'What's your name O' Brien asked, dismissively?

'Pat.'

'And your number?'

'42.'

'Right Pat, I want you to sit back and relax.'

What a strange sense of humour this man has,' though Pat. O 'Brien was large man in his forties with a shock of orange red hair and the look of a mad professor. Pat noticed the strange array of offensive looking implements on the white cloth that covered the table to the right of the chair. On the left he noticed a blood splattered white enamel bucket. He sat back nervously. The helpers moved to each side of the chair.

'Open wide Pat,' O'Brien said in a curt voice.

He opened his mouth as wide as he could. O'Brien adjusted the lamp for a better look.

'Mmhhhmmm. 'Cavities in both rear molars' he said indifferently.

An assistant wrote something into a book. O'Brien nodded to him. The assistant secured a large strap around Pat's waist and tightened it so tightly Pat could hardly get his breath. At that instant it dawned on Pat that this was it. There would be no painkiller. The blood drained from his face. The assistants strapped Pat's arms tightly to the arm rests. O'Brien picked up an implement. Pat tried desperately to wiggle free.

'Now look here,' said O'Brien, waving the implement in front of Pat's face 'this won't take

232

very long if you co-operate. If you make things difficult you'll be the one who suffers, not me. Do you understand?'

Pat nodded, terror-struck.

'Now open wide.'

Pat could see O' Brien's hairy nostrils as he bent down over him. He could feel the cold steel of the implement tighten on his tooth. He struggled to breathe as O'Brien's large hands tightly gripped the handle and began to exert pressure. A pain, so excruciating that he thought the top of his skull had exploded, ripped through his body. Then he fainted.

'Wake up. Wake up.' O'Brien was slapping him on the face. He opened his eyes.

'Spit into the bucket.'

Pat felt his jaw throbbing. He coughed almost choking on his own blood. The bucket was placed in front of him and Pat spat into it. Fresh blood-stains splattered the assistant's white coat. O'Brien handed him a glass filled with a blue liquid.

'Good boy, rinse your mouth out with this and spit it into the bucket.

Pat did as he was told.

'Sit back,' said O'Brien.

Pat was terrified. O'Brien adjusted the lamp above his head. Suddenly he realized his ordeal was still not over.

'Please' he begged, 'don't do that to me again.' 'O'Brien picked up the implement. Pat kicked and screamed.

'No.' Please.' No.'

***

Later at lunch break, Pat and Stephen sat on the concrete bench in the schoolyard. Each held a blood-stained cloth to their mouths. Though they were

233

hungry, they were unable to eat. The old football was again taking a battering from the children as they pushed and shoved each other around the schoolyard chasing it. Pat spoke through puffed lips.

'They had to put 'Tubby' in the sick bay. Did you see the state of him? They couldn't stop the bleeding.'

'I saw him' said Stephen, shaking his head, 'wasn't I sitting with you when they dragged him down the corridor?'

'Oh yeah,' said Pat, remembering.

Stephen tried to smile, but his face hurt too much.

'When I saw them haul you out, I was so scared I was about to make a run for it.'

'You should have.'

'I would have, if I thought I could have got away with it,' said Stephen.

'I thought he was trying to pull my head from my body,

'I fainted, twice.'

'That's nothing to be ashamed of. I nearly did too.'

'They woke me up after the first tooth.'

Stephen had a look of horror on his face.

'You had more than one pulled?'

Pat nodded.

'O'Brien began yanking the second tooth, I was struggling in the chair, the others were holding me down and I swear to God, I thought I was going to die from the pain, or suffocation, or both.'

Stephen spat out some blood on to the concrete in front of him.

'O'Brien doesn't give a shit about anybody, is it any wonder they call him 'the Butcher.' .He must have burst Tubby's gum.' 'It feels like he burst mine, too' said Stephen.

'Which teeth did he pull?'

'He pulled two, right at the back.'

Stephen wiped his mouth with the bloodied rag.
'Jaysus I'm lucky, I only got one of the smaller
ones pulled. Can you imagine pulling teeth,
without some sort of painkiller?'

'I bet you O' Brien gets a pain killer when he
goes to the dentist.'

'You can bet your life on it,' said Stephen.

For a moment they said nothing and watched
the children running around the yard kicking the ball.
Joseph stood talking with Bugs. He was throwing
threatening looks in their direction.

'That's typical of him' said Pat, always looking for
others to do his dirty work.'

'I'm not scared of him or his friends.'

'He'll try and get his own back on you.'

'Let him try,' said Stephen, spitting blood.

Pat shook his head dejectedly.

'I can't take this place any more. I'd prefer to be
dead.'

Stephen sensed the despair in Pat's voice.

'Maybe we should tell Father Dunn. He might be
able to help us.

Pat stared blankly ahead.

'You could show him what Sister Agnes has done
to you.'

Pat was unconvinced.

'I don't know if I'd be better or worse off, if I
squealed on her?'

'Everybody can still see the marks of the black eye
she gave you,' said Joseph.

'Yeah but everybody thinks I fell and banged my
face.'

'Well tell him the truth. Tell him who gave it to
you. Show him the marks on your back.'

Pat spat some blood onto the cloth and wiped his mouth.

'That cow beat me so badly with her cane; I had to sleep on my stomach for three nights.

'She's has to be stopped before she kills someone.'

'She even stole the ten shillings I got from Sister Claire. She told me she was keeping it to help pay for new sandals.'

'She's probably spent it on cigarettes.'

Pat shrugged his shoulders.

'There's nothing we can we do.'

'We could try telling Hopalong

'Hopalong' said Pat, disbelievingly.

'Yeah,' said Stephen, 'maybe she doesn't know what's going on.'

The ball rolled under Stephen's feet. He kicked it hard across the yard.

'Ya black bollix,' shouted Seamus.

Stephen ignored the jibe. Pat took the bloodied cloth from his mouth.

'She doesn't give a shit about us. She knew there was no painkiller being used this morning, that's why she hasn't been seen all day.'

'You're right, she's gone into hiding.'

Look' said Pat, 'they don't care about us, we're not real people in their eyes. You wouldn't treat animals the way they treat us. When Sister Claire or Noel began to ask questions, they got rid of them. It's as simple as that.'

'You're right,' said Stephen looking a little dejected.

'We don't have an awful lot going for us, do we?'

Pat scratched his head.

'No. we don't.'

'At least we've got Christmas to look forward to.'

'I'm not so sure any more.'

236

'What do you mean?

'I'm afraid it mightn't happen now.'

'Why not' asked Stephen?

'I can't contact Sister Claire.'

Stephen tried to lift Pat's spirits.

'But that doesn't mean she won't take you out.'

Pat wiped some more blood from his lips.

'Maybe you're right, but I'm not going to wait around to find out.'

The ball smacked Stephen in the side of the head. He stood up and kicked it over the farmyard wall.

'Serves you right ya stupid Golly Wog' shouted Joseph.'

'Ya black bastard,' shouted Bugs.

The children looked at him in disgust.

'Fuck'n nigger,' said Seamus as he got a leg up over the wall.

'Ignore them' said Pat, 'are you ok?'

'Yeah I'm fine, what's a mere smack on the head compared to a ruptured jaw?'

Pat tried to laugh but it hurt too much.

'What do you mean you're not going to stick around,' asked Stephen sitting back down.

Pat looked him in the eyes.

'Promise you won't say a word to anybody.'

'I Promise,' said, Stephen.

'I'm going to run away.'

Stephen gave him a sympathetic look and shook his head ever so gently.

'Do you not think you're in enough trouble already?'

Pat eyes widened.

'You can come with me if you want.'

'Don't be stupid there's nowhere for us to run to.'

'That's good, 'cause then they won't know where to look for us.

Stephen liked his logic.

'We would never get away with it.'

'How can you say something like that, if you haven't tried?'

Pat unfolded the bloodstained cloth looking for a clean spot. Stephen spoke softly.

'Pat, don't you understand we'd have nowhere to go. Where would we sleep? How would we eat? How could we survive? You don't even have your ten shillings anymore.'

'Thanks for reminding me,' he said wiping his mouth clean.

'We could get a job.'

'What jobs can two eight-years olds do?'

'We could make rosary beads.'

'Yeah, and sell them back to the nuns,' said Stephen. 'Don't make me laugh' said Pat, holding his jaw.

'Seriously though,' said Stephen, 'we'd never survive.'

'If we can survive here, we can survive anywhere.'

'What if we got caught?

'I have no intention of getting caught.'

The sky opened and it began to rain. The children stopped playing football and ran for cover underneath the galvanized shed. Stephen and Pat sheltered underneath the eaves of the building. Stephen tried his best to dissuade Pat.

'If they caught us, they'll kill us. The police would be looking for us, for God's sake. We'd end up like common criminals on the run. We wouldn't be safe anywhere. There are not too many black boys roaming around this part of the country. Two young lads, one with red hair and freckles the other looking like a 'golly wog' would stick out like a

238

sore thumb. Think about it. We'd be spotted a mile away.'

Rain pelted down from the overflowing gutter forming puddles at their feet. Pat knew Stephen was right, but tried to remain positive.

'Maybe we could join the circus or a carnival or something. I'm sure there are a lot of black people working with the circus.'

Stephen shook his head trying to see the funny side.

'Is that all I'm good for, a circus or a freak show.'

'I'm sorry I didn't mean it like that', said Pat.

'I know you didn't.

He spat more blood onto the ground, and watched the strange pattern it made as it mingled with the rain.

'Listen to me Pat, they would hunt us down, in Dublin, Cork, wherever we went. We'd never be able to relax. We'd be looking behind us all the time.'

Pat was desperate; he couldn't take any more, he wanted out, one way or the other and was determined nothing was going to stop him.

'Maybe, we could go Kiltealy. Perhaps Claire would help us?'

'Don't you see, that's the first place they'd look. You'll end up getting her in trouble, and then you definitely won't see her at Christmas. It's only seven weeks away Pat. Surely you can hold out till then?'

CHAPTER THIRTY- EIGHT

The dormitory was quiet. It was past twelve o'clock and all the children were sleeping. A single forty-watt bulb burned behind the partition leading to the nun's quarters, casting a dull yellow wash of light on the wall to the rear of the dormitory. Pat sat up in bed, checked that the coast was clear, and climbed out. Quickly he dressed himself putting on two jumpers to keep himself warm. Stephen sat up in his bed.

'Are you really going,' he whispered

'Jesus you frightened the life out of me, I thought you were fast asleep. Yes I am going. You can still come with me if you like.'

'I think you're mad,' whispered Stephen, resting his head on his hand.

'You're probably right.'

'In a way I wish I was as mad as you are.'

'Thanks a bunch,' said Pat, still unsure it was meant as a compliment or not.

He stuffed some of his other clothes under the bed covers and pulled them right up.

'I might visit Sister Claire just for an hour or so. Maybe she can help me.'

'That's on the other side of the country.'

'It's a small country, wish me luck.'

'I hope you find her. That would be fantastic. If you do, will you write?'

'Sure.'

Stephen reached out his hand. Pat clasped it tightly.

'Good luck mate, take care.'

'Thanks Stephen , I'll be seeing you.'

'I hope not, 'cause that would mean you'll have the shit kicked out of you.

'If I'm caught, they won't need to kick the shit out of me. I'll have done it myself.'

Stephen watched the indiscernible figure of Pat, hobnailed boots in hand, tippy-toe towards the stairs. He heard the familiar squeak and gentle clunk of the heavy door. Pat was gone.

***

The moon was veiled by a passing cloud as he ran through the darkness. He had fallen several times into ditches and bushes that had never been apparent to him in the light of day. He was breathless, and consumed with fear.

'It's too late now, no going back,' he told himself. He ran through the fields that led to the open road. Cattle scattered as he neared scaring him half to death. He could not afford to stop and kept running, his little heart pumping overtime. The moon peeped out and lit the surroundings in welcome silver light. He stopped, gasping for breath casting a glance back towards St. Joseph's. Thankfully it was still shrouded in darkness with not a single light to be seen. Relieved, he took a deep breath and hurried on his way.

Once he had reached the road he headed towards the village of Rathmore. It was the first time in his short life that he had ever been so alone, so distant from another human being and so far from prying eyes. The isolation and the strange eerie shadows on the road ahead, made the hairs on the back of his neck stand. On hearing the sound of a motor in the distance he turned to see its faint lights weave along the road behind him. Quickly he scampered over the nearest stone wall and lay low. He watched as the headlights neared and the engine noise grew louder.Everything seemed amplified in the stillness of the night. 'Could this be a search party' he wondered.

Had his escape been discovered so quickly?' Soon the hedgerows were lit by the beams of the headlights. He could not determine the make of the car or its occupants. He watched, peering through the darkness as the car rattled by, and faded into the distance.

Dark clouds crossed the moon shutting out the light. He was relieved he had not been seen. Yet, he felt the isolation grow. He was on the side of a mountain, in the middle of nowhere, alone and scared, and already tired and hungry. Perhaps he should have been braver. Perhaps he should have showed himself, and hitched a lift. Maybe now he could be sitting in the front of some salesman's car, heading far from here, far from Moyross, and the clutches of St Joseph's. He climbed back on to the road and inched forward, his hands outstretched like a child feeling his way in a game of blind man's buff.

Time passed slowly. He had been walking for nearly two hours, helped and hindered by the re-emerging moon. The first pink rays of light began breaking in the east. His spirits were lifted by this welcome sight. Soon the stillness was broken by something he had never heard before, the dawn chorus. The whole bird kingdom seemed to be waking up, singing in full throated joy, at the imminent birth of another day. In the distance he could see the sparse lights of Rathmore. To him they seemed warm and compelling, and as inviting as the fairy lights on a Christmas tree. He continued with a new-found vigour The morning sky was dull and overcast as Pat eventually reached the small village, typical of a thousand villages scattered around the country, just one long street with houses on both sides .Pat was tired and cold. Nothing stirred, not even a stray dog. It was as if the world had stopped. He made his way along the street, ever conscious of the grating sound

242

his hobnailed boots made on the concrete footpath. He thought of all those lucky souls lying in their warm beds wrapped up tightly, oblivious to the cold and damp outside.

He stopped at the window of a little shop and was transfixed. Never in his life had he seen such a display of colourful cardboard boxes, neatly stacked one behind the other, with sweets Pat had never seen before in his life. There were Trigger Bars, with a silhouetted cowboy on the wrapper. There was Turkish Delight, with exotic buildings on the box, 'Macaroni bars' and 'wine gums'. They even had candy cigarettes.

He cupped his face in his hands and leaned against the glass trying to peek inside. On the shelf he could see large jars with screw top lids, full of red 'gob-stoppers' 'bulls-eyes' 'acid drops' and 'licorice allsorts'. How he wished he had his ten shillings. He turned away, his tummy rumbling and walked a little further up the street, where he spotted the village pump and rushed over to it. Only now did he realize how thirsty he was. He pressed down hard on the long green handle. It squeaked and rattled before water eventually came gushing out onto the concrete at his feet.

He opened his mouth and gulped the water in a sucking motion. The coldness pained his torn gums. He wiped his mouth in the sleeve of his jumper and continued on. His attention was caught by something in the window of a butcher shop. He had never seen anything like it before. It was round and green, with neatly cut out triangular eyes, nose. and mouth. Inside a nightlight flickered dimly. He stood watching for some moments, fascinated. Written in large white letters on the window pane were the words 'Happy Halloween'. Curiously he rubbed his finger through

243

the letter 'H'. To his surprise the white came away on his finger. He rubbed the white chalk substance from his fingertip, before carrying on. Up ahead a small road branched off to the left.

A signpost read Ballina 36 miles straight ahead, the other to the left read, Foxford 23 miles, and behind 'Moyross' 6 miles. To his astonishment he had travelled only six miles. He was still much too close to the orphanage for comfort and too easily identifiable to be able to relax in any way. He knew Claire lived somewhere in Co. Wexford. He stood for the first time in his young life at a crossroads, not knowing which road he should take.

The morning turned nasty. Heavy rain and sleet swept in from the North. Pat took shelter under some woods on the outskirts of the village. He was soaked through. The thick heavy jumpers he wore acted like a sponge holding in the cold rains and chilling him to the bone. Slowly the village rose from its slumbers. Sounds of movement could be heard, the occasional starting of a distant motor or the barking of a local dog. Later the sound of church bells rang out, calling the parishioners to morning mass. He was caught in two minds. Should he take shelter in the church till the rains eased, risking the possibility of being spotted, or should he stick it out, cold and wet in the relative safety of the woods? He knew by now the alarm bells were ringing in St. Joseph's. Sister Agnes would be aware of his absence. He would be the talk of the school, a hero to some of the children, a fool to others and a headache to the nuns.

His thoughts were interrupted by the sound of a car. He ran towards the road. To his horror he realized it was a 'garda car' and he quickly dived on to the soaking grass.

'Christ, she must have called the police' he thought, as he lay face down in the muck.

To his relief the police car passed right on by. He picked himself up and tried to wipe the mud from his face and legs. For the next three agonizing hours Pat sat huddled beneath the trees in a shivering ball sheltering from the wind and rain. Though the odd car had passed, he was afraid to show his face. Stephen had been right. It was useless after all. Why had he been so stupid? Why had he not devised a plan, or at least drawn a map to show him which way to go. He had not even considered the fact that it might rain, yet he knew it always rained in Mayo. He had no money, no food, and was cold, dirty and hungry. Now that the police were on his trail, the locals would be keeping an eye out for him. He knew he would not be hard to spot, especially in his present condition. Stephen' was right; he did stick out like a sore thumb. The rattle of a lorry came trundling down the road. Pat looked up. He recognized the unmistakable sound. It was Miko in the milk lorry. For a moment he stood confused, not knowing what to do, then he ran to the roadway waving his arms. The lorry stopped. Pat ran to the driver's side. Miko was shocked to see Pat and the state he was in.

'Pat? What in God's name are you doing out here. Why aren't you in the orphanage? A Jesus, look at the state of you.'

'I need your help Miko. I ran away.'

'Climb in before you get your death of cold,' said Miko in a stern voice.

Pat was disappointed at the reception he was receiving. Perhaps he had made the wrong choice after all, but still he climbed into the cab. Outside the rain pelted down on the tin roof like a steel drum.

'You can't just run away like that,' he said, his voice now a little more sympathetic. 'Where are you going to go?'

Pat gazed through the split windscreen as the lorry pulled off. He watched as the wipers struggled to contain the deluge of water pouring down the glass.

'I'll find somewhere,' he said defiantly.

'Ah Pat. You're soaked, freezing and probably half starving into the bargain.'

He pointed to an old black crombie-coat in the back of the cab.

'Stick that on you before you die of cold.'

Pat wrapped the old coat around his shoulders. Miko reached behind him and pulled out a large brown paper bag.

'I have a bag of apples and nuts here, you can have the lot if you come back to the orphanage with me. What do you say?'

Pat was disgusted with Miko.

'You don't understand. I don't want to go back there. I've run away and I need your help.'

Miko spoke in a fatherly voice.

'Listen Pat, we all want to run away at different times in our life. We all get frustrated, angry and upset. Things get on top of us, and we think we can't take any more.'

He shook his head and looked sympathetically towards the shivering child

'The grass is no greener on the far side of the hill. If you run away now, what can you possibly do? At your age you're too young to work as a labourer or a farm hand. You are even too young to be an apprentice. What choices do you have? How would you get by?'

Pat had heard it all before. He sat quietly watching the windscreen wipers swishing to and fro, not wanting to listen to Miko's words. Though he didn't like them, he knew they were true. They confirmed what Stephen had said and what he himself had known in his heart all along. It was useless. Perhaps it was a cry for attention or a scream for a normal childhood.

'Suppose you did manage get to a city like Dublin', Miko continued; 'the only work you could get would be something menial, like selling newspapers on street corners or assisting some old chimney sweep. It would only be a matter of years before you took the inevitable boat journey to London, or Liverpool, to work as a labourer or a 'navvie'.'

Pat didn't know what 'navvie' meant, nor did he want to.

'I know what I'm talking about. I went down that road. For twenty years I lived in Manchester working my fingers to the bone, thinking that money would buy me happiness. I spent twenty of the most miserable and lonely years of my life there, before I realized I simply did not belong. You're too bright for that, you deserve better. Study while you can, son; take the opportunity of an education. If you do, then the world can be your oyster.'

This time he was curious.

'What's an 'oyster'?'

'It's a fish, a shellfish.'

Pat looked confused. '

'If I study, my world could be a shell fish?'

Miko's smile was full of pathos, as he reflected on the innocence of youth and the harshness of life. He offered the bag to Pat. For a moment Pat hesitated then took the apples and nuts from him. Miko gave him a warm smile.

'Good lad, when I'm finished delivering here, I'll drop you home.'

Pat turned to Miko, an angry expression on his face

'That's not my home Miko. I don't have one. St. Joseph's is the last place on earth I would call home.'

Miko felt touched, he understood the boy's dilemma.

CHAPTER THIRTY- NINE

The lorry chugged past the gate lodge that had once been Noel's home. Pat looked across at the boarded door and windows. He felt a knife-of-guilt pierce his heart.

'Stop the lorry Miko, I can't do it. Please stop.'

'What's the matter?'

'I can't go back there, she'll kill me.'

'Who? asked Miko.

'Sister Agnes.'

'Don't be silly Pat, she'll be as relieved as the rest to see you and know that you are safe.'

Pat pointed to the greenish hue beneath his left eye

'Who do you think I got this from?'

Miko stopped the lorry

'You told me yourself, you fell.'

Pat tossed off the 'crombie'-coat and pulled up his damp jumpers revealing his scars. Miko face dropped.

'Christ, what happened to your back?'

'Sister Agnes. She whipped me. She forced me tell her who was giving Sister Claire's letters to me. That's why Noel is no longer here. She got him sacked.'

'Good Jaysus, are you saying she's the reason Noel was evicted.'

Pat lowered his jumper once more.

'Sister Claire sent me letters through Noel. He minded them and gave them to me. She found the letters and beat the story out of me.'

Pat started to cry.

249

'I tried, I swear I tried not to tell her, but the more I tried, the harder she beat me.'

Miko was now visibly angry.

'You poor child.'

Though they were good friends, Noel had never divulged the real reason why he was leaving. He placed his hand on Pat's shoulder.

'I'll tell you what I'll do' he said reassuringly.

'If you come back with me now I'll go straight to Reverend Mother. Don't worry, I won't tell her you're with me. You can hide in the cab. I'll tell her I know where you are, nothing more. I'll tell her that if anybody lays another finger on you, they'll have me and the police to answer to. She knows only too well it's not difficult for me to keep an eye on you. If she doesn't agree I'll say nothing more and I'll drive you back out the gate of this place. I promise.'

He offered his hand to Pat.

'Do we have a gentleman's agreement?

Pat nodded reluctantly.

Reverend Mother sat behind her desk. Her face betrayed no emotion when Miko returned with Pat who was shivering from the cold and damp and fear.

'I found him just outside Rathmore. He was wandering around like a lost soul in the pouring rain. The poor little fellow could have caught his death of cold.'

Reverend Mother looked at the sorry state of the child in front of her.

'And what do you have to say for yourself?'

'I'm sorry, Reverend Mother.'

She stood up and approached him. Miko stepped forward and placed his hand protectively on Pat's shoulder.

250

'Once again you have let down the good name of St. Joseph's. It seems to be a hobby of yours. Just look at the state of you.'

She circled like a vulture closing in on its prey. Pat was glad Miko was there to protect him.

'To say I am disappointed is an understatement. This is not the first time I've had to deal with you, and your crazy notions. Perhaps I should have you assessed by a doctor. Maybe there's more to this than meets the eye.'

'Perhaps you should' said Miko in a hostile voice.

'Whatever do you mean by that' said reverend Mother indignantly?

Miko looked down at Pat reassuringly.

'Show your back to Reverend Mother, son'.

Pat hesitated.

'It's okay. Nothing is going to happen to you.'

Pat turned his back and lifted his clothes. Reverend Mother gasped.

'Would you care to explain this to me,' asked Miko?

Reverend Mother seemed lost for words

'He's a small child, for God's sake. I thought this sort of punishment went out with the 'Inquisition. I've a good mind to go straight to the police.'

She stopped by the window. Pat could see the avenue outside through the thick lenses of her glasses.

'That won't be necessary Mr. O' Sullivan, it's an internal matter and I'll make sure this never happens again.'

'Don't you worry Reverend Mother, I too will make sure it never happens again.'

Her face reddened with anger. She tried her best to remain calm, and turned to Pat.

'I'd like you to thank Mr. O'Sullivan for the kindness `he has shown you, and apologize to him for your outrageous conduct.'

Pat looked up at Miko who gave him a smile and a wink.

'Thank you, Mr. O' Sullivan, and I'm sorry for all the trouble I caused.'

Miko squeezed his shoulder gently.

'Think nothing of it son. Here don't forget your apple's and nuts'.

'I don't think rewarding misconduct is a good idea, Mr. O' Sullivan.

'They are a present from me and I insist he is allowed keep them.'

'As you wish,' said Reverend Mother pointing to the door.

'Now go to the laundry room and tell Sister Bernadette I sent you. Ask her to run a nice warm bath, it'll take the chill out of those bones of yours. Give yourself a good clean up and I'll send somebody up to get you when you're finished. Now off you go.'

'Yes, Reverend Mother.'

Miko gave him a final wink and he was gone. Reverend Mother turned to Miko despondently.

'He's got such a stubborn streak and sets such a bad example for the other children. He desperately needs to be taught some discipline.'

Miko looked her squarely in the face.

'Perhaps he does, but violence is not the way. I've seen what that's done to him, now let that be an end to it!'

She reached for the door handle, angry at Miko's admonishment.

'Good day Mr. O'Sullivan' she said dismissively. 'Don't worry I'm going, but if anybody lays a hand on him I'll be back and next time, it will be with the authorities. Good day to you Reverend Mother.'

Though Miko spoke softly, he left her under no allusion as to the sincerity of his words. He turned and headed down the hall while the infuriated nun slammed the door behind him.

CHAPTER FORTY

Pat quietly followed Sister Bernadette up the dull back stairs. She was a sweet old nun who no longer had much contact with the children. She puffed and wheezed her way up the stairs. Each step seemed like a new challenge. In his hand Pat held a large grey towel. He watched the wooden rosary beads dangling from her belt sway and rattle with each step and looked to the large cross hanging from the beads and to the figure of Christ impaled upon it spinning erratically with her every move. Sister Bernadette opened a door. Apart from Reverend Mother's it was the only bathroom in the school, the same bath Sister Claire had used. Sister Bernadette flicked the light switch and ushered him inside. The dim light from the bulb hardly registered. She placed the stopper in the plug hole. Pat watched as she struggled with her arthritic hands to turn on the large brass taps. First there was a gurgling sound followed by a gush of water. She let it run checking the temperature regularly with her hand. Pat noticed the strange ornate metal feet supporting the bathtub. They looked like the claws of some large bird and he found them a little scary. Steam began to rise and the bath began to fill. Pipes rattled, making strange eerie noises above him in the attic. Sister Bernadette took the towel from Pat and placed it upon on a convector heater in the corner. She pressed a switch and a bulb inside glowed red.

'It will be nice and warm for you when you get out.'

'Thanks Sister.

'Take off those wet clothes like a good boy,' she said turning her back to him. Pat did as he was told.
He looked thinner more delicate without his clothes, like a cat after having fallen into water.

'Now, in you get.'
Sister Bernadette turned around again and began picking up his soaking clothes.

'Look at the state of these, were you rolling around in muck or what?'
He lowered his head and said nothing as stood by side of the bath testing the water with his toe.

'Give yourself a good scrub and don't forget to wash behind your ears. There's plenty of soap so don't be………..'
She stopped mid-sentence.

'My God, you poor child, what happened your back?'
He did not know what to say, and began to climb into the bath. She threw his clothes into a wicker basket.

'What happened, did somebody beat you?' she enquired.
He nodded nervously

'Who?'
Pat remained silent, not wishing to jeopardize his tenuous situation any further. She stood looking down at him waiting for a reply but he dared not answer

'You're afraid to tell me, aren't you child?'
Pat nodded. She shook her head ruefully and picked up the basket.

'Don't forget to wash your hair it's filthy. I'll send somebody up in a little while with some dry things for you to wear.'
She opened the door to leave.

'No splashing do you hear. I'm leaving the door slightly ajar. If you need something call out, somebody will hear.'

255

Pat listened as Sister Bernadette's feet shuffled across the bare floor boards on the landing. He listened to her footsteps on the wooden stairs grow weaker and weaker; finally he could hear them no more. He was alone. For the first time he was completely alone in the orphanage. He glanced around the dull green walls and listened to the rain beat against the frosted window pane. He was excited and nervous. He had never been in a bath before, and had never seen so much hot water in his life. Carefully he lay back and lowered himself into the water. He could feel its soothing warmth caress him. He lowered his head till his ears were just below the surface and listened to the strange gurgling sounds as he moved his arms and legs. Gazing at the ceiling, he searched the cracks for hidden monsters.

***

Outside, Tommy the postman knocked on the main door. He was wearing a shiny black rain cape and leggings to protect him from the incessant rain. Sister Agnes opened the door.

'What a horrid day. Step inside.'

Tommy entered the hallway, lowered his hood and wiped his feet on the large mat.

'Indeed it is Sister. They don't come much worse than this' he said, wheezing louder than ever.

He reached beneath his cape, opened his glasses case and placed them on his wet nose.

'I have another letter for Noel. Has he got himself a new address yet' he asked, as he shook the rain from his hands and delved into his saturated post bag.

Sister Agnes smiled warmly.

'Not yet I'm afraid, he asked me to look after his mail till he gets a forwarding address.'

'How is he Sister?' enquired Tommy, as he sifted through the letters in his hand.

'He hasn't been in touch much lately.

'I presume he's busy looking for a new job and setting up a home for himself, and his family.'

'I thought he was happy here in St, Josephs?'

'Oh you know how young men are,' she smiled, 'wanted the bright lights of the city.'

She laughed weakly.

'We weren't good enough for him anymore.

Tommy handed a small bundle of damp letters to her.

'That doesn't sound right; he always struck me as the quiet sort.'

He removed his glasses and put them away.

'You know what they say, never judge a book by its cover.'

Tommy pulled the hood back over his head.

'I best be on my way, I've still got half my round to do.'

Sister Agnes opened the door to the swirling wind and rain. Tommy lowered his head protecting himself as he walked out into the deluge.

'Good day Sister.'

She quickly closed the door behind him and sorted through the mail stopping at an envelope addressed to: Noel Cummins, The Gate Lodge, St. Joseph's. Moyross. Co. Mayo. and pulled it from the pile. A smile broke across her face as she opened it. Inside was a letter to Noel, and one addressed to Pat. She opened the letter to Pat, and began to read.

CHAPTER FORTY-ONE

Claire stood by her bed. She packed some clothes into an overnight bag. Her hair had grown in the intervening months and she wore it in a bob. She had a determined look on her face as she stuffed the little bag with essentials. Her mother entered the room.

'Here, I thought you might like a cuppa.'

Claire smiled appreciatively.

'Thanks mammy, what would I do without you?'

Her mother sat on the bed beside her.

'Strange we've not had a single letter in over six weeks' her Mother said, as she watched Claire pack her overnight bag and zip it shut.

Claire sat on the side of the bed and sipped from the cup.

'Nothing. It's the third week of November and we still haven't heard a single word. I don't understand it, something's wrong, I know it, even Noel doesn't answer my letters anymore.'

'What time do you make it?'

Her mother looked at her watch.

'You have plenty of time the bus won't be here for at least another fifteen minutes.'

'I'd rather be safe than sorry, mammy' said Claire, sipping her tea.

She looked into her mother's pale blue eyes.

'I can't take this any longer. I have to go there and find out what's wrong.'

Her mother held her hand.

'Of course darling, I understand completely. I'll come with you, if you like?'

'No mammy, I appreciate the offer but perhaps it's better if I go there alone. I hope you understand?'

'It's a long journey and I thought perhaps you might be glad of the company.' Claire smiled warmly.

'That's all the more reason you shouldn't come.'

Her mother rebuked her.

'I'm not an invalid you know.'

'I know mammy, I just don't want to put you through an ordeal like that.'

Claire drank the rest of the tea and placed the cup on her dressing table. She went to the wardrobe and took out her overcoat.

'Wrap up well it's freezing outside.'

'I'll stay in Ballina tonight and get the bus to St. Joseph's in the morning.'

Her mother took her purse from her cardigan and opened it. She took out two five pound notes and pressed them into Claire's palm.

'Here take it; it's just a few pounds.'

'I'm fine mother, I have some money.'

Her mother insisted.

'Take it. Like you just said yourself, it's better to be safe than sorry.'

'Are you sure?'

Her mother smiled.

'Of course I'm sure. Buy some sweets for Pat.'

'Thanks, he'll be thrilled. I'll tell him they are from you.'

Claire folded the notes and placed them in her pocket. She kissed her mother on the cheek.

'I better get going.'

She grabbed her bag and headed for the door.

***

The bus came to a halt outside the Gates of St. Joseph's. Claire alighted, her blonde hair blowing in the bitter wind. She looked sad. She had enquired from the bus-driver about the conductor who six months

259

earlier had wished her well and placed a 'half crown' in her hand and was appalled to hear he had died from cancer. Had he known his plight back then, she wondered? She stood and said a little prayer for him as the bus slowly pulled away.

Again she entered under a wrought iron arch that led to 'Saint Joseph's Orphanage'. Memories, some good some bad, came flooding back.. The avenue was strewn with the leaves and bare branches overhung the driveway. She was shocked to see the gate lodge had been boarded up.

Suddenly everything was clear to her. Her letters could never reach Pat, nor could his reach her. . She walked apprehensively up the avenue towards the convent. The building seemed greyer than she had remembered. She stopped and listened to the children playing in the schoolyard and noticed how untidy the grounds appeared. Walking slowly towards the main door she rang the bell and waited nervously for some time before Sister Bernadette, opened the door. She peeked out distrustfully from behind the large timber frame.

'Good day, how can I help you?'

Claire was glad to see an old familiar face.

'Sister Bernadette it's me, do you remember?'

Sister Bernadette looked a little confused. Claire tried to help her.

'Clifden Bay. The red sandals. Bare feet?'

Sister Bernadette smiled.

'Ah yes, Sister Claire. Gosh how you've changed, I hardly recognized you. We were talking about you only the other night.'

'Kind words I hope?'

Sister Bernadette opened the door wide.

'Do come in.'

'Thank you Sister'

260

CHAPTER FORTY-TWO

Claire stood in Reverend Mother's office. It had changed little from the last time she had been there. It was cluttered and untidy with books and files still stacked upon the desk. Reverend Mother slid her thick glasses back up the bridge of her nose. She pointed to a cushioned chair.

'Please, sit down.'

Claire was shocked by how frail she appeared. Her face was drawn, thin and gaunt. The bulldog jowls had all but disappeared, only sagging skin remained. Claire sat on the chair. She felt ill at ease and uncomfortable in the room.

'Well this is a surprise,' she said sarcastically.

'To what do we owe this unexpected pleasure?'

'I was passing, Reverend Mother and thought I might drop in and say hello to the children.'

Reverend Mother's glasses slipped down her nose and she slid them back into place. She joined her hands, both index fingers pointing upwards and tapped them gently against her thin lips as if contemplating.

'I see,' she said eventually. 'I'm afraid it would not be a wise thing to do, under the circumstances.'

Claire remained composed.

'Why ever not,' she enquired, unnerved by the negativity in Reverend Mother's voice?'

'I feel perhaps, it might be disruptive to the children and could have an upsetting effect on them. I don't want anything to interfere with the good

261

relationship Sister Josephine has been building with them, since your abrupt departure.'

Claire could sense her hostility. '

'I don't wish to interrupt them in class, Reverend Mother. They are playing in the schoolyard as we speak. Perhaps, I could just say hello to them there?'

There was a knock on the door. Sister Agnes entered. Claire froze in her seat. She was relieved when Sister Agnes did not recognize her.

'I'm sorry Reverend Mother, I didn't realize you had company, excuse my interruption. I just need to collect some blotting paper.'.

'You'll find it on the middle shelf,' replied Reverend Mother.

Sister Agnes stood behind Claire searching through some boxes. Claire could feel a shiver running up her spine.

'It will only be for a couple of minutes Reverend Mother, just a quick hello and then I'll be off again.'

Sister Agnes recognized the voice. She stopped what she was doing and turned to look at the young woman sitting in the chair.

Reverend Mother, registering her surprise, interjected;

'Ah Sister Agnes, you remember Sister Claire, don't you?'

Claire reluctantly turned to face her.

'And I'm sure you remember, Sister Agnes?'

Claire looked her in the eyes and sensed her unease.

'Indeed I do, Reverend Mother. I dare say I'll never forget her.'

Sister Agnes smiled nervously.

'Well that's high praise indeed,' said Reverend Mother.

Sister Agnes grabbed the blotting paper and headed towards the door. She looked at Reverend Mother.

'I've got what I need; I won't disturb you any longer'. She cast a glance in Claire's direction. 'Goodbye.'

Claire did not respond, instead she watched with relief, as Sister Agnes swiftly left the room and shut the door behind her. Claire returned to her conversation.

'As I was saying, I would appreciate a quick word with them before they go back to class, that's all I ask, then I'll be on my way.'

Reverend Mother leaned back in her chair, her eyes steely.

'The children's welfare comes first and I'm afraid I have to disappoint you.

Claire felt the heartlessness of her words.

'Then I implore you, let me speak to just one child. We have become good friends and in fact my mother has applied to foster him this Christmas.'

Reverend Mother's face stiffened. She stood up and walked to the window clasping her hands tightly and rubbing them together, as if she was trying to warm herself.

'And who might that boy be,' she asked.

'Patrick Deegan. Pat 42, as he is known to the school'

Reverend Mother shut her eyes, sighed and adjusted her glasses.

'I'm afraid that won't be possible.'

Claire stood up, to implore her.

'Please you have to let me see him.

I've come all this way and I won't leave till I do.'

Reverend Mother continued to stare vacantly out the window, avoiding eye contact.

'I know I upset everybody here in St. Joseph's, but that's no reason to take your revenge out on a small child.'

She could no longer contain her frustration. Her voice trembled.

'Have a heart for God's sake.'

She walked across to confront Reverend Mother. She was desperate now, and past caring.

'Do you even know what a heart is,' she blurted out. Reverend Mother ignored her little outburst.

'It's nothing to do with you' she said coldly, as she hobbled past Claire and stepped behind her desk once more.

'Well then why won't you let me see him? A few minutes, that's all I'm asking.'

Reverend Mother turned to face her. Claire could now see the gaps in her wimple where her fleshy cheeks used to be.

'But why,' she implored.

Reverend Mother took a deep breath and sat back down in her chair.

'Because,' she hesitated a moment, 'Pat is dead.'

Claire stood transfixed, trying to come to terms with what she had just been told. The words impacted on her like she had been hit by a steam train. She felt she was spinning head over heels; not knowing which way was up. Her mind raced, her logic deserted her as she dropped into the chair trying to make sense of Reverend Mother's words.

'What. Oh no. No. You must be mistaken.'

'I'm afraid not,' said Reverend Mother, calmly.

'Pat died at Halloween.'

The words crushed Claire. She placed her hands over her mouth.

'No. No.' she cried.

Reverend Mother sat defiantly, offering neither sympathy nor support. Claire tried desperately to pull herself together.

'How,' she gasped?

'It was a terrible tragedy. The little fellow, drowned in the bath.'

Claire struggled to make sense of what she was hearing.

'Where?'

'He must have fallen asleep and slid under the warm water. We did everything to try to revive him, but it was too late.'

Nothing was making sense anymore. 'What was he doing in a bath? The children don't have baths.' Reverend Mother's voice was void of emotion. She shuffled past the seated Claire, limping towards the window once more.

'He ran away from the orphanage and was out all night. Mr. O' Sullivan the milkman found him wandering around Rathmore and brought him back. He was in a terrible state, covered in mud, soaked to the skin and shivering to the bone. I took pity on him and felt a hot bath might help.'

Claire turned towards Reverend Mother. Her face drained of blood wondering why he had run away. A tide of guilt engulfed her. Was she to blame for this tragedy, had Pat broken his 'pinkie promise', had things got so bad he could no longer carry on?

'Why was he left alone and unsupervised?' Reverend Mother turned towards her.

'There's more than one child to look after in this orphanage. Sister Bernadette went to find some dry clothes for him to wear. He was not alone for more than ten minutes.'

Claire found her explanation s disturbing.

'Who found him,' she demanded?'

Reverend Mother ignored the question.

'He was an unfortunate little fellow always getting into trouble.'

Claire, raised her voice.

'I asked you a question, who found him?

Reverend Mother though visibly shaken by Claire's outburst continued to stare out the window.

'Sister Agnes' she said timidly. Claire raised her hands to her face.

'Oh no, no, no', she repeated inconsolably.

Turning from the window Reverend Mother assured her.

'We did everything we could to revive him. Sister Agnes gave him the kiss of life. She tried desperately to save him, but it was too late. He was gone.'

'What did the doctor say?' she asked, fretfully.

Reverend Mother glanced out the window once more.

'He said that it was too late, nobody could have helped him.' '

Why didn't you let me know' she asked angrily.

'Why should I let you know? You no longer have anything to do with this school. It was an internal matter.'

'You could have informed me' she sobbed.

'You're not his next of kin.'

'Where is he now' asked Claire, emotionally shattered.

'We buried him just outside the walls of the Nun's graveyard.'

'That's not even consecrated ground. Why wasn't he buried in Rathmore cemetery?'

Reverend Mother stood silently, her back to Claire, a ghostly black figure silhouetted against the tall widow frame. Eventually she spoke.

'Father Dunn and Sister Agnes were of the opinion Pat took his own life.'

Claire had prayed she would never hear those words, now her worst nightmare had come true.

'Oh no.'

'Father Dunn held a lovely little service for the repose of his soul.'

She turned to Claire.

'It's too late now, for feelings of remorse. You weren't here when he needed you. Perhaps if you had been, this tragedy might never have happened.'

Claire felt her words cut like a dagger through her heart.

The school bell rang. Claire could hear the patter of the children's feet in the corridor outside as they noisily gathered for class.

'We did our best. I have nothing further to say on the matter.'

CHAPTER FORTY-THREE

A shattered Claire wound her way through the overgrown grass towards the quaint little graveyard hidden behind the walls of an ancient church ruins. A chill north easterly wind whipped across the barren landscape. She felt numb, not from the cold but from the news she had just heard. Her head was spinning and her heart was aching. Christmas was only a few weeks away, why couldn't he have waited? It angered her that he had not held out till then. Perhaps, she could have given him the strength to carry on. Why had he run away and where was he running to? What caused him to resort to such drastic actions?

She yearned to know the truth and why Noel no longer worked for the orphanage. A hundred thousand questions raced through her mind as she approached the grave. Against the perimeter wall she found the simple wooden cross. Nothing adorned the grave not even a single withered flower. Weeds had begun to flourish in the upturned soil. The grave itself stood in the shade of a yew tree close to an ivy covered window Through the window Claire could see the nun's cemetery and the distant purple hue of the snow capped mountains. She wept uncontrollably as she read the simple hand painted inscription;

Pat Deegan
1955 -1963
R.I.P.

Brushing some nettles aside, she knelt down and prayed. Later she began to remove some weeds.

'What happened Pat?' she asked utterly distraught. A little robin with a puffed red chest, perched on the ivy wall nearby. Claire watched it flit from branch to branch as if observing her every move. 'Why Pat? Why did you break our 'pinkie promise?'

She gazed across the bog lands to the 'Nephin Beag Mountains' shrouded with dark cloud, as if they had donned a veil of mourning. Feeling chilled to the bone she rubbed her arms in search of warmth and comfort.

'Where were you running to? You had ten shillings you could have come to me.'
She lifted the collar of her coat and pulled it tightly around her neck.

'It's strange, I can feel you all around and I know you're up there, smiling down on me.'
She ran her hand along the grain of the simple timber cross.

'You've found a home at last,' she said standing up.
'Perhaps now, you can rest in your mother's arms.'
She pulled a handkerchief from her pocket and wiped away a tear.

'I'm sorry, I'll never get a chance to show you Dublin, or do all the nice things we had planned. But I will never forget that day in Clifden Bay. We had such fun. I can still see your smiling freckled face as you held the string tightly and watched the little red kite, bobbing and darting through the blue sky. Are there skies in Heaven? There must be, and oceans too.'
The robin, drawing ever closer, perched on top of the timber cross.

'I see you have found a little friend.'
Claire looked at the little bird, its feathers buffeted by the biting wind.

'Keep an eye on him for me,' she said softly.

The robin hopped down onto the arm of the cross then flew away.

'No more school for you. What will you do all day in Heaven? Perhaps you can learn to swim; you have nothing to fear any more. Why don't you build me a sandcastle, with turrets and towers, just like the one we made down here, that day?'

The harsh reality that she would never again lay eyes on Pat's freckled face was slowly sinking in and it frightened her. When Claire stood by her Fathers graveside two years previously and watched him being lowered into the earth she could not come to terms with the concept of eternity. The priest had prayed for the eternal life for her father but knowing her dad as well as she did, she doubted he would have wanted it and was sure he would tire of it after a few short years. Forever and ever was beyond Claire's comprehension.

Her father had a soft Wexford accent, yet in the two years since his death, she had never once heard a voice that sounded like his and knew she never would, nor would she hear Pat's voice again. She recalled his last words to her on the avenue.

'Goodbye Sister.'

Those words now carried so much pathos. Her father's death was part of the cycle of life and though it hurt her terribly, she accepted it. Pat's death was a tragedy, a tragedy in which she had played a part. It was something she would never come to terms with.

'I brought you something.'

She reached into her coat pocket, pulled out a brown paper bag and placed it underneath the wooden cross.

'I got them for you this morning, in Ballina. Licorice Allsorts, I thought you might like them.'

The robin returned.

'Perhaps your little friend might like one too.'

270

She spread her handkerchief on the grave, gathered a fistful of soil and placed it in the centre of the cloth, then with fingers, stiff from the cold, she pulled the four corners together and tied them into a knot. Carefully she placed the bundle in her coat pocket.

'I'll plant a flower in this, when I get home, so you'll always be in my heart.'

She stood up, backed slowly away from the grave and blessed herself before blowing a final kiss.

'Say a prayer for me every night before you go to bed,' she said, as she turned and walked slowly away.

CHAPTER FORTY- FOUR

Claire knocked on Sister Agnes's door.

'Come in.'

The room was dull and smokey. Sister Agnes, cigarette in her mouth, sat behind her desk filling out forms, she was visibly surprised to see Claire standing in front of her.

'How can I help?' she asked caustically.

'I need to ask you some questions.'

'What sort of questions?'

'I'd like to ask about Pat's death.'

Sister Agnes pulled on her cigarette.

'Well well, have you found a new vocation, inspector Claire? I hope it's a little more successful than your last one, not that you ever had one, in the first place.'

Claire ignored the jibes.

'I want to know how Pat died'.

Sister Agnes pointed to an empty chair. Claire ignored her offer..

'Did Reverend Mother, not tell you?'

'I want to hear it from you.'

'I'm afraid there is nothing I can tell you, that you don't already know.'

'Reverend Mother tells me, you found him?'

'That's true, I did.'

'What were you doing in the bathroom?'

Sister Agnes inhaled deeply before stubbing the remainder of her cigarette in the ashtray in front of her.

'I'm sorry, I wasn't aware the bathroom was off limits to me.'

'You know what I mean.'

'I was bringing him some dry clothes. I didn't want poor Sister Bernadette climbing those stairs again especially at her age.'

'So you say Pat was lying under the water when you got there?'

'Your thoroughness astounds me.'

'Please answer my question.'

'That's correct.'

Sister Agnes lowered her head and continued.

'Poor thing, he was so unstable of late. I rushed in and pulled him out of the water as quickly as I could. I lay him on his side and began pumping his chest. Water poured from his mouth and nose but he did not respond. I tried mouth-to-mouth but it was too late the poor little mite was gone.'

Claire began to weep softly, as she listened to her harrowing tale, not wanting to believe what she was hearing.

'He looked so peaceful, lying on the floor; as if he was sleeping.'

'What happened then?'

'Naturally I called Reverend Mother. She called Father Dunn. He administered the last rites and we all said some prayers. We told the children about the unfortunate accident and how Pat had fallen asleep.'

As Claire listened, each word added to her feelings of guilt.

'What happen to Noel? Why is he no longer in the gate lodge?'

Sister Agnes looked at Claire with her soul-less brown eyes.

'You ask a lot of questions for somebody who has absolutely nothing to do with this orphanage.'

'You got rid of him, didn't you?

'I haven't the faintest idea what you are talking about?'

'Don't lie to me.'

Sister Agnes gave her a spiteful look.

'Get a hold of yourself and stop acting like some demented moron.'

Claire bit her lip.

'And I know why.'

'Do you, now?'

Sister Agnes stood up and moved swiftly from behind her desk.

'And what might that be?'

Claire stood toe-to-toe with her.

'You got rid of him, because he helped Pat and I keep in touch.'

'Don't be ridiculous. I have absolutely no idea what you're talking about?'

'You got rid of him, to get back at me.'

'I 'm beginning to doubt your sanity.

'There's only one maniac in this room, and it's not me.'

'How dare you darken the doorway of this school.'

Claire wiped Sister Agnes'e spittle from her face.

'You despise me, don't you. Is it because I had the courage to say no?'

Sister Agnes turned away.

'Don't flatter yourself.'

'Did you have anything to do with Pat's death?'

'You had better watch what you are saying young woman, otherwise I'll have you sued for slander.'

Claire stood her ground.

'Someday I'll get to the bottom of this.'

Sister Agnes opened the door.

'Get out of my sight, you brazen hussy.

CHAPTER FOURTY- FIVE
(Enniskerry, 2005)

Claire finished relating her story. Bill sat in silence letting her words sink in.

'Good God. The poor child' he uttered involuntarily.

Once more he became aware of the chirping birds, the rippling water, and the beautiful surroundings The warm sun on his face was a stark contrast to the chill he felt inside. Claire stood up.

'I'm going to make some fresh coffee, would you care for some?'

'Yes please that would be great,' he said, relieved the moment was broken.

He was about to stand up but she stopped him.

'Stay here. I'll bring it out to you.'

Bill watched Claire as she walked beneath the rustic arch adorned with roses and back towards the house. He liked her. He liked her openness and her honesty, but he still was puzzled as to why Sister Agnes had taken her own life, especially after so many years. He realized now, the mixed emotions Claire must have felt when he first spoke to her at the door. Her antagonist was gone, but so many questions still remained unanswered. Claire returned with the silver tray in her hands. She poured some coffee. Bill thanked her and added milk and sugar. Carefully she rested the tray on the seat and sat down beside him.

'You never did find out what happened?'

Claire shook her head weakly.

'No.' Sister Agnes will take her secrets with her to the grave.'

She spotted a butterfly and watched as it dipped and rose through imperceptible air currents. Finally it landed on a pink rhododendron bush a short distance away.

'What beautiful little creatures they are,' she remarked.

'They are, aren't they?'

'It's nature's fairy-tale.'

'I'm sorry, I don't quite follow?'

She smiled.

'You know, Ugly Duckling becomes beautiful Swan, or 'Cinderella' becomes a Princess.

He chuckled.

'What a lovely concept, 'nature's fairy-tale'.

She offered him some chocolate cake. This time he took a slice.

'They say beauty is fleeting. Think about that butterfly's life-journey. First it's an egg, then a caterpillar, munching its way through several times its own body weight each day'.

Bill interrupted.

'I know a couple of guys back in the office who would make fantastic caterpillars.'

She smiled and sipped some coffee.

'It sheds its skin several times. Then the poor thing has to spin its own cocoon, go into hibernation shedding its skin yet again, and after all that, it's still just a pupa.'

Bill sensed the spirituality of the woman as she spoke.

'Finally after a winter in hibernation, the metamorphosis is complete and we have a butterfly. What we see before us, is the result of that fantastic life-journey.'

'We all need to adapt, to be able to re-invent ourselves.

'It's quite amazing really. I know now, what you mean, when you say 'nature's fairy-tale'.'

She picked a morsel of cake from her plate.

'Do you know how long a butterfly lives for,' she asked, before placing it in her mouth

'A summer I suppose?'

She sipped on her coffee and watched as the butterfly flew away.

'Less than two weeks,' she replied.

Bill was surprised, he hadn't known that.

'Two short weeks, that's it, snatched in its prime, taken before it really has a chance to live.'

Bill sensed that there were more questions than answers, in her words. He licked the chocolate from his fingers and drank from his coffee.cup

'If the caterpillar knew, beforehand do you think it would bother' she asked?

'Probably not, but do any of us really want to see our future, or know what lies ahead?'

'I suppose not,' she added quietly.

Bill observed her a moment before speaking.

'Sometimes, I wonder what it's all about.'

She turned to him.

'It is one of the great mysteries' she said, rubbing some crumbs from her fingers 'perhaps there's nothing more to it, than procreation and the survival of the species. A good friend of mine once said; 'We're born, we work our butts off, then we die, that's it.' That's life.'

She gave a wry smile and stared blankly out into the shrubbery.

'I'm afraid if that's what it's all about, then I have failed miserably.'

Bill sensed sadness and honesty in her words. She changed the subject.

'Do you believe in a God,' she asked?

277

Bill was a little surprised by the question.

'If you mean three divine persons and all that stuff, then no, I probably don't. I do feel there is something more powerful than us, but I don't know what it is?'

She admired his candor.

'I ask myself the same questions.'

He was surprised.

'But you joined a convent; you were going to takes vows.'

'Life is one big learning curve. What we chose to accept or reject, is subject to where we are on that curve. As a young woman, I didn't have enough experience to even ask the questions. Now as I grow older, the questions confronted me every day. They become bigger and bigger and impossible to ignore.'

She placed her cup on the tray. Her voice was lighter.

'If you think I am the first person to join a religious order and have misgivings, then I'm sorry to say, my misgivings include your intellect.'

'Lot of people doubt my intellect,' laughed Bill.

'Are you married' she asked?

He smiled.

'No not yet. I don't think I'm in any great rush to be honest. You know, statistically less than one in three marriages survive. The odds seem pretty poor and I'm not even a gambler.'

Claire poured more coffee, amused at his remark.

'Is there someone special?'

'No. Not at the moment.'

'Do you have family here in Dublin?'

'My mother and Father live in Sutton, on the north side of the city. I have a younger sister Niamh; she's studying architecture and still living at home. Myself, I rent a small flat near the Canal Basin'

'That sounds nice.'

'Nice price too. They charge an arm and a leg for it.'

'Property in Ireland is outrageously expensive' she agreed. 'I don't know how young people ever get the money to buy their own homes.'

'Half my mates still live with their parents.

'You should make it your business to visit your family as often as possible. Some day they won't be there. You know what they say, 'you never miss the water'

He interrupted her.

'I do, and yes, I pop home regularly.'

Bill's face broke into a mischievous smile.

'It's the only place where I get a decent meal.'

'Men, you're all the same' she said in mock disgust.

'Speaking of family, did Pat have any?'

Claire took a slow deep intake of breath.

'None, I could find. I searched for records of his admission, but like so many things in so many institutions, they seemed to have been misplaced', or burned in mysterious fires.'

'The tribunal must have been a nightmare for you?

Claire stroked her fingers through her grey hair.

'Yes it was, yet in another way it was a closure of sorts.'

'What do you mean?'

Claire looked him in the eyes. Bill could still see beauty in her tired face.

'Did you know that over two hundred and fifty children died whilst in the care in 'Dublin's Artane' orphanage alone?

Bill looked skeptically at her. Her voice grew passionate her eyes fixed.

'Can you imagine so many young children between the ages of three and sixteen dying while in the care of the church and state?

He shook his head.

'There are over a hundred and fifty cases nationwide, of children dying under suspicious circumstances.

Bill was shocked.

'Many of those deaths have never even been registered. Many of the graves remain unmarked.

She turned to him,

'I 'm sorry, I get so angry when I think about it.'

'I can understand why.'

Her tone softened.

'Did I tell you I went back to the orphanage to visit Pat's grave when I first returned to Ireland?'

'No you didn't.'

She continued her story.

CHAPTER FORTY- SIX
(West of Ireland 2001)

'It was several weeks before I felt strong enough to visit Pat's grave. I had just bought my car and was a little apprehensive about driving. I still wasn't used to the state of the Irish roads and the fact that you drove on the wrong side.'

Bill liked her sense of humour

'It took me a little while to get used to a stick shift, having spent so many years driving automatic cars in the States. This was to be my first adventure, my first journey through the heartland of Ireland since my return. The weather was crisp and sunny as I drove across to Galway,'

I spent the day there; I could not get over the atmosphere and vibrancy of the city'.

It's one of my favourite places in Ireland' interjected Bill.

'I was amazed; it was winter and Shop Street seemed to have as many pedestrians walking through it, as you would find on a pavement in Manhattan. I found Kenny's bookshop and spent ages browsing.'

'It's such a beautiful old shop, isn't it?'

'I sipped coffee and watched the world go . I could hear so many different languages; French, Spanish, Italian, German, Romanian, and God knows what? We Europeans share such a unique heritage. It's incredible that here on the edge of Europe, on the west coast of Ireland in the most westerly city in Europe, I could hear a greater variety of language, than I ever heard in the streets of New York.'

'It's crazy', agreed Bill.

'I spent that night in the wonderful surroundings of Ashford Castle.'

'Lucky you.'

'Though I was traveling alone, I simply loved the adventure. The next morning at breakfast I could look out on to the swans as they glided across the shimmering waters of ......'

'Lough Corrib' he informed her.

'That's it, Lough Corrib. I felt such inner peace, such tranquility, such …a sense of belonging.'

She looked at him.

'Do you know that in all those years in America, I had never had that feeling? Why had I waited so long to discover what I always knew? I was Irish, born and bred. I had grown up in a rural community. Rural life was in my blood. Though I had spent most of my life in New York, I had always felt like a fish out of water. Now I felt myself immersing slowly and blissfully back into my own genetic pool. After breakfast, I drove along the narrow roads skirting the lake. The beauty was inspiring. In a weird way everything seemed magnified, and strangely, everything seemed diminished. What I once considered a good road, I now considered a narrow boreen. What I once perceived as pretty, I now considered awe inspiring. Stop me if I'm rattling on too much' she said a little embarrassed.

'You're fine' he assured her.

Twenty-eight years in America can have that affect on you. I decided to drive through 'Mamm Cross'. The scenery was stunning. The 'Twelve Pins' looked awesome as I drove through the mountain passes. One minute the sky was dark and the heavens opened, the next minute I was driving in glorious sunshine along the sodden landscape glistening in the stark winter light.'

'That's Ireland for you. Four seasons in a single afternoon' he said with a shrug of his shoulders. 'When I eventually reached the top of the pass, I parked the car in a lay-by. There was a wonderful view of the Atlantic Ocean and the rugged coastline below. I couldn't imagine a starker contrast, than that of the bleakness before me and the bustling city of New York on the other side of the pond. Two centuries earlier crossing that ocean was like crossing from one life into the next. Now it is little more than a five hour inconvenience.'

Anyway as I was saying, I continued on and descended towards the ocean. After much searching, I came across a road sign for Clifden Bay.'

'That's where you went with the children wasn't it?

'You were listening' she said, with a grin.

'The old teahouse was in ruins. All that remained was a few weather beaten blocks and old rusting galvanized sheets strewn in a pile amongst the overgrown weeds. I stepped out of the car and wrapped myself in my warm coat. The wind was chill and whipped across the dunes.' She folded her arms as she spoke.

'I could hear the waves pounding on the shore as I headed towards the beach. I walked along the waters edge as I had done all those years before. The place looked different. Everything looked so stark. The sea was angry; the sky an ominous grey.

She sipped some coffee and tried to explain.

'It was like each step I took was a step backward, a step into my past. I could hear the shrill sound of the gulls overhead calling me back in time. I could hear the children's cries echoing on the wind. In my mind's eye I could see the little red kite twist and turn in a blue sky, and the children's happy faces gazing up as. I ran my ice-cold fingers through my hair and breathed deeply, my head filled with the memories. 'How time alters things, I thought to myself.'

She gave a melancholy smile.

'Nothing remains the same. Time sees to that, this very moment, is already history. The words I speak right now are already placed in the confines of the past. The whole universe is in flux even as we speak, trees are growing, walls are crumbling, children are being born, while stars are dying.'

He could sense the pathos in her voice. She questioned him.

'Why are we are so reluctant to admit this?

He paused before he spoke.

'Perhaps we don't want to confront change We want the comfort of familiarity.'

She continued.

'If someone had told me all those years ago that, I would live in New York and work as a lawyer', I would have laughed. If someone had said, I would not remain a nun, I would have cried. If someone had said, 'I would fall in love and be engaged to an American man, yet would never marry I would have doubted his or her sanity. If somebody had told me, Pat would be dead in five short months, I would have been outraged..'

She exhaled deeply.

'Life is like a series of roads', said Bill 'we never know what's lurking around the next corner, that's what makes it so fascinating.'

She shivered as she continued. '

I must have walked for the best part of an hour along that beach lost in memories. I spotted a white

284

shell, bent down, picked it from the sand and washed it clean before putting it in my pocket and heading back to my car. The gates to St. Joseph's were open as I approached. Thorn bushes had intertwined themselves through the rusty iron gates, and the pillars were overgrown with ivy. The gate lodge was in ruins. Four crumbling walls were all that remained. It was a gloomy sight. Slowly I drove beneath the leafless trees and along the grass-covered avenue. I was shocked by the state of the grounds. Tall weeds replaced what were once manicured lawns. The garden seats were rotten and falling apart. The school itself looked bleak and forgotten. The downstairs windows were shuttered and daubed in graffiti. Some of the upstairs windows were smashed. I was horrified at what I saw. A single car was parked outside. I got out and knocked on the front door.

A man in a peaked cap answered. He was in his seventies and unshaven, his face long and gaunt.

'Hello,' he said in a rich Mayo accent.

'Good day,' I said in a friendly voice.

'I was wondering if any of the nuns might still be here?'

The man smiled, exposing the gap in his discoloured front teeth.

'Jaysus you a bit late,' he said scratching the back of his head. The orphanage is closed this long time. The last few nuns left about eight years ago. The place belongs to the Mayo Co. Council now.'

'What's going to happen to it,' I asked him curiously?

'Jaysus', your guess is as good as mine, I'm only the caretaker here, I haven't a clue what they've got planned for the place.'

'I used to teach here many years ago,' I told him. 'I was wondering if you would mind me taking a look around.'

He opened the door wider.

'Of course, by all means, come in.'

'Would you like a cup of tea?' he enquired.

I looked at the state of the poor man and thought it safer to abstain.

'No. Thank you very much for the kind offer.' 'Well if you need me, I'll be in the kitchen. You know where that is, I take it?' 'Yes. I think I still remember.' 'Take your time, just be careful on the stairs, some of the steps are a bit rotten.

I walked down the dust-covered hall. It was dark and spooky. The place smelled of decay. Eventually I made my way down the corridor and stopped outside Reverend Mother's door. It was not locked and I entered.

'The shutters were drawn and the room was in darkness. I searched for the switch and to my surprise the light came on. The room was strewn with dust covered files and papers. Dusty old chairs littered the corners. I felt uneasy, as if I had entered a vault and disturbed the dead. I quickly left flicking the switch and closing the door behind me. Then I carefully climbed the stairs avoiding the broken and rotten boards. As I neared the landing, a pigeon, lofting beneath the roof, flew noisily through one of the many holes in the stained glass window scaring me half to death. The headless statue of the Blessed Virgin, where Pat had spent the night still stood on its plinth. I noticed the cobwebs on her redundant outstretched arms. The smell of polish had long gone, replaced by mould and damp. I ventured towards the dormitory. It was empty and scarcely recognizable. The vast room was littered with the remnants of the broken beds. I felt as if I was in some strange time warp, looking back on a 'Dickensian' scene. It was like being part of a dream, a distant dream and I had to question whether I had ever actually lived here. I made my way to the back stairs and to the nun's quarters. It was dark and desolate. Slowly I walked towards the bathroom. The door was shut. I turned the handle and pushed it open. Cobwebs broke away as I did so. My heart pounded when I saw the bath. I walked towards it with apprehension. It was littered with bits of plaster that had fallen from the ceiling. I ran my hand along the cold metal rim. It chilled me to the bone. The window was broken and the wind whistled through the room with an eerie crying sound. Through the window I could just about make out the old walls of the grave yard. I blessed myself and hurried out the door. I thanked the caretaker for his kindness and went outside to investigate further, relieved to be back in the cold fresh air, free from the confines of decay'. She turned to Bill. 'Do you know I was surprised by the lack of emotion I felt when I returned to the convent after all that time?' 'Perhaps 'time' was playing one of its many tricks. 'I fought my way through the tall grass towards the nun's graveyard. It too was overgrown and neglected. I noticed there were some additional headstones so I went inside. I found the graves of Sister Carmel and Sister Bernadette side by side. As they had been in life, so were they in death. Both had died within a month of each other in November 1964. I blessed myself and said a little prayer'.

'In another corner I found the grave of Reverend Mother. She had died less than eight months after Pat. I searched, but could find no gravestone for Sister Agnes's. At that time I didn't know whether she was dead or alive and wondered what had become of her. Eventually I left the little graveyard and went to find

Pat's grave. I walked through the tall grass along the outer wall of the graveyard trampling the nettles under my feet as best I could. I came upon the yew tree. It was dead; its branches brittle and choked in ivy. It was the only tree on this side of the wall. I knew it had to be in the right spot, but I couldn't see the window or the grave. I eventually discovered the window completely concealed beneath the ivy and began searching for the grave. I stooped down and began combing my hands through the high grass. All I found was a rotten piece of timber. I picked it up and examined it. That was all that marked his grave. I began to cry.'

She turned her anguished face towards Bill.

'Can you believe that, they didn't even have the decency to give him a headstone, or properly mark his grave? As far as the rest of the world was concerned, Pat never existed. Nobody knew who he was, where he came from, where he was buried, or how he died, what was worse, nobody seemed to care.'

Her voice trembled as she spoke.

'I promised myself a long time ago, I would find out the truth, but I never did.'

'You tried your best' Bill assured her.'

'I reached into my pocket and placed the shell I had picked that morning beside the wall.

'It's from Clifden Bay, I told him. Now we both have one'.

Later having composed myself, I returned to the caretaker.

'I have a request' I said.

'What's that,' he enquired.

'I told him I had seen the garden seat. It was broken, and the timbers were rotten. I asked him if he would mind me taking the cast iron frames'.

288

He was happy to oblige and cut away the remaining timbers with a small saw and helped me place the cast iron frames into the trunk of the car. Then I asked him if he had a hammer and nail. He said he had a toolbox in the kitchen.'

'When he returned, I asked him if he could make a simple cross for me. He made one with the best bits of timber he could find. Together we went and placed it above Pat's grave. When I bought this house, I had the seat restored and that's what where're sitting on right now'.

Bill rubbed his hand along the white ornate cast iron frame.

'It's a beautiful seat it really suits your garden. 'Thank you. I'm very pleased with the way it turned out.'

'How did you actually become involved with the victim support groups' asked Bill

'I decided to attend one of the meetings in Dublin, for Victims of Child Abuse. Most of the 'abused' were in the forty to seventy age bracket. I sat watching and listening, as people told their stories. I listened with revulsion to accounts of rape and buggery. I watched people break down, and turn to shivering wrecks as they tried to relate their previously unspoken horrors. I listened to mentally scarred women, who had committed the unthinkable; becoming unmarried mothers in their teens. They told of how they were shamed and hidden from society in the 'institutions' ending up as 'laundry girls' incarcerated like common criminals, to be used as slave-labour, sometimes for the rest of their lives. I listened to countless stories of how 'the religious' who were responsible for these crimes were protected. The poor unfortunates, were now fighting the Church and the State in the courts, seeking compensation, but above all seeking justice and transparency. I vowed to do all in my power to help them'.

'For the last few years I've worked tirelessly for the Victims of Child Abuse. Despite the introduction by the Government, of the 'Freedom of Information act' records are still ridiculously hard to come by. School after school claims their files are missing or have been destroyed in mysterious fires. One day quite by accident, I came across some files on St. Joseph's. I carefully sifted through the papers. To my surprise and dismay, I discovered Pat's death was never registered. Through further research, I discovered that after the tragedy no doctor had been sent for. There was no post mortem, no cause of death, and no death certificate ever issued.'

Bill looked at her. He was in shock

'Jesus Christ, that's unbelievable.'

'As you know the Government set up 'The Lafoy Commission' to investigate the allegations, and a redress board was formed to deal with the specifics of each case in relation to abuse and monetary compensation. 'Religious' were called upon to counter claims made against them.

Though some were guilty of horrendous offences, under the agreement made between the church and state, no individuals could be imprisoned, or punished for his or her crimes. I became one of the most outspoken campaigners. Everywhere I went I tried to bring the plight of the victims to the fore, often to the annoyance of 'Catholics' of an older generation. I discovered that Sister Agnes was still alive and living in a retirement home in Co. Cork. She too was summoned before the tribunal as one of the accused. I was apprehensive about seeing her. Yesterday I saw her again for the first time in nearly forty years'. Bill observed her as she spoke. 'When I did see her I was shocked. I instantly recognized the souless brown eyes, but was shocked to see how frail she had become.

She was not wearing a habit. She did not appear to recognize me. Her grey hair was styled with a permanent wave flicked back off her gaunt face. She wore a grey suit. On her arm she held a light grey overcoat'.

'That's exactly what she was wearing at the roundabout,' exclaimed Bill.

She continued.

'Once, she actually looked in my direction. I wasn't sure if I could ascertain a smile of recognition or not. I watched her gingerly take her place on the podium. I found it hard to believe, forty years previously; this feeble woman had terrorized and abused so many children. I watched as she answered the questions thrown at her by the legal teams. Though she was frail, her mind seemed as sharp as ever. Whenever she was asked something that might be in any way incriminating, she, like all the other defendants, used to great effect and frustration, the term; 'I forget. Shortly before lunch Sister Agnes's testimony was complete. As she stepped down she smiled across at me and left the room.' 'It had been another frustrating day for me. Everybody was strongly denying any part in the wrong doing. The victims were left feeling they were on trial. I started becoming despondent and began to feel it was a waste of time, and that justice would never be done. Some victims were so worn out by the trauma of their ordeal, they were past caring. 'To me the whole tribunal seemed nothing more than a charade, orchestrated by Church and State to pacify the electorate. Then yesterday afternoon we heard the

291

good news, the Government had agreed to compensation.'

CHAPTER FORTY- SEVEN
(Dublin 2005)

Little was Claire to know that shortly after Sister Agnes left the tribunal she returned alone to her hotel, 'The Berkley Court' where she sat down in the resident's lounge and ordered a coffee. Using the hotel stationary, she began to write a letter. Having placed the letter in an envelope, she sealed it and searched through her pockets. She pulled out a piece of paper on which she had written an address. Carefully she transcribed the address on to the envelope before discarding the paper. Later, she handed the letter to the concierge to post, and asked him to order her a taxi. Shortly afterwards a taxi arrived at the front door and she climbed in.

'Where to luv', asked the taxi driver in a thick Dublin accent?

'The airport please,' replied Sister Agnes.

'You off on a holiday then,' asked the balding, red faced driver?

Sister Agnes did not reply.

He raised his voice, and lowered the radio.

'Are you off on a holiday,' he repeated, looking in the rear view mirror.

'Yes,' was her curt reply.

'Anywhere nice?'

'I hope so!

'Will it be your first time?'

'Yes,' she answered grudgingly.

'As long as it's nice and warm you're laughing.'

She ignored him and wound down the window letting the cool air blow across her face.

'This city is the pits, half the bleeding country is dug up. No wonder there's so much chaos on the roads. If you ask me, the government should be taken out and shot.'

She wasn't listening.. The driver, glancing in his rearview mirror, realized he was not going to get any more conversation from the woman and raised the volume on his radio. The taxi by now had reached the outskirts of the city and was now nearing the airport. Sister Agnes looked around her.

'Pull in, just up there near the roundabout.'

The taxi driver laughed, and lowered the volume on the radio once more.

'Ah Jaysus luv we're still a good bit from the terminal.'

'This will do me just fine,' she said, in her more usual gruff manner.

He glanced back at her in disbelief.

'I'm not supposed to stop on the motorway. Are you feeling sick?'

Sister Agnes nodded her head.

'Please, just do as I say and stop the car.'

The taxi pulled into the hard shoulder, with its warning lights flashing.

'Thank you. Now how much do I owe.'

The taxi driver turned to Sister Agnes who was opening the door of the car.

'Ah now, hang on, you can't get out here.'

'Don't worry. This is perfect, now how much?'

'I could loose me license for this,' he said, in a disgruntled tone.

Sister Agnes opened her purse and pulled out a fifty euro note. The driver looked at the fifty, then at Sister Agnes.

'I shouldn't really.'

'Keep the change, I don't need it' she said, and stepped out on to the grass verge.

The cabby capitulated, took the money and stuffed it into his shirt pocket. He lowered the electric window on the passenger's side and leaned across the front seat.

'Are you sure your okay? Do you want me to call a doctor or friend?'

Sister Agnes folded her grey coat.

'No thank you. I'll be absolutely fine.'

The taxi driver sat uneasily for a moment watching as Sister Agnes walked along the grass margin, worried about her mental state. Even if he called her back now, he couldn't force her into his cab. A call came through on his radio. In a crackling voice a female gave him the address of his next pick-up. He indicated and pulled out into the heavy stream traffic bemused by the whole affair.

CHAPTER FORTY- EIGHT
(Enniskerry 2005)

Claire and Bill sat on the garden seat, still engaged in conversation. The sound of a motor could be heard in the distance. It came to a halt outside the gates of Claire's cottage. The gate squeaked as it opened. A postman walked towards the house.

'I'm over here Sean,' waved Claire.

Sean smiled and walked towards them.

'I saw you on the telly last night. You were great.'

'Thank you Sean,' she said humbly.

'This is Bill O'Malley, he works for R.T.E.'

Bill offered him his hand.

'Don't tell me they're going to film your life story already?'

'It's nothing like that I'm afraid,' laughed Claire.

Sean handed some letters to Claire.

'What a beautiful day,' he said energetically.

Claire sifted through the letters.

'It's the ideal weather for a sail or a game of golf,' she said absentmindedly.

Sean's face broke into a wide grin.

'Now you're talking my language. When I finish this round, I'm off to Powerscourt for another.'

'Pardon,' said Bill not understanding.

'Golf. A round of golf,' he explained.

'Powerscourt can be expensive.'

'Not half as expensive as sailing.'

'Point taken,' said Bill.

'A good walk ruined,' interjected Claire.

Sean laughed.

'You should try it. I guarantee you, you'd love it. Well I'll be off. I don't want to miss my tee off time.'

As he turned, Claire mischievously shouted after him.

'Good luck Sean, enjoy your interrupted walk'

Sean cast her cynicism aside with a wave of his hand.

Claire sat down. The sound of Sean's van could be heard vanishing in the distance

'Seem like a nice guy,' said Bill.

Claire was distracted. Her attention was drawn to one of the letters in her hand. Slowly she opened the envelope and began to read the letter.

'Oh my God,' she said, lifting her hand to her mouth. It's from her!'

'Sorry,' said Bill completely lost.

'It's from Sister Agnes.'

She began to read the letter aloud.

Dear Sister Claire,

When you read this letter I will not be around anymore. You have fought a brave fight, and I congratulate you on your courage. These past few years have been Hell for me. I have been forced to do a lot of soul searching, and I am ashamed at what I have found out. I am ashamed at the way I have been protected by the might of the State and the Church. I wanted to pay for my sins. I wanted to wipe the slate clean but I was not allowed to do so. If I had tried, they would have certified me insane. So nothing has changed really. We still have the cover-up. Every time a victim spoke at the tribunal today I felt they were talking about me personally, even though I had never seen most of them before in my life.

Each word was like a knife piercing my soul, exposing the badness within. Sadly, it is a black soul, and we all know where black souls go. I know I forced you to leave the convent. Had I not, perhaps the victims would have lost a formidable ally, so maybe some good did come of my actions. I am sorry from the bottom of my heart for what happened to Pat. I tried to keep him from you. I wanted to punish you but I ended up punishing him. He missed you. I hated that. He loved you. I hated that too. I saw him in the bath and sensed his fear when I entered, His back was black and blue from the beating I had given him, I wanted to rub some ointment on the wounds but he would not let me near him. I got angry. We struggled, and God forgive me I held him under the water till he stopped moving, When I realized what I had done I panicked. I lifted him from the bath and tried to revive him. I told Reverend Mother and Father Dunn, when I entered the bathroom Pat was lying beneath the water, and that knowing the tormented child he was, he had probably taken his own life. Father Dunn spoke to the local police and nothing more was said about it. I lied my way out of it. I have lived that lie ever since. It hangs like a millstone around my neck. I can carry it no longer. Please show this letter to the authorities, and have Pat's death properly documented. He deserves at the very least a burial on consecrated ground. I am sorry, truly sorry. I cannot face it any more,

Each day seems to exacerbate the pain I feel inside. I don't want to be part of another great lie. God forgive me. If you find it in your heart, say a prayer for me.

Sister Agnes.

Tears fell upon the open page. For years Claire carried the burden of guilt, feeling she was in some way responsible for Pat's death, despite their 'pinkie promise'. She had always harboured a suspicion it was not suicide, at last, she knew for certain. The weight of forty-years had lifted like a cloud from her shoulders,

298

she had been vindicated. The letter she held in her hand was the confession she had always wanted. Pat's memory was no longer tarnished and at last he could be given a dignified burial in Rathmore cemetery. At least he would be able to take his place amongst the common people, even if it was only, in death. Strangely she felt no euphoria, nor sense of closure. The fact was, she felt nothing, nothing at all, nothing but a dull aching emptiness in the pit of her stomach.

CHAPTER FORTY- NINE
(Sheepshead Peninsula, Ireland 2006)

It was warm and humid. The little country graveyard of St, Fiachna's in the parish of Gurteen stood high on a remote hillside overlooking Bantry Bay. Though the graveyard was in County Cork, Claire gazed across the glistening water to the Kerry coast, to Bere Island and the fishing port of Castletownbere, basking in the glorious mid-day sun. Claire stood by a graveside dressed in a simple black suit. There was a poor turn-out, for the funeral just a few unfamiliar faces gathered in a circle, possibly ten or twelve people in all. Claire looked to the headstone standing above the open grave. It bore the inscription Joseph O Neill 'Gurteen' 1903-1958 and Mary (nee Burke) 1911 – 1960. She noticed that the adjacent gravestone also bore the inscription 'O'Neill' and presumed they were in some way related. Strangely, this headstone bore only one name, that of William O' Neill 1909 - 1944.

The priest sprinkled holy water over the casket that held the remains of Sister Agnes.

'Ashes to ashes and dust to dust' he said, as he blessed the coffin.

Sister Agnes's brother, a man in his mid-sixties seemed to be the only surviving relative present. Despite his ashen color, he had a warm face and a head of thick white hair. Claire watched him wipe a tear as the coffin, its crucifix glinting in the bright sunlight, was lowered into the ground. She felt a lump in her throat, and was forced to avert her gaze out to sea. There was an eerie stillness in the air, broken only by the distant cry of gulls above the craggy rocks on the headland. She listened to the strange dull thump of fresh clay fall upon the coffin lid, covering it in a soft moist shroud of finality. The priest concluded the last few prayers and closed his missal.

'In the name of the Father, Son, and Holy Ghost, Amen'.

The mourners began dispersing slowly. Claire went to Sister Agnes's brother to offer her condolences.

'I'm so sorry for you troubles,' she said.

The poor man was lost in grief. She held out her hand. He shook it and as he did so she could feel how badly disfigured his fingers were.

'Thank you' he said in a gentle voice, 'and you are?'

'Claire. Your sister knew me as Sister Claire.'

As he looked her in the eyes, she could see his suffering.

'Thank you Claire. I'm Sean, Kitty's younger brother.'

He turned away and began to hobble back towards the mourner's car,

'May I accompany you,' she asked politely.

The old man nodded and waited for her. Claire gently held his arm.

'Sometimes', he said, 'the auld arthritis play's hell with me'.

She helped him along the uneven pathway. 'Rheumatoid' he said smiling bravely; 'it destroys the joints you know.'

'God love you, the pain must be excruciating?'

'Some days are better than others.'

She was moved by his acceptance of his lot.

'How did you know my sister?'

'I spent some time, in St Josephs'.

He stopped and turned to face her.

'You knew Kitty at the orphanage?'

301

'Yes.'

'Did she ever tell you how she got there?'

'No, she never spoke of it to me.'

'So she said nothing at all to you?'

'No' replied Claire, 'nothing.'

'Did you know my father sent her there when she was only a child of fourteen?'

Clare looked into his warm face. She did not understand.

'Sent her there? What do you mean?'

He took a shallow breath.

'I was only an infant at the time.'

'But she had a family' said Claire?

'Yes' he said remorsefully, 'she was sent there as a kitchen help'

'But why would your father do that' asked Claire, more confused by the second.

They had now reached the mourners car. The driver sat waiting in his black uniform and cap. Some mourners came to offer their condolences and Claire stepped aside.

He spoke briefly with them, thanked them, and they left. Claire went to Sean once more.

'I'm sorry; I hope you don't mind me bothering you again.'

'You're fine,' he said quietly.

He leant back against the black car.

'Where was I' he asked, trying to recollect where they had left off?

'I was asking you why Kitty was sent to 'St. Joseph's.'

'Ah yes.'

Sean heaved a long agonizing sigh.

'She was pregnant.'

Claire's face dropped.

'At fourteen years of age?'

302

'Yes and her infant was born in St. Joseph's'.

Claire could not believe her ears.

'She pleaded with the nuns for permission to keep her baby but it was impossible. She wrote to my mother begging to be allowed home with her newborn infant. It broke my poor mother's heart that she had no option but to refuse. So Kitty was a mother at fifteen years-of-age, abandoned and homeless.'

'But why did your parents not help her' asked Claire.

'You forget, we are talking about rural Ireland of the forties. Unmarried girls, simply did not have babies. In a small community, such a scandal brought shame on an entire family, doubly so, if the baby was fathered through incest.'

Claire could see the pain etched across Sean's face.

'I'm sorry, I don't understand?'

'My uncle attacked her, even broke her nose and forced himself upon her. He was supposed to be looking after her.'

He fought back tears as he spoke.

'My father had gone with my mother to a nursing home in Cork, where I was born.'

Claire raised her hands to her mouth in disbelief.

'Oh my God, her uncle?'

He glanced back down towards the graves. 'My father was a proud and simple man. He reacted in the only way he knew how and for the first seven years of my life I didn't see him. He was incarcerated in Mountjoy prison, for his actions. After his release he returned home a broken man. I remember him walking through the gate and not knowing who he was. Can you believe that, I had to be introduced to my own father?'

'You mean'…. she could not finish what she was about to ask?

The old man nodded.

'Yes. That's his grave next to my father's.

Claire listened in disbelief.

'My father shot his only brother.'

'William O'Neill, was uncle Bill? Was he the one who saved Kitty from drowning as a child?'

His face registered surprise.

'Yes I believe so, it was before my time. My mother mentioned the irony of it to me some years later. Did Kitty tell you that story?'

'Only that he had saved her from drowning and that she wished he hadn't. At the time it didn't make any sense me.'

He looked out towards the bay.

'With my father in prison and uncle Bill dead, there was nobody to help around the farm. The locals ostracized our family. My poor mother worked her fingers to the bone to try and make ends meet, God love her. It sent her to an early grave. Nobody wanted to help us. Times were hard. We barely survived. To make matters worse we had to sell land to the same farmers who ostracized us. When my father returned he couldn't cope and soon took to the poitin. Things went from bad to worse.'

Claire swallowed hard.

'Kitty' as we called her, eventually joined the convent. She never wrote to my parents. Several times my father tried to rekindle their relationship, but it was no use. She never forgave him for sending her away, or my mother for forcing her to have her baby adopted. I wrote to her when my father was on his deathbed asking her to come and see him before he died. She didn't even bother replying. The poor man died with her name on his lips, having spent seven years of his

304

life behind bars, because of his love for her. Today I buried a sister I scarcely knew.'

'Oh my God, I am so sorry' said Claire, holding back her tears.

Sean tried to open the car door. Claire helped him.

'At least I know she'll be lying in my mother and fathers arms tonight. For the first time in nearly seventy years they are all together again. Soon I'll be joining them and we'll be a normal family for the very first time.'

The old man sat into the car. Claire was numbed by what she had just heard. She was about to close the door but hesitated.

'May I ask, did Kitty have a baby a boy or girl?'

'It was a little baby girl' he said in a crushed voice.

Claire eyes welled.

'You're not alone Sean. You can still find your family; perhaps I can help? You have a niece, possibly a grand niece and nephew out there somewhere waiting to meet you. Perhaps one day they'll knock on your door and lighten your life.'

He smiled forlornly.

'God bless you Sean, I'm so glad to have met you.' She closed the door and the car pulled off. Claire stood watching as the empty hearse, followed by the mourners car, drove slowly through the maze of leaning headstones and out through the rusty iron gates. She watched the black cars, glinting in the sunlight drive into the distance, dipping from view as they glided behind the dry stone walls skirting the undulating road along the shore line of the bay.

She looked back towards the graveyard and its magnificent backdrop. The grave diggers with their weather-beaten faces rolled their shirt sleeves, spat on

305

their hands and began to fill the open grave. Claire blessed herself.

'May God have mercy on your soul Kitty, may you rest in peace. I forgive you.'

She turned and walked away, her emotions as jagged as the rocks on the cliff face far below.

CHAPTER FIFTY
(DUBLIN 2007)

It was a rare sweltering day in June and a sweet bouquet of jasmine drifted on the warm airs of the Phoenix Park as it lay resplendent in a mantle of blossoming shrubs and blooming flowers, confirmation that at last summer had finally arrived. Parents tried in vain to control their excited children as they headed for the Zoological Gardens. Families sat on rugs, picnicking on the lush green grass. Mothers fought a losing battle with sticky hands and faces as ice cream seemed the order of the day. Young lovers sat on benches beneath the shade of beech trees kissing and cuddling lost in their own fairytale.

Away from the main avenue, beneath the Papal Cross, in a quieter corner of the park several hundred people had gathered in front of a small podium erected in the middle of a newly built Memorial Garden. Today was to be the official opening. Behind the podium two large red curtains shielded the veiled sculpture erected and dedicated to the memory of all the children who had died whilst in the care of the state and the institutions. Radio and television were in attendance as were political figures, and members of the church. A large screen had been erected to the left of the podium, on it the Army Band were performing a medley of slow Irish airs. Claire sat next to Mike and Gina Borinsky. They had just arrived the day before from New York. It was a wonderful surprise for Claire who was delighted to see her old friends and as usual had insisted they stay with her in Enniskerry. The garden was laid out in rows of

307

seating. Claire and her friends sat several rows back. It was not yet three o' clock and the seats around them were beginning to fill as more and more people arrived for the official opening.

'Gees, this place makes Central Park look like a garden' said Gina.

Claire smiled. She loved Gina's zany Italian ways. She was now in her sixtieth year but looked better than half of the women twenty years her junior. For the last five years she had been successfully running her own boutique in 'Queen's' so needless to say every stitch she wore was the creation of some well known designer.

'If it wasn't for her boutique, the clothes on her back would have bankrupted me years ago,' Mike moaned.

It was probably true. In lots of ways she and Claire were chalk and cheese Gina loved the glitz and the glamour. Clare liked the simpler things in life. Perhaps that's why they got on so well. They saw things from very different perspectives and their discussions were always, to say the least, interesting. Mike sat reading a sailing magazine, happy to get some respite from Gina's constant waffle.

'So, tell me about my god-daughter?

Gina fanned her face with her bejeweled hand.

'Can you believe it, Sophia is in her final year in Berkley. Last Easter she brought this lovely guy home with her. His name is Ezra and he's studying macrobiotics.'

Claire listened as Gina gesticulated wildly with her hands. She loved her Latin flair.

'I think there might be some real chemistry going on there' she said with a saucy grin.

'That's terrific' said Claire.

'The guy is a waster if you ask me' interrupted Mike, not bothering to lift his head from his magazine.

Gina sought Claire's support.

'That's just typical, always the cynic.'

'It's part of my charm dear.'

'And what's wrong with Ezra' asked Gina?

'Nothing, apart from the fact he's a bum.'

Gina looked at him in disgust.

'He's a lovely young man.'

Mike closed the magazine. Now it was he who looked to Claire for support, but Claire was wise enough never to taking sides.

'What do you think of a young man who lets his girlfriend borrow five thousand dollars from her mother to finance their trip to Europe?'

Claire gave Gina a surprised look.

'What. You lent him five thousand dollars and you hardly know the guy?'

Gina sat back in her chair, an indignant look on her face. She gave Mike a cutting look.

'Anyway I didn't lend it to him, I lent it to Sophia.'

Mike gesticulated.

'Yeah, so now it's Sophia who has to pay the five thousand dollars for the bum's trip around Europe.'

'Hold on a minute' said Claire, 'surely they're going together?'

'Yeah' said Mike, 'but it was his idea. He said he would take her.'

'He's a student for God's sake' said Gina; 'he'll pay her back when he graduates.'

'By that time,' said Mike, 'she'll have got sense and booted him out of her life.'

Several people entered the row and their little confrontation abruptly ceased. Claire was thankful. She stood up to let them pass.

'Sister Claire, it is you, isn't it?'

Claire looked at the tall well-dressed black man who had called her name.

'Yes.'

She corrected herself.

'I mean I was Sister Claire, for a short time.

'I know! St. Joseph's Orphanage, I was there.'

Claire's eyes opened wide,

'Stephen?'

'Yes Sister.'

He smiled broadly, delighted she had remembered his name.

'Please sit down and join us.'

Stephen sat down.

'I can only stay a moment, I'm with my wife and child. I thought I recognized you, so I decided to pop over and congratulate you on this wonderful memorial.'

Claire introduced him to Mike and Gina who were once more on their best behaviour. Claire looked him up and down.

'It's so great to see you Stephen. My, what a handsome young man you turned out to be?'

'Thank you, Sister.'

'You must point your family out to me,' she said excitedly.

Stephen pointed to an attractive blonde girl sitting a few rows back with a beautiful young half-caste boy of about two sitting on her lap. Claire waved. The little boy shyly waved back.

'What a beautiful boy, what a beautiful family, you must be proud.

Stephen nodded,

'I am.'

'Are any of the others here?'

'From St. Joseph's, you mean?'

310

'Yes,' said Claire hopefully.

'I see Thomas regularly. We were talking only last week. Apart from him I haven't laid eyes on the rest of them for years. He said he would do his best to get here.'

Claire was eager for news.

'How is he?

'He's in great form. He joined the police when he finished with the institutions. He's a detective now, stationed in the Bridewell.

'What about Joseph have you seen him?'

Stephen's smile faded.

'I saw Joseph about eight years ago. He was in a bad state and could hardly speak. He was begging on the pavement outside Heuston Station wrapped up in a dirty overcoat with a piece of cardboard beneath him to keep out the cold. I went over to him but I could tell he didn't recognize me. He looked terrible, filthy and unshaven. He had a little shoe at his feet with a few coins in it. I noticed the sole was hanging from one of his boots and his toes were showing. I felt sorry for him and placed a twenty-pound note in his hand. He looked at it for a moment before lifting his head and smiling. God love him, his eyes were sunken in his head, his front teeth were missing and his forehead was badly cut.

He just gave me a glazed stare.

'God bless you sir' he said in a broken voice.

'I wanted to make conversation, but I knew he was incapable. I was upset and walked away, saddened by his plight. That was the last time I saw him. I passed that way a week later with a bag of clothes I wanted to give him, but he wasn't there. I enquired at the ticket office about him. They told me he was found dead on the pavement, two nights earlier.'

Claire shook her head.

'A heroin overdose, they say he was dead on admission to hospital.'

Claire sighed deeply.

'His body was cremated and his ashes scattered in the Liffey.'

Stephen held her hand gently.

'I better get back to the family. It was lovely to meet you again Sister. Thanks for all the victim support and congratulations again on this wonderful day. Pat would be proud of you.'

Claire smiled.

'Thank you Stephen, you don't know how much that means to me. If you see Tommy, tell him I said hello.'

Stephen kissed Claire on the cheek and handed her his business card.

'Call in any time, bring Mike and Gina. The treat is on me.'

Claire thanked him

'It was lovely to meet you again after all these years, Sister'.

'The pleasure was mine' she said warmly.

'Perhaps you could give me a call?'

'I'd love to.'

He bade them goodbye and left. Claire looked at the business card in her hand.'

'Le Petite Marseilles'
Restaurant (French Cuisine)
Georges Street. Dublin
Proprietor. Stephen Ward.

She smiled.

'He seems such a lovely young man' said Gina. Mike interrupted.

'From somebody else, those words might be a compliment, but having just witnessed you giving the same accolade to a bum, I'm not quite sure?'
Gina looked up to the Heavens,
'Gees, Claire, he gets crankier by the day.'
Mike smiled like a naughty schoolboy.
'She's probably right' he conceded.
'Work ain't no fun anymore. I'm thinking of calling it a day, packing the whole thing in.'
Claire was shocked.
'Is it true' she asked Gina
'We've been talking about it for a while now' she admitted. '
I ain't getting any younger, Claire.' '
But what are you going to do Mike You're not the sort of guy who can sit around the house all day.'
'Gees I'm not an invalid. I can still play a round of golf.
He lifted the sailing magazine on his lap.
'This is my latest passion.'
Gina rolled her eyes
'Boats' said Claire?,
'Not boats Claire, yachts. I just bought myself a sloop.'
'Forgive my ignorance, what's a sloop?'
'Women' he muttered.
'Sometimes he's worse than a child.'
'All men are boys at heart' laughed Claire.
Gina shrugged her shoulders. She clasped Claire's hand in hers.
'Mike and I have a business proposition for you. We think you might like it.'
'Oh yeah'.
'Its part of the reason we're here', said Mike.
The crackle of the microphone distracted them from their conversation.

313

'We can discuss it later' said Gina.

Claire smiled, she hadn't a clue what they were talking about, but she knew she soon would. On the screen the Presidential car was arriving, having made its short journey from Aras an Uachtarain A voice came over the public address.

'Ladies and Gentlemen, please welcome the President', Mary Mc Aleese'.

The crowd clapped politely as she took the stand. The floor manager gave a cue and cameras moved into position. The band began to play the national anthem and the crowd stood to attention. When it was over they applauded, cameras flashed as she began her speech. Claire listened to her words. She pondered on her last few years in Ireland. It had been a struggle, much harder than she had ever anticipated. Everywhere she turned she had met a wall of silence. It transpired 'Freedom of Information' did not mean what she had hoped it would. She now knew that it meant no more than, the freedom to seek information. What good were such freedoms if the 'information' was no longer available, or had been hidden or worse still, destroyed? She had spoken with numerous survivors who had been witness to horrific beatings. The victims of such atrocities were often never seen again, nor were their names ever mentioned, they had disappeared, without trace. She knew she had only managed to scratch the surface of a festering wound in Irish society. The Church and State contended those innocent children who had died under suspicious circumstances, were unfortunate casualties, victims of ill health and disease and nothing more. An excellent job had been done in concealing the truth, files had mysteriously vanished and the guilty had walked free, their tracks covered by the soil of numerous unmarked graves across the length and breadth of this country. Hapless children, caught in the institutional trap were left unprotected, like flies, baiting the surface of a religious river of shame, while the perpetrators lay in the murkiness below, waiting for their moment to pounce. Not only had the Church and State deprive the children of their dignity in life, they had stripped them of their identity in death. Some poor souls it seemed had never existed.

She was glad of one thing; at least she had found the proof she needed. Pat's young life had been taken whilst in care. She was happy he had been re-interred in the consecrated ground of Rathmore cemetery. It was the closure she had always wanted and an opportunity to seal a painful chapter in her life. At his burial she wrapped the 'Chocolate Flamed Venus' in her scarf and placed it on Pat's casket and watched as the damp soil covered them both, reuniting them for eternity. She had finally let him go, she had said her last goodbye. Tragically his young life had been plucked by the hands of one, who herself had suffered and fallen victim to an oppressed and corrupt Ireland. Claire knew that Pat's was just one of the many innocent lives taken, yet she knew the remaining suspicious deaths would never be proved as anything other, than suspicious deaths. Those words from the commuter train returned to haunt her.

'There never was nor will there ever be, justice in this world.'

Thomas arrived and sat next to Stephen, 'Sorry I'm late. We had to deal with another gangland murder this morning. That's a total of nine this month.'

315

'Christ this place is getting worse than America' said Stephen.

'Tell me about it'.

President Mc Aleese was about to end her speech.

'Before I conclude I would like to thank all those people who invested their time, and their hard work to this worthy project. I would especially like to thank Claire Conlon. Without her, we would not be here today. It was through her ceaseless campaigning, that the Government finally relented and agreed to finance this wonderful memorial garden to the children of Ireland. Before I officially open it I would like to call on Claire Conlon to unveil the sculpture dedicated to all the children who died whilst in institutional care'.

The audience applauded loudly. Gina squeezed Claire's arm.

'We're proud of you.'

Mike winked in solidarity. Claire stood up. The President continued,

'May this wonderful monument remind us of the innocence and vulnerability of childhood. May it make us more aware of the dangers our children have to face from the ever changing society we live in. May it, through your vigilance, ensure 'child abuse' becomes a thing of the past, not only here in Ireland, but all over the world.'

Claire spotted Bill as she headed for the podium. He raised his voice above the applause.

'Congratulations Claire. You're one hell of a woman.'

She smiled and shook his hand.

'Thanks Bill.'

Nervously she stepped on to the platform. The cameras flashed as she stood shaking the President's hand.

'She's such a special person' said Thomas' clapping wildly.

'She certainly is. I spoke to her before you arrived. She told me to say hello.'

President Mc Aleese led Claire to the large red velvet drapes. The band began to play 'An Irish Lullaby'. The president retreated into the shadow cast by the Papal Cross. Claire pulled the red satin rope and the curtains dropped revealing two life size bronze statues. The image flashed across the screen. One was of a young girl with a skipping rope, the other of a boy with a string in his hand. He was looking up. On the end of the string was a kite floating on the breeze. On the base of the statue was the inscription;

When I feel upset and lonely,
I think of you, and it helps me to be strong.
To the memory of all the children
who died in Irish Institutions

The crowd stood and applauded. Thomas turned to Stephen.

'The inscription is a line from a letter Pat wrote to Sister Claire.'

Stephen interjected.

'It was the last letter he ever wrote.

'Do you know I never knew his family name?'

'He didn't either, till he received the first letter from Sister Claire.

Thomas smiled.

'Pat 42'. It sounds like the identification number for a policeman or a soldier.'

'You know', said Stephen 'it was a war. That memorial is the proof. We're gathered here today to honour those who were lost in the struggle.'

'I never thought I'd live to see this day,' said Stephen wiping a tear.

'Neither, did I,' said Thomas.

Stephen lifted his young son onto his shoulders. The little boy giggled with delight.

'You wouldn't have, if it hadn't been for the courage of that woman standing in front of you now.'

The End

21247889R00186

Made in the USA
Charleston, SC
10 August 2013